Cowgirl Country

Patricia Probert Gott

Cover Picture:
Cover designed by Patricia Probert Gott and
Illustrated by Laura Wiley Ashton

Photo Credits:
Front Cover, iStockphoto.com
Page 250, Arlene McConnell

Although based on a true story, this book is a work of fiction.
Rimrock *is* a real dude ranch in Cody, Wyoming and it was owned
and operated by Glenn and Alice Fales. Some character names have
been changed. Any resemblance to actual persons, living
or dead, events or locales is coincidental.

Previously published as *So You Wanna be a Cowgirl* and *Cowgirl Days*

ISBN: 978-0-9845898-7-6

PUBLISHED by PRGOTT BOOKS
www.prgottbooks.net

Printed in the United States

ALSO by PATRICIA PROBERT GOTT

Novels

Me and Sitting Bull
The DAYES of Wyoming
Searching for a Magpie

Travel Novellas

Ancient Egypt and the Nile
Volunteer to Empower

Children's Horse Stories

Horse Tails by Shasta
Horse Tails by Mookie the Mustang
Horse Tails by Rafiji the Safari Horse
Horse Tails by Horses in Harness
Horse Tails by Famous Fred
Horse Tails by Appaloosa Duke
Horse Tails by Shiloh

Prologue

Many young girls dream of horses. Some take lessons and learn to ride; the rest of us live and breathe all aspects of horses—drawing, painting, scrap-booking, playing horse games, and forever scheming to own one. Any horse will do, just so we can brush, braid, hug, and ride. We read *The Black Stallion* series with fervor. We imagine being a cowgirl riding the backcountry of Wyoming, after reading *My Friend Flicka* or *Thunderhead.* Some take it a little farther than dreaming, as I did.

During the summer of my eighth year, my dad bought a farm outside of town and I got an old Shetland pony. All I had to do was promise to stop biting my fingernails, and to be responsible for the pony's barn chores and taking care of him. No problem—I was in seventh heaven.

From that old pony, I progressed through my senior year in high school free-leasing or buying horses. First was a retired draft horse, then a sway-backed old Thoroughbred mare, a Welch pony, a Morgan horse and lastly, a two-year-old pinto Quarter-horse gelding which I trained into a fine western trail horse.

As most kids do when left to their own ingenuity around horses, we taught our horses to rear, like Lone Ranger's horse, Silver, sometimes staying on, sometimes falling off. We vaulted over their rumps onto their backs Roy Rogers's style, and raced each other to see who had the fastest horse that day. When we weren't racing, we were playing Cowgirls and Indians. Because I rode bareback, I often played an Indian, even riding with a war bridle—a rope looped around the horse's jaw instead of a bit, the rope continuing along his neck, used as a guide rein. When playing a cowgirl, I taught all my steeds to halt whenever I threw the reins, and to ground-tie like good cowponies.

This wasn't exactly my idea of being a cowgirl but it would do until the real thing came along.

Many years (and many horses) later, the real thing did come along. I had the chance to work summers at a dude ranch outside Cody, Wyoming as a ranch wrangler and trail guide.

I was going be a real cowgirl . . . this is my story.

PART ONE

Chapter 1

With my car window rolled down, I stared in awe at my surroundings in the Wapiti Valley, northwest Wyoming. The air rushing in was much cooler than I had expected. After all, I remembered, it's still May, and I'd been warned that in this part of Wyoming it was apt to be chilly with possible cold rains or snow through mid-June. I pulled off the road and got out of my car to get a better view. It had been a long four-day drive from my home in Maine to Cody, Wyoming, but this scene, perfect as a postcard, showed that this trip was going to be well worth it.

On my left, a large herd of horses grazed peacefully on irrigated pasture grass alongside the highway, while in the background, sagebrush and prickly-pear cacti sunbathed on the arid soil of rolling hills. Snow-capped mountains formed the northern horizon to my right. I later learned they were the Absaroka Range of the Rocky Mountains. The Shoshone River, lined with pine and cottonwood trees, wound west/east through the valley, and puffy white clouds, so near you could almost reach up and touch them, dotted the brilliant blue sky overhead. The clarity of the air helped make the view spectacular.

The scenery was even more resplendent than I'd ever dared dream when Glenn Fales had said that my horse and I were hired to work at Rimrock Dude Ranch for the summer. I was a 40-year-old divorced businesswoman from Maine going to work as a ranch wrangler, and my seven-year-old Arabian gelding would be one of my guide horses.

Razan, my horse, traveled via commercial horse carrier from Maine to Rimrock Ranch. I called Alice Fales, Glenn's wife, when I arrived in Cody, asking for driving directions to Rimrock and she told me my horse had arrived safely a couple of days ago, thankfully. He was being isolated in a small corral getting acquainted through the fence with the other 125 ranch horses and pack mules. I had worried about Razan's wellbeing while he was traveling in the care of others. Would he drink enough to keep hydrated, or load and unload without problems at stopovers? I had raised Razan from a yearling, training him myself, and as other horse owners/horse lovers tended to do, treated him like a family member.

Looking ahead, I could see what I supposed was The Rim, jutting out nearly a mile in length and rising 500 feet above a ranch I assumed was Rimrock. The ranch was located 26 miles west of Cody, on the North Fork Highway leading to Yellowstone. Teddy Roosevelt once said that this drive following the North Fork of the Shoshone River from Cody to Yellowstone Park was, "The most scenic 52 miles in America." I could not agree with him more.

With eager anticipation, I got back into my car and drove on toward The Rim. It was time I introduced myself to Glenn, Alice, and my fellow wranglers. I had met Glenn and Alice briefly 4 years ago when I'd been a guest on a horse-pack trip going from Cody to Jackson Hole with Rimrock as the outfitter. The Fales had hosted a pre-departure dinner for six other guest-riders and me the night before we were to begin our ten-day, hundred-mile adventure, riding over the Rocky Mountains. Alice told us we'd never forget it—how right she was!

* * * *

I knew a little about the couple from pack-trip campfire chatter and telephone conversations with Glenn over the past winter. Glenn and Alice, now in their 70's, had owned Rimrock Ranch for 35 years. Glenn had been a rodeo bronc rider in his younger days and now, years later, suffered the consequences of being thrown to the ground time after time by bucking horses. Although he was a little stiff and arthritic, he still rode his horse, Ronnie, with his friends when they came to the ranch as guests. His horse was named after President Ronald Reagan who'd been a guest at Rimrock Ranch in the 80's. Glenn's domain was anything to do with the horses, corrals, wranglers, day rides, and pack trips. His priority was pleasing his guests in any way possible, and many returned year after year because of his accommodating ways. He ran his ranch hands-on style, according to his employees: his word was law. They called him Chief out of respect.

Alice oversaw the bookkeeping, cleaning, cooking, waitress, and yard staff, handled reservations, ordered supplies, and scheduled outside ranch activities, i.e. weekly rafting trips down the Shoshone, day trips to Yellowstone Park. Yet, she somehow managed to find time to occasionally ride her Arabian horse, Casper. She was well respected by employees and guests alike.

Chapter 2

Rimrock Ranch's driveway was a mile long. I drove over the proverbial slatted western cattle/horse guard that ensured animals did not go beyond that point. Westerners honored a 'fence-out' law, while Easterners, a 'fence-in' law. I passed Glenn and Alice's home on the left, set back from the ranch road for privacy. A little further on, there were two small pastures. A couple of horses appearing to have medical problems were grazing in one, and the other pasture grazed some young horses, maybe yearlings.

Then came the ranch pond that I later learned was amply stocked with trout for guests to catch and release. The large rodeo arena was vacant, but the stock corrals were full of horses—and there was Razan, I noticed, looking not-so-content in his small adjacent corral. What stood out right away was that most of the horses were chestnuts or bays with very few pintos or appaloosas. I knew that brown horses tended to accept other brown horses fairly easily, and I was pretty sure that Razan, being a chestnut and also a non-aggressive type, would readily acquiesce and fit in. He'd be content at the bottom of the pecking order as long as he was with the other horses. I would integrate him with the rest as soon as I had a chance to consult with Glenn.

As I drove straight ahead to the main ranch house, I could see the snow-topped peak of Ptarmigan Mountain in the background, framed between Green Creek Ridge and The Rim.

What a magnificent picture! I took several photos with my new camera.

The ranch house was a log-style lodge surrounded by an open porch. I noticed a stone chimney protruding from the roof and the backside that looked like it might be for a huge, homey fireplace—it was. The huge lodge contained the dining room and kitchen besides a small office and lounge area.

I had a fleeting moment of uncertainty about my drastic decision to come 2500 miles west to work, especially bringing my own horse with me and exposing him to all kind of unknown conditions, i.e. weather, feed, and terrain. The ranch was at a mile high elevation where simply breathing was going to take getting used to. Oh well, Glenn hadn't discouraged me. I was already here and it was too late to back out now.

Putting my sudden anxiety aside, I parked my red Chevy Beretta, now more than a few miles past any good trade-in value, in the guests' parking lot. I took my time looking around before entering the lodge. There were nine rustic-looking log cabins, for guests apparently. Glenn had said that the ranch could accommodate 46 guests at peak season. What looked like a feed shed and another large building were tucked behind and under some cottonwood trees. I correctly supposed all the horse tack and supplies were stored in this larger building because several hitching rails stood adjacent to it. Next to the parking area set a long three-sided shed, maybe for maintenance and for the repairmen to use. I wondered where the employees' quarters were and what my accommodations would be like.

No time like the present to find out.

I walked up the porch steps and knocked on the door. A good-looking, and noticeably, long-legged cowboy answered the door. I gulped, stared at his gorgeous dark eyes, twinkling under his Stetson's brim, and thought simply: *Wow!*

"Hi, I'm Pat Gott," I managed to say. "I'm going to be working here this summer and I'm supposed to meet either Glenn or Alice Fales. They're expecting me."

"Howdy ma'am, I'm Dustin," the cowboy smiled and replied. "I used to work for Glenn but I run my own outfit these days up near Pahaska, packing into Yellowstone. I just stopped by to say 'Hi' on my way into town.

"Glenn's gone with a couple of the wranglers checking trails, but Alice is down back in one of the cabins. I just talked to her so she should be along soon. I was on my way out, but you can wait in here if you want."

"I'd like to get unpacked but I don't know where to park my car, or myself. I guess I could wander around until I find Alice."

"Yes, but first, why don't you pull your car around back, that's where the employees park. I'd offer to help you carry your stuff but I don't know which bunkhouse you'll be in."

"That's okay. Thanks for the offer and nice meeting you. Maybe I'll see you around this summer."

"Same here, ma'am."

Hmmm, that was interesting. Things were looking good —literally.

I drove my car around back like Dustin had said and found a parking spot not far from the bunkhouses. There were three single-story buildings, each about the size of a house trailer, and two smaller ones. I found and pocketed the map of Rimrock's ranch and land that Glenn had sent me, put on my hiking boots, and set off to explore, find Alice, and check on Razan—not necessarily in that order.

Chapter 3

On my way to the corrals, I spotted a building called The Store. No one was there, but there was a lot of merchandise, e.g. souvenir type goods of woven Indian rugs, postcards, key chains and western accessories of every kind, limited only by sizes and quantity. There were socks, T-shirts, gloves, caps, rain ponchos, belts, and bandanas, along with necessities like Band-Aids, aspirin, and tampons. I wondered who these items are for. Are they ranch supplies, or merchandise for sale, and how would I purchase something? I figured I'd just add these to my many other questions for Glenn or Alice, when I finally met them.

I nosed around down by the hitching rails and found the wranglers' saddle shed and horse shoeing area. It looked like they'd been busy picking tails and clipping bridle paths as horse hair was abundant on the ground—as were several piles of recent manure. A keg of new horseshoes of various sizes and shoeing nails were just inside the feed room door. I noticed that all the shoes were cocked—*must be so they won't slip while climbing up and down these rugged mountains*, I thought.

Down at the corral Razan whinnied when he saw me. "Good boy," I said as I patted his sleek neck. "How are you? You look pretty good." But he wasn't happy. He fretted nervously back and forth wanting to join the other horses. I looked around to make sure he had water. He did—his drinking source was Canyon Creek that ran through Rimrock's 1500 acres, furnishing water not only for the horses but also for irrigating nearby pasturelands. I could also see he'd been given plenty of alfalfa hay but wasn't eating much of it.

Just then, I heard a truck pull up the drive and stop. A couple of cowboys got out along with an older man I figured was Glenn. *Finally,* I thought, *I'll get some answers and get us settled in.* Glenn waved to me and shuffled stiffly to the corrals. He wore cowboy boots, jeans, long-sleeved shirt with sheepskin vest, cowboy hat, and a smile. Glenn had a twinkle in his eye. Throughout the summer, he would kid me about my Arabian horse, 'Raisin', as Glenn called him, and my use of western language—or lack of it. "The Wyoming word for field is 'meadow'," he'd say, "and it's a 'creek' not a brook, and you 'tie' your horse, not hitch him."

"Howdy, guess you're Pat."

"Right, and you must be Glenn. Pleased to meet you." He had a real firm handshake.

"So what are we going to do with that Arab of yours? He's not eating much but he looks okay and he's not colicky."

"I'd like to put him in with the others if that's okay with you."

"We can try it. We were waiting until you got here to see what you wanted to do with him. Go open his gate and we'll see how he adjusts."

Thus Razan was set free from his enclosure and joined the Rimrock horse herd. There were a few squeals, tail swishes, threats to kick, and necks snaking out to bite, but within a few minutes all had quieted down. Razan kept his attention on the most dominant horses. That was particularly difficult when he was eating hay from the bins with his rear toward the herd. After receiving a few nips and bites over the next few days, he learned to wait until most of the others had their fill, then go to a hay bin that wasn't crowded.

* * * *

Glenn said he and Alice had decided that because of my different job and work hours, I would bunk separately from the other female help. Being a loner, this was just fine with me. A young man named Frank, not exactly the rugged, masculine type like I imagined most ranch hands to be, but nice, came from the kitchen and helped me unload and carry my suitcases and gear to my small cabin. He said he was a pack-trip cook but helped Mary, the ranch cook, until the mountain trips started in July. Frank told me that lunch was at noon. He or Mary would clang a bell when it was time to eat—and "Do not be late." Food was plentiful, but hungry help and guests did not wait for anyone.

I took in my surroundings. Opposite my cabin porch was the men's shower and toilet facility; I was not too impressed with that sight. My room was about 12-foot square and held a full size bed, chest of drawers, lots of wall hooks, and a separate nook containing a toilet and wash sink. *I wonder where I bathe or shower?* I sure hoped I didn't have to share the men's showers—now that's something to think about. I unpacked, putting my waterproof and insulated LLBean boots and my cowboy boots by the door. I hung my jeans, jacket and rain slicker on the wall hooks, and put my shirts, socks, and undies inside the chest of drawers. There was room for my coffeepot on top. Besides my toiletries, I kept the rest of my belongings in my suitcase, which I slid under the bed. Curtains covered a small window over the bed and a picture window looked out across Canyon Creek and the log cabins beyond. All-in-all, the cabin was sufficient and I was making it my home. I could live here comfortably for however long.

Chapter 4

Frank was right; the lunch bell rang promptly at noon—right outside my cabin. On my way to the dining room, I met two more employees, a cabin girl named Ann and waitress named Debby. Ann, a sweet girl from Virginia, had just graduated from an equestrienne college. Debby was a friendly transient also interested in horsemanship. Their quarters were in the ladies bunkhouse across the yard from me. They told me I could use their shower facility. It would be especially convenient before dinners, as all the ladies worked during that time and their rooms would be vacant.

The dining room was larger than it looked from the outside, containing six round tables and two long rectangle tables that would sit 10-12 people. A luncheon buffet of cold meats, an assortment of cheeses, a couple of cold salads, cold drinks, and cookies and/or chocolate pudding for dessert was set up in the center.

I was hungry. I filled my plate and sat at the first round table for eight that I came to. Sitting at the table already were Glenn and the two other cowboys I had seen with him in the truck. Actually, I quickly learned they were *wranglers* not cowboys. Cowboys dealt with cows, wranglers with horses.

Glenn introduced me to Tom, who was the head wrangler, and to Ryan, a fellow ranch wrangler like myself. Ryan was a good-looking young man with a beautiful smile. He attended Montana State College and had worked for Glenn in past summers, last year as the head wrangler. Glenn treated him as his son; I liked him immediately. We struck up a good mother/son relationship over the summer. Ryan came to me for personal advice. He was only 18 years old and was like my own son. He'd thoughtfully lift the heavier saddles onto the taller horses for me if he saw I was struggling.

Tom was older and my first impression was that he either did not like me personally, or did not like me working for him as a wrangler. Maybe he was just unhappy with his job. Glenn asked him to saddle Phyllis, the ranch's college-trained buckskin mare, and take "Raisin" and I out on the trails in the afternoon and show us the ranch land.

"Meet me at the corrals at one o'clock," Tom growled and got up from the table.

"Do you need a saddle and bridle?" Glenn asked.

"No thanks, I brought my own. It's in the trunk of my car, but I'll get it down to the saddling area. See you at one, Tom."

Glenn told me that there were three more wranglers coming to work tomorrow, Sunday, as well as seven guests for the week. He explained that most guests booked reservations mid-June through the last of August while schools are closed.

"We always have a guest orientation Sunday evenings after our outdoor cookout," Glenn said. "My speech at that time should answer many of your questions. And I've scheduled a wrangler meeting after breakfast on Monday at the wranglers' shed.

"Tom should be able to familiarize you with the ranch on your ride this afternoon."

Dressed in my favorite Akubra Australian hat, long-sleeved shirt, denim vest, wrangler jeans, cowgirl boots, and leather riding gloves, I saddled my horse, donned my chaps and was ready to ride. I'd acquired my most of my western gear over the past five years doing pack trips in Wyoming, Arizona, and Colorado. The chaps were new.

Razan and I followed Tom and Phyllis past the feed

shed to a trail that immediately crossed the East Fork of Canyon Creek and then climbed switchbacks up, and up, and up. Razan was doing a little puffing, I was trying not to look back and/or down, and Tom was silently riding ahead astride Phyllis. *Was this some kind of endurance test for my horse and/or a test of my own fortitude,* I wondered.

We rode for another fifteen minutes toward some high cliffs over the flat top of the bluff we'd just climbed. The trail turned south and we rode nearly a half-mile along the base of the cliffs where golden eagles frequently nested. I wanted to know more about the land, and if Tom wasn't going to volunteer information I'd just have to ask.

"Are we still on Glenn's land?" I asked.

"Yep," was all Tom offered.

"How many acres of horse pasture does he own?" I tried again.

"About 600," Tom replied.

"Is that all? Looks like more."

"Most of what you see west and south is the Shoshone National Forest separated by the East and West Forks of Canyon Creek. We'll turn back and head a mile or so east to Green Creek. At the creek, Rimrock's land runs into the Washakie National Forest. With the National Forests bordering three sides of Glenn's land he doesn't have to own much trail land," Tom explained.

"Do the horses have free run of all this land for pasture?"

"No, the horses graze this land close to the ranch only when it's still green in the spring. Glenn leases the irrigated pastures along both sides of the main highway during the dry summers."

"How do you find all the horses out here?" I asked.

Tom turned around and said with a smirk, "That's what you're here for. You wranglers round up the horses every morning. They stay in the corrals or are ridden during the day, then you drive them back to a pasture every evening."

Okay, that might have been more information than I needed right now. I'd have to think about that for a while.

We rode quietly east toward Green Creek, Razan following Phyllis up and down steep slopes and across a flooded high meadow. At times, the trail ascended so steeply that I had to reach forward and hold onto Razan's mane. I leaned back in the saddle a little and pressed my stirrups forward to help my horse balance when going down steep narrow inclines. I found myself sometimes holding my breath but Razan seemed to be doing fine.

Back at the corrals a couple hours later, Tom said, "That was your introductory ride. You're on your own from now on."

Chapter 5

The next day being Sunday, no one worked in the morning so I knew my services wouldn't be required. I saddled my horse and set out on my own to explore the ranch trails. I figured there were enough points of reference to keep my directional bearings intact, i.e. The Rim to the west, Ptarmigan Mountain to the south, and the Eagle Cliffs to the east.

I started following a trail I had seen behind the bunkhouses. It, too, crossed Canyon Creek then ascended slightly through aspens and cottonwoods that grew along the creek. Out in the open, the land was sage and grass prairie and was easy to cover at a nice trot. Razan was a little apprehensive without Phyllis to follow, especially when we came to where the trail dipped down a side-slope, with a fifty-foot drop-off to the right. A stream of water running across the trail had washed out some parts of it, making it difficult for my horse to maintain his footing.

Rounding a corner and coming out of a group of cedars, I saw a moose drinking from a small pond off to my left. Coming from Maine I was familiar with moose and knew by its size that it was no more than a yearling. However, I didn't know how long a young moose stayed with its mother and didn't want to hang around to see if the cow was nearby. I trotted off through an open area of mainly sagebrush before the trail disappeared into a group of evergreens. This trail, with the Eagle Cliffs on my right, must be one of the trails that Tom and I were on yesterday before we traversed to Green Creek. Recognizing my surroundings increased my confidence.

Content with the quiet of the forest's tranquility, I didn't see two mule deer partially hidden in a shelter of spruce trees. They startled my horse as they suddenly leaped across the trail ahead of me and continued through the conifers. I noticed the forests were different here in the west. Unlike Maine, there was no thick underbrush to contend with so I could go off-trail without difficulty—which I did.

I reined Razan left to where the deer had come from and discovered a fair-sized secluded pond, seemingly spring-fed as I couldn't see any inlet. From the pond, I had a clear view across to The Rim and spotted a bighorn sheep near the top of a steep trail—maybe a horse trail, as there were indications of switchbacks. What a nice spot! I wondered if we could swim here when it got warmer. *If someone cleaned the pond and dammed the outlet, it would make a natural swimming pool,* I thought. Later, when I approached Glenn with the idea, I learned that water is so scarce in Wyoming that it is unlawful to vary a natural water supply, no matter how trivial it may seem. So much for that idea!

We ascended another very steep slope climbing upward toward the peaks. Before reaching the apex, I saw a pair of golden eagles land in the cliffs above. I figured they were making a nest there as I'd been told the cliffs were called Eagle Cliffs.

After exploring for an hour, I dismounted to give my horse a break and took some pictures at the same time. I chuckled to myself because Razan was looking around at the spectacular scenery as if he was a tourist himself. "Guess we'd better gaze to our hearts content now, ol' friend," I said, "and not when we're guiding guests on trail rides. We don't want to act like tourist ourselves; that sure wouldn't instill much confidence in our ability."

I looked north toward Jim Mountain; snow still blanketed its high meadows as it hovered protectively over the Shoshone and Wapiti Valley. The panoramic view was breathtaking. I could see as far east as the Buffalo Bill Reservoir fifteen miles away. The multi-million dollar, 353-foot dam housed a huge reservoir of irrigation water for farmers in the lowlands and was popular for fishing and boating.

During the last half of the loop back to the ranch, the trail wound down over slopes and beside dry ravines. It was arid land with only sagebrush and prairie grass growing. Jackrabbits were everywhere, and, needless-to-say, so were red tailed hawks and coyotes whose main menu was rabbit. I spotted a coyote entering a den in the side of a ravine. This would be a good guest topic later in the summer when the pups emerged.

I made it back to the ranch just in time for lunch. Three more wranglers had arrived and were waiting in the chow line. Scott, Trampus, and Cortney, all from the Cody-Powell, Wyoming area, were college friends of Ryan's. They were all nice-looking young men, dressed in colorful western shirts, jeans and cowboy boots. I learned that Glenn required his help to wear western attire at all times while at the ranch. I wondered where their Stetson's were, then saw them all hung on antler hat racks above the archway, including Glenn's. Alice did not allow hats at the dining tables.

All three shook my hand, appearing gracious and pleased to meet me. Scott and Cort (short for Cortney) were first-time wranglers at Rimrock the same as I. Scott brought a smile and could sing and play guitar. His idol was country-music singer Chris LeDoux, and he looked like Garth Brooks. Cort brought his boyish charm and sense of humor. Tall, lean Trampus, who had worked at Rimrock last year, was a flirt. I liked them all.

The guests arrived during the afternoon and Tom fitted them to saddles. There were two families: one, a middle-aged couple with an adult daughter, the other, two sisters and their husbands. I waited until the evening outdoor cookout to mingle.

At the guest orientation, I joined the other employees singing The Rimrock Song to the tune of "My Heroes Have

Always Been Cowboys," accompanied by Frank and Scott playing their guitars. Introductions were made all the way around, and Glenn assigned horses to the guests according to their riding abilities. He gave a brief outline of the coming week's activities and told the guests Rimrock assumed they would participate unless they signed out at least four hours in advance.

I learned that The Store was for the convenience of employees and guests—and operated with no attendant. It operated on the honor system. Purchases were brought to the lodge's front desk for payment. There was no TV on the property and only one telephone, a pay phone outside the kitchen door.

Glenn said for guests to gather at the corrals no later than nine o'clock tomorrow morning to meet their horses and prepare for their Monday morning introductory ride.

Chapter 6

I awoke to a dreary, misty, cold morning. After a hearty breakfast of buckwheat pancakes and lean bacon, orange juice and coffee, all wranglers met with Glenn—Chief—at the wranglers' shed.

I had looked forward to the meeting and learning what a wrangler's (my) responsibilities were. I had thought about bringing a clipboard to take notes but didn't think that would look too cool. I planned to hurry back to my cabin to write it all down after the meeting, though.

Just as the meeting started it began to rain so all seven of us moved into the small shed—close quarters.

Chief began by assigning a horse to each wrangler for the summer. Mine was a small but very lively pinto named Navaho. He could (and would) move instantly, whether chasing a straying horse back into the herd or climbing a riverbank to rescue a guest in trouble. No question, Navaho was quick.

Ryan was happy to have King, a seasoned alpha male chestnut gelding with an attitude. Cort was assigned Cody, a swift blue-roan gelding. Trampus would ride an airhead chestnut named Deuce. Scott was assigned another alpha male sorrel, Penny, and Tom kept Adobe, a big-boned, dark-gray mustang he'd been riding. Other horses we could use to wrangle were: Fiddler, Nemo, Ace, Patrick, Taxi and Reno. However, Glenn said that every horse was to be ridden at least once to get their winter kinks out and checked for soundness before they were assigned to guests.

The most important tasks at hand over the next two weeks would be not only to ride each horse but ensure every horse was shoed, wormed, checked for scratches or sores, bridle path clipped, and tails groomed and picked. That was quite an undertaking as Rimrock had 14 pack mules, 6 draft/pack horses, 100 riding horses, and 5 young mustangs.

On top of that, fences needed to be checked and mended, trails cleared, and irrigation ditches dug. Thankfully, two more wranglers would be arriving during the week. There was plenty of work for all.

Tom spoke up and said that he'd like to go over what he expected from the wranglers. Chief said, "I still run the ranch so *I'll* tell them what I expect and you can make sure it's carried out."

Ouch, I thought. *That won't help Tom's disposition any.*

Glenn stressed that he liked the boys to maintain a clean-cut cowboy image by not swearing, using foul language, or being rude. "And, please train or discipline horses in private— not in front of the guests," he added.

In addition, he said, "When you bring the horses in from the pasture, a steady trot will keep them moving together and get them here in good condition. You don't race them into the corrals.

"Remember that guests are most important, and it's good for you to mingle and get to know them.

"Any questions?"

"How do we know when we are supposed to wrangle? And what time do we start?" Cortney asked.

"Next week, after all wranglers have reported to work, Tom will assign wrangle partners for the summer. Until then, check with him every evening. The wranglers assigned for that day arrive at the corrals by 6:15am. Horses are taken back out to pasture when we're all through with them, usually about 4:30-5:00pm," Glenn replied.

"Oh, and whenever possible, I'd like you to rope the

horses when you catch them in the round pen. Guests love to see cowboys use their lariat."

Well that leaves me out, I thought. *I wonder if I can learn to rope a horse in one easy lesson!*

"Ryan, anything else to add?" Glenn asked.

"Just that, as in the past, wranglers are responsible for keeping tack cleaned and repaired. And I don't know if most of you do this or not, but Rimrock uses double blankets and a breast collar on each horse. While you're saddling up, make sure the bridle and saddle fit. Last year we had some problems with saddles slipping because narrow-tree saddles were put onto round-backed horses. And wide trees on high-withered horses won't work either. So pay attention while you saddle up, and tell Tom if there's a problem with the fit."

Chief agreed.

The rain was still pouring down when the meeting broke up at 8:30. Glenn went to the lodge to see if, or how many, guests still wanted to ride. Meanwhile I scooted back to my cabin to write down what I'd just learned about my job. I felt pretty confident about my knowledge and ability to handle horses but I still didn't know what *wrangle* meant. I'd find out soon enough.

* * * *

Two of Glenn's longtime pack-trip guides, John and Gerald had arrived to shoe horses all day. However, it looked like it would continue to rain, so they hooked the large horse trailer to their pickup instead. They would drive to Montana and bring back another load of horses to get shoed, groomed and guest ready.

Rimrock used to have a horse-roundup every spring, and employees and volunteers would help drive the herd 100 miles from their winter pasture in Montana to the ranch in Wapiti Valley. They would drive them down Sheridan Avenue (the main street) in Cody, creating an annual tourist attraction. Unfortunately, after a 50-mile strip of Montana highway was paved along their route, Glenn decided it was too hard on the horses' hooves and legs—too many lame horses. They now hauled them in trailers. It was nowhere near as exciting.

Glenn told the wranglers that the guests had decided not to ride today as long as it kept raining. They would entertain themselves in the recreation room playing pool or ping-pong this morning.

The rain continued.

"The ranch's yellow Suburban will load up at 2:00 to take you into Cody to the Buffalo Bill Historical Center for the afternoon. Pat, you'll drive." Alice announced at lunch. I thought, *Good, at least I'm being productive.*

And the rain continued.

When the spring rains fall in Wyoming, it's cold. Razan had shed his winter coat and with no place to get under cover, he was standing with his head down, back hunched up and shivering. I felt sorry for him. I'd gotten him into this and it was up to me to help him out. I decided that I would purchase a waterproof blanket for him while I was in town.

I told the boys at the lunch table what I planned to do. After they got through snickering, (I guess no one blanketed horses in the west) Ryan told me to go to Corral West. "Not the store on Sheridan, but to the outlet near the post office, on the way to the airport. They have a better selection of ranch supplies," he said. I figured I'd found my way 2500 miles from Maine, I could find the Corral West Outlet, after I found Cody, and the museum.

Cody was the epitome of what a modern, western town ought to be and that is: not touristy. It looked like, and was, a real functioning western town, population around 8000. Although Cody was the largest city and county seat of Park County, its residents were down-home friendly, even to strangers.

The first attraction after passing the Buffalo Bill Reservoir Dam and Shoshone Power Plant, was the Cody Nite Rodeo. Opening night was next week, June 1st, and the whole ranch would attend every Thursday night all summer. I couldn't wait—*ya-hoo and yee-haw*—I'd never seen a real live rodeo.

After passing a few motels, restaurants, and an attraction called Old Trail Town (I'd have to check that out later), I spotted the Buffalo Bill Historical Center. I pulled into the parking lot to let the guests out and said, "I'll be parked right around here, and we'll head back to the ranch promptly at 4:30." I found the Corral West Outlet, after a fashion, where I purchased a horse blanket for Razan. I was back to the center in time to do a little touring myself. I read the center's directory, which included the Buffalo Bill Museum, Whitney Gallery of Western Art, Plains Indian Museum, Cody Firearms Museum and the Harold McCracken Research Library. The complex was a collection of four excellent museums under one roof. I went to the Indian section first then wandered around the Gallery of Western Art. I looked at my watch and it was almost 4:30. *Shoot*, I thought, *guess I'll have to tour here again on another rainy day.* Time to go.

* * * *

Well, Rimrock's corral now supported the only bright-blue-blanketed horse in Wapiti Valley, maybe in all Wyoming. I smiled at the absurdity of it all and knew neither Glenn nor the other wranglers would let me forget this, but I was genuinely pleased with the result. With his waterproof cover, although he sure was noticeable, even to the other horses, Razan was warm, dry and eating again.

Chapter 7

Usually, Tuesday meant everyone got up early to ride to an outdoor cowboy breakfast. However, it was still raining so the ranch went to Plan B, which was to have a cookout in the front yard and eat on the covered porch. Glenn still served up his blueberry hotcakes, and everyone was happy.

After breakfast, Glenn assigned me the job of making a large three-by-four-foot horse chart on an erasable board that would hang in the saddling area. I listed all the horses' and mules' names leaving two blank spaces next to each. Glenn or Tom would fill in the name of whoever was assigned to that horse and his/her saddle number. Everyone could use the chart to see what horses were being used, by whom, and which ones were available.

The rain had finally stopped. Alice announced the guests would be taking the usual ranch sponsored Shoshone River Float Trip that afternoon. I was to drive the guests into Cody, again, and escort them, with the Wyoming River Trip guides, down the river in rafts. The river trip was in moderate white water with class II rapids. It would be cold this time of year, exciting, but relatively safe for all ages.

The Wyoming River Trip guides transported all guests via busses from their office in the Holiday Inn complex to the Shoshone River near the old DeMaris Hot Springs. I quickly smelled the offensive sulfur odor from the hot springs but kept my comments to myself.

While rafting, the seven guests as well as myself got wet when we hit the 'washing machine' and the 'little Colorado' rapids but dried off while drifting through the Red Rock Canyon. One lady dropped her paddle and reached for it just as we hit the 'roller coaster' rapids. She fell over the side, but a fast-acting guide pulled her back into the raft in a hurry. I was having a great time—and getting paid for it. However, I wondered if I was ever going to get to *wrangle*— whatever that was.

Upon returning to the rafting headquarters, everyone changed into dry clothes and waited to collect their rafting pictures that the company had taken during their fun river trip.

While the guests and I were in Cody, another wrangler arrived at the ranch. Grady drove all the way from Utah in his beat-up old truck. He was a student at Brigham Young University studying Theology to become a Mormon minister. He claimed to be an experienced horseman.

How much Grady or I knew about being a wrangler would soon be tested.

The forecast for the remainder of the week was for clear skies; guests would definitely be riding. The head wrangler Tom said, "Pat and Grady, you'll wrangle tomorrow. I kept Beauty in the corral for you to ride, Pat. Grady, you'll ride Reno."

Gerald was going to be around shoeing horses all day, and I was thankful when he volunteered to accompany us novices. He would ride Cowtown, the horse he always used as his guide horse on pack trips.

Beauty was a spirited black mare of average build, about 15.3 hands tall, who loved to race. Gerald, Grady and I set off across Canyon Creek and took the trail winding up the left side of the high bluff. About ten minutes into the ride Gerald spotted a small group of 12-15 horses and said he would round them up and take them back to the ranch himself. He said that when we came upon the main bunch, one wrangler should act as herd leader and ride in front, while the other person should round up the strays and push the bunch to follow the leader.

Grady and I reached the crest and spotted the herd scatted all over the flat top. I galloped Beauty toward the headwall intending to lead the horses around the steep slope of the bluff and come into the ranch corrals from the side. The horses, being more familiar with the wrangle routine than I, took control and decided to go straight to the ranch, over the bluff's headwall, at a gallop. At that point I had two choices: one, I could wimp out, going around the slope and come in a half hour after the herd arrived, or I could go for it and gallop down over the headwall with the rest. I decided to go for it, hoped Beauty was athletic enough to handle the steep grade with me on her back, and said a silent prayer before hurdling over the brim.

All horse lovers have seen or read *The Man from Snowy River* and his big scene chasing brumbies down the steep mountain side. Well, to me, this was exactly the same scenario. Beauty, as well as the other horses, leaped over the brim, slid on their haunches or galloped sideways until reaching the bottom a couple hundred feet below. Was I scared?—not exactly. Was I thrilled?—yes.

Grady wasn't far behind. A few of the older horses had trotted down the switchback trail rather than gallop over the headwall. After they were all in, Grady closed the corral gate and he and I went to breakfast. No one said anything about our downhill gallop so I figured it was a normal event in wrangling, and I didn't mention it to anyone.

Later in the week, however, I overhead Grady as he expounded to Gerald about how exciting and dangerous it was galloping the horses down the headwall. Gerald said he wished he'd returned to help us. "Sounds like I missed a once in a lifetime ride," he said.

Only then did I realize that this incident was very much out of the normal realm of wrangling and I should be proud of myself.

I was becoming a real cowgirl.

Later I discerned that because of Beauty's tendency to

race, she was not usually used as a wrangle horse. Tom must have known this and had intentionally put me on her thinking, hoping, I couldn't handle her. This would have served to show that I couldn't do the job. What a jerk! Maybe that's why he was gone within the next week, either fired or quit. I didn't care. Glenn appointed Ryan to be the head wrangler again for this year. I was happy with the choice. I liked Ryan. He had integrity.

Chapter 8

When Glenn suggested I take the afternoon off, I was delighted. I had kept my horse in the corrals instead of sending him out to pasture, hoping that I'd get a chance to ride him soon.

Debby and Ann had approached me earlier and asked if they could ride with me sometime. Both being accomplished equestriennes, they came to be employed at the ranch thinking they'd get to do some horseback riding. Once there they learned that they could ride *only* if there were horses available and a wrangler willing to escort them. Luckily at this time of year, horses were available to ride, and I had some spare time to escort.

They wanted to ride to the pastures near the highway to do some loping. This was fine with me as I hadn't ridden in that area yet. After a nice lope over the grassy meadows, Debby looked up and said, "Look at that building up there that resembles a Chinese pagoda. Let's ride up the hill to see it."

I found a trail that led up from the pastures and passed the pagoda. *What an odd looking structure*, I thought. Rumor was that a man built it for his lover; when scorned, he hanged himself. The building now stood empty. How sad!

We trotted along a grass-filled road, which eventually led to a dirt road and a sign saying, Green Creek Road. Following that dirt road, we passed a rock wall containing some kind of ancient hieroglyphics. I would have to find out what those were about so I could inform guests. Finally the road led across a creek that I recognized from my ride with Tom. I knew my way back to the ranch from there. Nice ride; good company. We agreed to ride together again and explore up Canyon Creek.

* * * *

Glenn told me my next day off wasn't until Sunday, so I asked him if I could turn Razan out with the herd at night instead of his remaining in the corral. Glenn said, "If you think Raisin can handle the wrangling back and forth you can try it this evening when the wranglers run the horses to the front pasture."

It didn't turn out exactly as planned. At first, Razan was excited to be running free with the herd, but after a mile, he turned around and ran back to the corral. He wanted food, and to him the corral was where he'd been fed. After a good laugh at his individuality, I ponied him beside Navaho to the horse pasture. When he found good grass to eat there, he was content to stay.

For the remainder of the week, we wranglers wormed horses, cut bridle paths, and picked tails, while Tom lead the seven guests on local trail rides around the ranch.

The next week Tom left, so Ryan and Cort took turns guiding the twelve guests on trail rides. When they weren't leading rides, they helped Glenn and Grady finish clearing debris from the horse trails. Trampus got the job of digging and unblocking irrigation ditches, while Scott, Jack and Gerald shoed the remaining barefoot horses.

Tuesday and Wednesday, I drove the guests into Cody again, to the museum and float trip, though I didn't do the trips myself. I became familiar with the city and now knew where the post office, grocery store, best art galleries, souvenir shops and clothing shops were.

In between guest trips to Cody, I checked fences on horseback and made necessary repairs. I carried the wire cutters, claw hammer, and fencing staples in a leather saddlebag thrown over the back of a buckskin gelding named Taxi, who was content to graze nearby as I mended fences.

Another new wrangler, Pier, arrived during the week. He was a veterinary student from Northern Italy and was as handsome as they come. He had beautiful eyes and a naive smile that could melt the hearts of ladies from five to seventy-five. The guest ladies and girls would love him. He'd be good for business.

Ryan, Scott, Cort, and Trampus occupied the four-man side of a bunkhouse; Pier moved into the smaller two-man side with Frank. Scott, Pier and Frank all played guitar and sang country western songs, and on many evenings their music soothed the ranch to sleep.

Glenn free-leased three young Appaloosas that summer under the condition that only wranglers ride and train them. They were *not* to be guest horses. Pier chose a handsome sorrel Appaloosa with a white blanket, named Clyde, for his wrangle horse. I picked a beautiful dark-gray, three-year-old Arab/Appy cross, named Washakie, to train and use as my extra guide horse. The third Appy was a waste of time and money. The wranglers gave up trying to teach him anything.

* * * *

The boys were horsing around roping each other down by the corrals one evening after supper. I got my arms roped to my sides by Trampus, then Ryan threw a rope and caught one of my feet. They were about to hog-tie me when I yelled, "Stop. Can you please teach me to throw a lasso so I can defend myself?"

The boys all raised their eyebrows.

"Sure, I can show you how. Watch," Ryan said, "then practice for a few years."

Ryan held the lariat loop with his right hand at his side, brought it across his front to his left, up his left shoulder, circled his head to his right shoulder then threw it out and down over a stump.

I tried the same thing a couple of times before I got the

hang of it and got the loop out into the air. I tried it several more times and finally managed to get the loop over a corral post.

"Guess I won't be roping a moving horse anytime soon," I said, annoyed at myself.

"Don't worry about roping horses," Ryan replied. "We only do that when Chief is around." He explained that loops whirling in the air upset the horses and made them hard to catch. It was also dangerous for wranglers to be in the small corral with 40-50 nervous and upset horses running and bumping into each other.

I decided I'd be content to rope a good-looking wrangler!

Chapter 9

Business picked up the next week, with 20 guests to entertain. By mid-June, there were 28, and now, the last week of June, business was booming with 40 guests. Between cabin girls, waitresses, maintenance man, yard boy, cooks, wranglers and guides, there were 23 employees.

Ryan, as head wrangler, assigned wrangle partners: he and Grady, Cortney and Scott, Pier and I. I was really happy to have Pier as my partner for the summer. Together we vetted the sick and injured horses and took special care of the very young and the very old. He was kind to animals. I liked that.

Partners wrangled every third day, so I only had to rise really early and round up the horses twice a week. That wasn't too bad. I liked to lead the herd, and Pier had the fun of rounding them up. He got all the dust in his face but said he didn't mind. I figured he was being nice.

As a mountain wrangler, Trampus helped Gerald get the black packhorses and camp gear ready for overnight pack trips that would begin July 1st. The pack horses Elvira, Ellie, and sisters Dolly and Molly, were gorgeous black Percherons, with abundant manes, long forelocks over wide foreheads, lively eyes, long necks, powerful forearms and thighs. They looked as if armor-plated knights from the Middle Ages should be riding them into battle. Heavily built Ebony, Sambo, Sankey, Satan and Nemo made up the remainder of the black pack string. Frank was their pack cook.

The head guide, John, had hired a mountain wrangler, Greg, and together with his wife, who was their pack cook, they pack tripped with Glenn's string of ten white mules. They were busy readying the mules, tents and camping equipment for weekly mountain trips in July and August. Rimrock's white mules were rare and famous. They'd been the lead attraction in Cody's Fourth of July Parade for many years.

* * * *

This weekend was Cody's Annual Plains Indian Powwow, sponsored by the Buffalo Bill Historical Center, and set up on the south end of its parking lot. Cheyenne, Comanche, Kiowa, Crow, Blackfeet, and Sioux, along with Arapaho, Apache, Navaho, Shoshone, Nez Percé, Ute and Pawnee tribes were represented.

Visitors from far and near, including Rimrock Ranch guests and workers, were drawn to the rainbow of colors and the Indians singing and dancing to the rhythmical beating of drums. Many special activities like hoop, snake and owl dances added to the festivities of the weekend.

I drove into Cody on Sunday morning and wondered at the enormity of the crowd enjoying the powwow as I tried to find a parking spot nearby. I marveled at the explosion of colored beadwork of red, yellow, orange, blue, green and purple, and the feather-work of the Indian fancy-dancers. The honored traditional dancers followed, adorned in black and white feathers and carrying the flags of two worlds, portraying the warriors of old in their classic dance movements. The traditional shawl-women dancers and the younger children paraded into the arena next.

On the outskirts of the dance arena, booths selling Indian beads, jewelry, clothing and accessories were set up for visitors to purchase.

* * * *

During the week, I drove guests into Cody less frequently now as each of us six wranglers took turns driving. More guests also meant all activities and trail rides went as scheduled. We wranglers were busy.

Every morning after breakfast, except Sunday, wranglers headed for the corrals to get our horses and the guest horses ready to ride. Today was Monday, and I was to guide the Introductory Ride with Razan. I pulled him out of the corral first and tied him to a rail. When the rest of the herd was run into the small round corral, it was real tight quarters and too easy for a new horse to be kicked or bitten by more aggressive horses. I didn't want this happening to Razan.

Ryan was busy writing each guest's name and saddle number beside their assigned horse on the chart that I had made. He yelled to me across the saddling area, "Did you notice Two Tone still limping when you wrangled this morning? He's supposed to be assigned to Marion for the week."

"Yes, he was," I replied. "Maybe we can put her on Arapaho? Still a paint and same disposition."

"Probably, but hold up on catching either one until I check with Chief. Scott, here's the list of the horses we need for this week. Grady, you start putting out saddles. Pat, you start grooming. I'll be right back to help saddle." With that, Ryan headed up to the ranch house.

Scott, Cort, and Pier were busy catching and haltering horses then bringing them to the gate for me. I led them two at a time to the hitching rails.

Cort warned me, "Be careful with Bonfire and Macho. They're 'pullbacks' so make sure they're not tied when you work around them. They may panic at any time and pull on their lead rope until they break something, like their halter or a hitching post."

"Thanks for the heads-up. Do I tie them at all?" I asked.

"Bonfire gets tied to the tree next to the saddle shed, and just flip Macho's lead rope over the rails; he'll stay right there," Cort replied.

When I had a dozen horses tied to the rails, I got out the currycomb and brushes and started grooming. When there were 20 or more horses to groom, I cleaned only the strategic areas—under the saddle and girth—and barely touched their rump, neck or legs unless they were really dirty—it took too much time.

Ryan was back and agreed with substituting Arapaho for Two Tone. He said, "Grady, are you riding Adobe again today?"

"Yes, I love that big guy and want him for my wrangle horse."

"Ok, then you'd better go catch him yourself because the boys can't seem to get him.

"Scott, would you come finish putting out the saddles?" Ryan yelled.

With only a few more horses to catch, Cort suddenly said, "Here comes Chief."

"Then let's quickly rope these last ones, get out of there, and everyone start saddling." Being head wrangler was a busy job. Ryan did it well.

After grooming, two saddle pads were placed on each horse's back, with the fleece pad nearest their hide. Saddles were then checked for proper fit and breast collars were attached to the saddles. Cinches were pulled just tight enough to enable the saddles to stay on. They were pulled tighter just before guests mounted up. Bridles were fitted and put on over the horses' halters. Snaffle bits with shanks and curb straps were used on all guest horses and most wrangle horses as well.

Nine o'clock arrived, as did the guests; there were still horses being saddled. Glenn said for Ryan and Cort to come help get guests mounted, while Grady, Scott, Pier and I finished saddling the horses. On an average, each wrangler saddled and bridled seven to nine horses each morning.

I usually tried to saddle the small and medium-size

horses, but occasionally I was stuck saddling a tall one. I was always thankful when Ryan came around to lift a man's heavy saddle onto a tall horse for me. Later in the summer, I found I could lift any saddle onto any horse by myself.

The Introductory Ride followed the same trail as Razan and I had explored my first Sunday at the ranch. Once groups of ten to twelve guests were mounted, Glenn gave them basic instructions in the small corral on reining their horse left, right, and to "Whoa." Ryan chose one wrangler to lead the group and another to ride last to be sure everyone was keeping up. Glenn watched them closely as they left the corral to make sure the guests could handle their horses satisfactorily. I led my group with Razan. Whereas he had walked this trail before, he acted like he was a seasoned guide horse.

Soon all guests and wranglers were on the trail. This first ride had all levels of riders on it, so we walked, got used to the horses and enjoyed the scenery. No moose or deer—too much noise. We stopped for a rest at the apex, the same as I had done. It was the proverbial picture taking spot.

When the last group made it back to the saddling area, the wranglers loosened all the horses' saddle cinches and put grain-filled feedbags on them, giving additional amounts to the aging horses.

At lunch, Glenn announced that all guests would be taking a three-hour trail ride in the afternoon, meeting at the saddling area promptly at 1:00. Everyone was to ride in one big group. Whereas only five wranglers were needed, Glenn told me to take the afternoon off. *Gladly*, I thought. *I've been up since 5:00 am, rode for four miles before breakfast wrangling horses, groomed thirty horses, saddled seven of them, and led a morning two-hour trail ride.*

I was ready for a nap.

Chapter 10

Square dancing was in the Ramuda Room (better known as the rec room) every Monday evening, and all employees participated per orders of the chief. Glenn called the dancing to old 78-rpm records playing western music. There were circle dances, where everyone changed partners on each round, and square dances, where partners got to swing with other partners. On the old time Virginia Reel and Lady of The Lake, ladies and gentlemen got to swing or do-si-do until their heads reeled. Maybe it was the absurdity of it all, or the fact that it put young and old, male and female, on the same level. Whatever it was, everyone had fun, much to our surprise. It was a wonderful way to mix guests and employees; and Glenn, being the all-knowing wise Chief, knew how to host a good time.

By the time the dancing ended at 9:30, I was glad I'd taken a nap because I was tired again. Glenn announced that all guests had to be at the corral at 7:30 the next morning.— everyone was riding to breakfast. That meant wranglers needed to start saddling by 6:00 a.m. *Well*, I thought, *at least I don't have to get up before sunrise and wrangle tomorrow.*

Blueberry pancakes, here we come! The guests were mounted and wranglers intermingled in the line of forty horses and riders. Ryan led the group. I was riding about six horses back. I was just starting to cross Canyon Creek when Navaho stumbled down onto his knees in the water. I stayed on, pulled up on the reins to help him get back on his feet, and off we went again as if nothing happened—except my feet were now soaked. Ryan yelled back, "Hey Pat, you okay? Or are you just entertaining the guests this morning?"

"Yes, I'm okay," I replied to his jest. "I didn't have time to shower this morning so I thought I'd bathe in the creek instead."

We climbed switchbacks up steep slopes then headed into the forest following the trail along Green Creek a couple of miles before the aroma of bacon and coffee filled the air. There in a small meadow, Glenn, and his helper Frank, cooked over a campfire. Coffee was ready.

While the wranglers tied, hobbled, and let other horses graze freely, the guests 'chowed down' on blueberry hot cakes, eggs and bacon, with orange juice on the side. Tales of Navaho's not-so-graceful trip through the creek was retold a few times, as well as rumors of Cortney's having spotted mountain lion spoor during Monday's ride up Canyon Creek. Mountain lions are notoriously elusive so there was no way a wrangler or guest was going to see one, but Cort confirmed that the tracks were fresh. Soon the big cats would head for higher, summer hunting grounds.

The large group split into three smaller groups on the ride back to the ranch. The novice group of walkers returned via the same route as they had come up.

A second group took a longer round-about route down Green Creek Road. When we got to some level ground, we trotted the horses for a while before heading back down the trail to the ranch.

The third group started on the same road as the second, then the roughnecks, rowdies and daredevils veered off and headed up a sagebrush-covered hill. When they reached the top, Ryan and Grady told everyone that they could ride back down to the dirt road—as fast as they wanted. No trail, just rocks of various sizes, gully-wales, a few small fir trees and lots of sagebrush in the way.

Ryan yelled, "Last one to the bottom buys drinks." And off he and Grady raced.

Guests tried to follow. Some made it, breathless but intact, while others were totally unprepared to ride off-trail at a fast pace—downhill—and ended up in the sagebrush. No one was hurt, and for some it was their riding highlight of the week. It gave them bragging rights because they'd done something the other guests didn't do.

After lunch Scott and Cortney drove the vans into Cody. While the guests went rafting, they met in the park and caught a couple hours of sleep under the shade trees. It was Grady's and Ryan's afternoon off, and they'd gone to visit Ryan's parents.

Pier and I stayed at the ranch and doctored the two horses in the hospital pasture. Buck had a stick puncture in his left hindquarter that Pier cleaned out and stitched up, then gave him a shot of antibiotics. Coke had gravel in the sole of his right front hoof. His cornet band was swollen with inflammation. I soaked it with warm water and Epsom salts to help bring out the abscess. I'd have to continue soaking his hoof daily for the next week to see results. In the meantime, he hobbled on three legs, as he couldn't put weight on that hoof.

* * * *

There were still a couple of hours until supper so I saddled Razan and went for a late afternoon ride up into the canyon. I hadn't gone more than a half mile beyond the creek when my horse stopped suddenly. I looked ahead and saw what appeared to be a large dog sitting in the trail. Upon second glance, I could see it was a bear squatting. Each stared at one another for a few seconds, then not knowing what to do, I headed back to the ranch to tell Chief. Razan was anxious but didn't seem scared. Probably there were so many different scents around that the bear's smell didn't stand out.

"Chief, I just saw a bear on the trail not far past the creek."

"Must be a young adult brown bear that's just been kicked out of the den by a mother who has a newborn cub. They wander around for a while not knowing what to do or where to go. They're usually harmless, but go tell the boys to run it up into the canyon," Glenn said, "and don't let the guests know about it or they'll be chasing the bear all over the ranch and someone will get hurt."

I rode to the corral where Pier was cleaning his saddle and Ryan and Grady were just ready to wrangle the horses back to pasture.

"Hey guys, there's a bear up on the Canyon Trail and Chief said to head it back up into the canyon before it gets any closer. And not to alarm the guests."

"Pier, throw your saddle on Fiddler," said Ryan. "Let's go boys; we'll follow you, Pat."

Great, I thought, *Razan was real good the first time; wonder what his reaction to the bear will be, second time around.*

The bear wasn't on the trail where I had first seen him, but Grady spotted it down by the creek. The boys went galloping after it whooping and yelling, "Yahoo" and "Yee-haw." Look out bear, I thought. I'll bet it won't be back to this ranch for a while.

Razan was excited now, not so much by the bear, but the yelling, running and hollering was beyond his comprehension. Dancing in place, he couldn't decide whether he wanted to run with the other horses or run away from all the noise. Not wanting to press my luck, I turned him back toward the ranch.

Chapter 11

Did you ever see softball players wearing cowboy boots and hats? It's a hilarious sight. Rimrock employees and guests played ball every Wednesday morning in a sagebrush and cactus field. And yes, wranglers wore their cowboy boots and hats. Glenn picked the captains, who in turn chose players, and the game was on.

Whoever chose Cortney had a definite advantage as he'd played some minor league baseball, and compared to the rest of us, he was awesome. I played softball in a women's league years ago, so I was familiar with the game. I played roving shortstop for the ranch and even made a few good hits during the summer, much to the male wranglers' surprise. Of course I tripped over sagebrush and got 'thorned' by prickly pear cactus a few times also, but so did everyone else. It was all part of the game.

Not every rule was fair. Chief umpired and gave the youngest kids unlimited strikes until they finally hit the ball. He called fair balls, out, on the winning team if they were too far ahead. All the rule bending eliminated the chance of hard feelings, except for Grady, who had to keep his temper in check if his team lost.

Back at the ranch, Alice told us The Wapiti Lodge had called saying some horses were grazing on the side of the highway nearby. She had driven down and determined that seven of the mountain horses had escaped through an old pasture gate. All six of us wranglers saddled up and headed out to round up the wandering strays before they got hit by a car.

When a few like-minded employees get together on their own, sometimes they become inventive—too inventive, maybe. As we wranglers loped up and down slopes, galloped across pastureland and leaped irrigation ditches, there was bound to be competition going on. Too much testosterone dictated that someone had to be the fastest.

Grady hollered over to Cort, "Race you to the highway gate."

Cort replied, "Eat my dust." And the race was on: Cortney riding Cody and Grady riding Adobe. The rest of us brought up the rear but weren't far behind. We knew Chief would never approve of racing. Ryan only hoped neither our horses nor ourselves got injured in our folly.

No one was at the highway gate to call a winner, and, of course, neither would concede defeat. They were going to race again, with the wranglers officiating at the finish line this time, when Scott said, "There're the horses up there near The Red Barn."

Calmly we rode up to the strays. Ryan roped Zane and began leading him alongside the highway. The rest of us surrounded the other horses on three sides and moved them in behind Zane, being careful to keep them out of traffic. This sight provided a photo opportunity for tourists; many cars stopped to take pictures—real wranglers, real horses, real west.

* * * *

Wednesday afternoon's Wine & Cheese Ride was a three-hour ride. The trail began at the driveway opposite the yearling's pasture, then climbed about a third of the way up and around the side of The Rim, crossing some ledges that looked down on the highway. I was astride Navaho and held my breath while riding over the ledges, hoping that he wouldn't choose this place to stumble again. I'd lost some faith in him with that tripping move in the creek, but I came to learn that he didn't stumble in strategic places, only when he wasn't paying attention.

The trail descended a bank into the West Fork of Canyon Creek and then followed the creek for a couple miles before stopping to rest in a small grove under evergreen trees. Everyone over 18 drank a small cup of wine and ate cheese and crackers; those under 18 drank pop.

After remounting, we climbed semi-steep switchbacks up the backside of the canyon's rim. The guests didn't know that the wine was to help make them mellow for their ride down the other side!

As I stood at the top looking down, I said to Ryan, who was standing nearby, "Don't tell me that's the trail we have to descend."

"It's the easiest of two trails. Don't worry, the horses know how to handle the steepness and the rough terrain. It's when guests try to tell their horses what to do that can be problematic."

With that, Ryan gave the guests some riding instructions: "These horses know how to step down from cliff to cliff and rock to rock. They are familiar with the trail, so do not try to tell them how to do it. Let them do it themselves. You just sit quiet and balanced. Don't hold the reins too tight; the reins are not brakes. And don't let them stop; keep them moving."

And down we went—guests' faces white, no talking, no picture taking, silence, concentrating, mostly scared. Guests have been known to wet themselves on that ride down The Rim.

In mid-summer, I initiated a very successful alternative Soda Pop Ride for the not-so-brave. The ride would cross the East Branch of Canyon Creek and make a loop up and over some hilly terrain—not steep. We'd stop for soda pop in an area where many old animal bones could be found, and the wranglers would give prizes for the most bones found and the largest. As the guests couldn't carry most bones back with them to the ranch, the last wrangler stayed behind and scattered the bones around the sagebrush and woods again, to be found by next week's guests.

* * * *

Jim Bama, a distinguished artist and friend of the Fales' who lived in Wapiti Valley, was a guest at dinner that evening. He'd painted a large picture of their horse, Phyllis, and a cowboy, which hung in the ranch dining room, and he had exhibits in the Western Art Museum in Cody. Everyone feasted on roast pork, mashed potatoes, applesauce, carrots and peas—my favorite meal. Mr. Bama stayed through the evening's cowboy-sing-a-long, featuring Pier, Frank and Scott.

I slipped away from the sing-a-long soon after I'd heard Pier sing Old Paint, and Frank's rendition of Desperado—both songs I loved. I went back to my cabin to sleep . . . I thought. Unfortunately, a mouse decided to share my room and disrupt my sleep by running up my arm. The boys had been having trouble with mice in their room, and I suspected Ryan was instrumental in putting this one in mine. I pulled the covers over my head to keep the too-friendly mouse off my body and decided that tomorrow I'd think of some way to get back at Ryan, and ask Frank to de-mouse my room.

The next morning it was my turn to wrangle so I got to the wrangle shed a little earlier than necessary. Overnight I had thought of a way to even with Ryan for his 'mouse-trick.'— I would 'short-stirrup' his saddle. It's similar to short-sheeting a bed: the near stirrup is left alone, but when Ryan swings his right leg over the saddle, he'll find the off-stirrup above his knee, instead of down by his foot. *Ha, ha.*

When it was time to begin the ride that morning, Ryan mounted up, and in front of waiting guests, he had to dismount, go to the horse's off-side to adjust his right stirrup, and mount up again. He looked disgruntled and a little embarrassed, but never said a word.

Chapter 12

I had saddled Razan to ride to Table Mountain on the Thursday All-day Ride. I was at the end of the line, bringing up the rear, and as it turned out, I was lucky to be there. A pack animal always accompanied the riders on Thursdays to carry soda pop and food to cook over an open fire for lunch.

Pier had packed Pecos today. Pecos was a bay mustang, formerly a wild horse rounded up and sold to Rimrock. He was not a guest horse as he was apt to be spooky. I owned Arabs—I knew spooky. I had ridden Pecos as a guide horse and found him surefooted and willing to lead, although he was a little flighty. He was *never* supposed to be a pack animal. Can you imagine a spooky horse with pack gear strapped to his back? Not a good idea!

Ryan, leading the line, was nearly up to the first switchback, guests were just crossing Canyon Creek, when pandemonium ensued. Something in Pecos' pack had started rattling while he was crossing the creek, and that's all it took for him to panic. He tore his lead rope away from Pier and went bucking and charging through the guests and horses in front of him, scattering them down the creek bank to the left and up the slope to the right. Horses kicking, rearing, people falling off, screaming. What a fiasco! It made for a funny story when related around the campfire later over lunch, but at the time, it was total chaos. Pier returned to the corrals, and with Gerald's help, transferred the pack to Jeff the mule.

The Table Mountain riders had just passed the breakfast area when Pier and the pack mule caught up. The group crossed Green Creek then started to climb. After a couple hours in the saddle, we reached a level spot and took a fifteen-minute rest stop for horses and guests.

Pier led the pack mule past the guests and continued to travel on alone. He planned to have the fire going and hot coffee for the guests when they reached Table Mountain. The only problem was that Pier didn't realize there were two trails to the top. He took one; the rest of us took the other.

Switchbacks were getting steeper and more dangerous; trees were getting smaller; the air was chilly as there was still snow on the ground in places. In the distance, a strange call came from a wild animal. Razan was beginning to fret and dance around. He kept looking about, worried that something might be coming up behind him. He did not like being at the end of the line.

After another mile of riding through stunted conifers, we arrived at the high meadow where Pier was supposed to have the fire going and coffee ready—no Pier.

Ryan said, "Cort, why don't you ride up to the summit to see if Pier took the wrong trail and he's waiting for us up there."

"I hope he hasn't headed back down again," Cort replied and he went loping toward the top.

The wranglers loosened all the horses' cinches and tied their reins around their necks intertwined in the throatlatch so the reins wouldn't slip over their necks. The guest horses were let loose to graze the long meadow. The wranglers' horses (all except Razan) were tied to trees to ensure they could be caught. I knew I could catch my horse, so I let him graze with the others.

I looked up and saw Cort, Pier, and the pack mule coming down from the summit. "Hey, how about that warm fire and hot coffee," I shouted.

"If you guys had told me which trail to take it would have been ready," Pier replied.

Soon hamburgers and hot dogs were sizzling on the grill, and guests and wranglers were enjoying coffee or hot chocolate.

The guests had a spectacular view while eating lunch. The ranch and all of Wapiti Valley were visible. Ryan said the elevation was about 9500 feet above sea level.

After lunch and a rest, I called Razan and we rounded up the other horses. The guests re-mounted, and the climb to the summit began. The horses were puffing as they climbed the last few hundred feet in the very thin air. Once on top, it was safe for groups of five or six to lope up small inclines. The theory being: at that elevation the horses weren't going to run far, and loping uphill was fairly safe as bucking was unlikely. Of course, there were always guests who loped too close to one another even after being warned to keep a horse-distance apart, thus falling off as their horse shied away from another's kick.

I led the way back down a different trail than we had climbed up to Table Mountain. My horse slid on his haunches descending steep sandy banks and crossed exposed ledges cautiously, perhaps feeling my anxiety. This side of the mountain was more open, and the view of Green Creek Canyon and Ptarmigan Mountain was breathtaking.

I was enjoying the scenery and the ride down when I heard Ryan yell, "Hey, slow that Arab down a little, this isn't a race to the bottom." I hadn't noticed that Razan was hurrying and walking too fast. He was hurrying away from elk, bear and moose smells that permeated the open meadows on top. From then on, I stopped frequently, letting the others catch up. Everyone stopped for a rest and potty break at the breakfast area, and then continued back to the ranch, arriving late afternoon.

It was my turn to wrangle and I wasn't riding my wrangle horse. "Scott, would you wrangle for me?" I asked. "I can't wrangle with Razan and don't want to bother to catch Navaho."

"Sure if you'll wrangle for me tomorrow night. Then I can have all tomorrow afternoon and evening off."

"Deal," I replied and headed up to my cabin to change

and cleanup for the Cody Nite Rodeo.

While Scott and Pier were wrangling the horses out to pasture, mischief was in the making. Ryan put a rope around the neck of a huge stuffed bear his girlfriend, Tara, had given him. Then he and Cort hid it behind a large rock next to the small corral. When Scott came riding back into the saddling area, they pulled the bear out from its hiding place right in front of Scott's horse. Penny, his horse, not having a tolerant disposition, spun around, bucked three times, and Scott hit the ground, cussing. *They* all laughed and thought it was funny. When I heard about it, I thought, *I don't think it's amusing at all, especially if they do that to me.*

* * * *

The All-day Ride was a very long ride for youngsters, and as the summer went on, Glenn and I started taking kids under ten years old on a Half-day Hotdog Ride up the canyon. We took a pack mule with us just like the big guys and made a campfire alongside Canyon Creek. We showed the kids how to cut sticks for cooking hotdogs and marshmallows over the open fire. After lunch, Chief showed them how to have a boat race, pretending the broken sticks were boats and letting them drift down the creek.

On the way back to the ranch, Glenn pointed out a split in the trail. He said that the trail heading to the right toward Ptarmigan Mountain led to the remains of Jeremiah Johnson's cabin. Jeremiah Johnson, being a notorious mountain man of the west, interested me. I thought maybe this would make a good exploratory ride for Debby, Ann, and me to take the next time we rode together.

Chapter 13

"Let's go rodeo," was the chant as wranglers and guests, dressed in their best cowboy/cowgirl attire, loaded into waiting Rimrock vans.

Cody was often referred to as the Rodeo Capital of the World because nowhere else was a full rodeo staged nightly for three months in a row from June through August. Rodeo stock took on cowboys from across the country in bareback, saddle bronc, bull riding, calf roping, team roping and bulldogging events. Having fallen off many horses, many times in my life, I liked the saddle bronc riding the best. I could identify with their sincere desire to stay on the bucking horses and not get thrown off.

Other traditional events of the Cody Nite Rodeo included barrel racing for cowgirls, and steer riding for younger cowboys. For children who attended the rodeo, there were fun events including the calf scramble and stick-horse race. Adults attending envied the crowd's adulation of the cowboys and some even fancied participating themselves. Our guests didn't know they'd get their chance to play cowboy or cowgirl on Saturday at Rimrock's Guest Rodeo.

Glenn discouraged Rimrock wranglers from participating in the rodeo as he didn't want his employees injured, mangled, mutilated or disabled. He let it be known that if you get hurt at the rodeo, you would be fired because you wouldn't be able to do your work. The boys, knowing they couldn't participate and filled with envy, did the best thing and always sat near the chutes below the Buzzards Roost, talking with the cowboys and watching them perform. I had wanted to enter Phyllis in the barrel racing competition, but Chief and Alice both said an emphatic, "NO." So I sat and watched with the guests.

At half time, I was buying a drink when I ran into Dustin, who I'd met at the ranch the day I arrived.

"Howdy, ma'am. Pat isn't it?" he said. "Nice to see you again."

"Same here, are you watching or partaking?"

"Just watching tonight, although I'm entered in the Wild Horse Race here next weekend, during the Cody Stampede."

"I think I've heard some of the Rimrock boys talking about entering. Apparently it's a once-a-year event, and they're raring to try for the challenge."

"And the prize money too, I'm sure," Dustin replied. "Are you sitting with anyone, or would you like to join me in the stands?"

"I'm chaperoning the ranch guests tonight, so I'd better sit with them. But I think I'm free tomorrow evening. Are you coming into town?"

"Yep, let's meet up at Cassie's around nine. I know from experience Glenn and Alice frown on your eating out, but we could go dancing. Do you know how to do the western swing?"

"No, but I'm trainable. See you about nine tomorrow night then," I said, trying not to sound too enthusiastic when what I really wanted to say was, *YEESSS. I need a night out with a handsome cowboy like you.*

Chapter 14

Rimrock employees took turns driving the ranch vans filled with guests into Yellowstone Park on Fridays. They drove to the famous Old Faithful Geyser, Upper and Lower Falls, Artists Point, Mud Volcanoes, and viewed huge buffalo herds grazing in Hayden Valley. The kitchen prepared bag lunches for all to eat when they stopped to rest at Canyon Village.

Only a few guests stayed behind to take advantage of morning customized riding trips and free time in the afternoon. Wranglers that didn't have to drive guests usually had the afternoon off, but this afternoon Glenn had a special project for Ryan, Grady, and me.

Glenn and Alice had purchased Rimrock Ranch from Earl Martin. He'd passed away a few years earlier, stating in his will his wishes to have his ashes spread over Rimrock's land. Mr. Martin's daughter, Susan, and son-in-law, Steven, arrived at the ranch early Friday morning requesting Glenn's assistance. He planned for Ryan, being head wrangler, Grady, studying to be a minister, and me, as public relations person, to accompany Susan and Steven on a ride to the top of Eagle Cliffs.

Chief and Ryan selected two sure-footed horses, Hugo and Macho, for the guests to ride. Chief chose Crystal for me to ride. He said she belonged to his granddaughter and assured me she had climbed the cliffs many times. Ryan and Grady rode their regular wrangle horses, King and Adobe.

The trail to and from the peak consisted of switchbacks

climbing over and around exposed ledges. Eventually the trail came to a high meadow that led into the forest a few hundred yards before ending atop Eagle Cliffs. Grady said a prayer before Earl Martin's ashes were released to the wind to float and fall over Rimrock's land. Susan handed the metal container to Ryan. He passed it to me with a terrified look on his face, as if to say, *What am I supposed to do with this?* I took a handful of ashes and threw them into the wind; Grady and Ryan then did the same. None of us had realized there were bones in with the ashes of cremated remains. We thought it was a little eerie.

The ride down the switchbacks was no easier or less stressful than riding up had been. Finally back to the ranch, I breathed a sigh of relief. Riding steep inclines or declines over exposed ledges was not my idea of fun. My idea of fun would be my date with Dustin tonight.

As it turned out, some of the other employees from Rimrock were also headed to Cassie's for a little dancing. I thought it wouldn't be a bad idea to have some friends around while I was with Dustin—after all I hardly knew him. I'd changed out of my blue jeans into a denim peasant skirt with a silver Concho belt that showed off my slim waist. I put on my good Justin boots, a long-sleeved fringed v-neck red pullover, and silver dangle earrings. I felt confident and even got a wolf whistle from Pier.

Ann, Debby, Ryan and Pier rode in my car. They said they could ride back with Cortney, who was already in town. The bouncer was checking ID's. As Ryan wasn't yet twenty-one, Wyoming's legal drinking age, I told him I'd say I was his mother and would make sure he wouldn't drink anything alcoholic. Surprisingly, they checked *my* ID, while Ryan walked right in. That caused a good laugh among our group.

The Rimrock bunch sat at one long table. I checked out the bar. There was Dustin. What a handsome hunk of cowboy he was: long legs, good build, and tanned rugged face, grinning back at me.

"Howdy, cowboy, buy a girl a drink?" I said, walking up to him.

"Sho' 'nough, what's your pleasure, ma'am?" he drawled.

"I'll take a Coors Light, please."

"Would you like to dance this one?" he asked as the band started playing *A Country Girl Can Survive.*

"I'd love to; lead on."

We did an easy two-step around the floor; Ryan gave me a discreet 'thumbs-up.'

We found a small table off to the side and sat down. I learned Dustin's last name was Lee; he was 35 years old and grew up in Montana. His parents owned a horse ranch between Belfry and Bridger, not far from the Montana/Wyoming border. They raised Quarter horses and adopted wild mustangs whenever there was a government roundup.

Dustin said he'd done some rodeo saddle-bronc riding when he was younger and now sometimes did team roping with a buddy of his, but mostly watched from the stands these days. He had an easy-going manner, seemed to talk straight without trying to impress me with bravado and bullshit.

He said, "You ready to swing dance?"

We danced the western swing (similar to the jitterbug, only faster) to *Should've Been A Cowboy,* and only bumped into one couple—Pier and Ann. We slow-danced to *I Can Still Make Cheyenne,* sat a little, talked a little, drank a little, and it was nearly midnight before I knew it.

"I turn into a pumpkin at midnight" I told him. "Think I'd better get back to the ranch."

Dustin walked me out to my car and asked about my plans for the upcoming Cody Stampede.

I said, "I've heard that Rimrock takes all guests and employees to the parade Thursday morning. I don't know any more than that."

"I have a pack trip leaving tomorrow, but I'll be back Wednesday. I'm entered in the Wild Horse Race Thursday afternoon at one o'clock. Could we meet somewhere after that?"

"We'll probably stay in town through the afternoon, especially if the Rimrock wranglers are in the Wild Horse Race. If I hang with them in the chute area, can you find me there?"

"Sure will. 'Til then . . ." he held my face in his hands and kissed me once lightly, and then again, not so lightly, encircling me with his muscular arms. *Oh my*, I thought, as I returned his embrace.

I was left almost speechless but managed to squeak out, "See ya," before getting in my car and driving off. I should have asked the others if they wanted a ride, but it was too late now. They'd have to ride back with Cortney. I wanted some time alone with my thoughts.

Chapter 15

Time passed quickly for me. The ranch had a full house, 45 guests, which meant 45 horses for the wranglers to catch, groom, and saddle every day. No one would be riding this Thursday because of the 4th of July Cody Stampede in town. Alice had cancelled the regular Tuesday afternoon float trip and everyone rode instead to Table Mountain after eating breakfast at Green Creek.

All the talk at the ranch centered on the upcoming Cody Stampede. Everyone wanted in on the festivities, including me. I was looking forward to Thursday and seeing Dustin. I'd learned that Rimrock provided a picnic in the park for guests and workers after the morning parade. Then employees were on their own until Friday night. Cody stayed open for forty-eight hours straight, featuring concerts and barbecues in City Park, street dancing, fireworks displayed at dusk and, of course, the Nite Rodeo. With all restaurants and bars staying open, I figured Dustin and I could find a lot to do.

After an earlier than usual breakfast, Glenn called out, "All aboard for the Stampede Parade," as he climbed into one of the ranch vans. A few of us opted to drive our own cars. We followed the ranch vans, forming a caravan into Cody. Pier and Ann, not having their own vehicles, rode with me.

We found space to sit under a couple of shade trees to keep out of the hot sun and watched the parade with Rimrock guests and the other employees. The Stampede Parade was one of the best in Wyoming and highlighted Cody's special Independence Day Celebration.

And what a parade is was! It began at 9:30 and took nearly two hours to parade the more than 150 entries. There was a large collection of horse-drawn carriages and wagons, and cowboys and cowgirls on horseback showing their best silver-plated saddle outfits.

"Pat, look at this Arab coming up," Cortney exclaimed.

"Wow, what a *gorgeous* animal," I replied, as a magnificent black Arabian stallion, adorned with red tassels on his headstall, breastplate and show blanket, pranced by us leading an All-Arabian Horse Club. The Arabs paraded proudly dressed in their native costumes.

"Too bad they don't have brains to go with their beauty," Cort said.

"Oh, you're just jealous 'cause you don't own one," I chided back. His mother owned an Arab that he liked, so I knew he was just teasing me.

There were mule trains, mountain men, and Indians walking or riding their painted ponies. I loved the brightly beaded Indian costumes. Antique vehicles, clowns, several bands, and numerous commercial and organizational floats, all depicting the parade theme Heading West, marched down Sheridan Avenue.

Talk about a 'photo op'. I took a whole roll of pictures. I couldn't decide which entry I liked the best; each entry seemed better than the last. The other wranglers, of course, liked the cowboys roping various guests standing alongside the parade route.

After the parade, Rimrock served up a chicken barbecue with accompanying cold salads, rolls and watermelon at one end of City Park. All the ranch guests and employees took advantage of the shade trees to eat under.

When I saw Ryan, Grady, Cortney and Trampus get up and leave, I followed.

"Hey, you guys headed to the rodeo?"

"Yeah, we have to get ready for the wild horses," Ryan replied. "The race begins at one."

"I'm meeting Dustin there. Can I hang out with you guys in the chute area?"

"Sure, follow us; we'll park in the contestants' lot."

During the past week, the boys had been practicing for the upcoming Wild Horse Race, in their spare time. They used their own wrangle horses, which wasn't a very realistic situation as they were too well trained and cooperated too easily. The horses used for the competition were raised wild, recently rounded up from the open range, never having been touched by humans until being hog-tied, haltered, and hauled to the rodeo this week, scared and fighting.

As I understood it, the teams each consisted of three members. Cort was the 'anchor' who would open the chute gate and hang onto the horse's lead rope. The second member, Grady, would be the 'mugger,' holding the horse's head in his arms, trying to keep it still. The third member, Ryan, would strap a saddle onto the wild, bucking, scared-to-death horse, mount him and then try to ride the wild, bucking, and still scared horse to the finish line at one end of the rodeo arena.

This sounded to me like it was dangerous, exciting and terribly abusive to horses. And my cowboy friend Dustin was also entered in this competition!

The Rimrock boys were in chute three, right in the middle of the fracas, but nearer the finish line than Dustin, whose team had drawn chute six at the opposite end from the finish line. I kept a low profile as there were not many females in the competitors' area. I stayed by chute three, keeping out of the boys' way. They had drawn a large white Appaloosa, blanketed all over with red spots. The competition was about to begin. I held my breath.

The starter's gun sounded, the chute gates opened, and the horses broke loose into the arena, leaping high in the air, biting, kicking and throwing themselves to the ground in their frenzied scramble to get away. The scene was exciting, but sad.

Cort got rope burns; Grady got bit; the Appaloosa fell on Ryan's leg pinning him to the ground for a few seconds, but he stayed on and rode across the finish line. They came in second out of six entries.

"Good job, Rimrock," I cheered.

Dustin's team, situated at the far end of the arena, came in third. He'd been the anchor man holding the wild horse's lead. I hoped he hadn't been hurt. I looked anxiously around the grounds for him.

Just then someone came up behind me and put an arm around my shoulders. "Howdy, ma'am. You sure are looking sweet. Are you lookin' for someone special?" His drawl, ready smile and twinkle in his eyes set my heart to fluttering.

"Howdy, yourself, cowboy. I'm glad to see you survived that fiasco called a race. Are you okay?"

"Just a little dry and dirty. Hey, let me wash up a bit in the men's room, then let's go for a beer, okay?"

"Yeah, I'm thirsty too. Meet me at my car? It's in the contestants' lot, second row back. The boys showed me where to park."

"Be there in five."

Dustin and I found parking space outside the Silver Dollar Bar. The bar and restaurant had swinging doors just like an old western saloon. I thought I'd just regressed into the nineteenth century. I hoped it didn't come equipped with a 'shootout,' et al.

"So what's on the agenda for the rest of the afternoon?" Dustin asked, after he'd ordered a couple of beers.

"The Rimrock gang wants to meet at five for an old-time photo as a gift for Alice and Glenn. The place is somewhere on East Sheridan. Do you know where it is?"

"I think it's a temporary setup down by the Olde General Store. It's almost 4:30 now, do you want to head that way after we finish these beers?"

"Yes, if you don't mind. I'd like to have my picture taken with the rest of the gang—for posterity and such. I understand we get dressed up in old western-style clothes and everything, to make it authentic looking."

"Sounds like a plan, let's do it."

Chapter 16

Nineteen Rimrock employees gathered to have our old-time photo taken in period costumes. Frank dressed like a dandy, Kyla, a madam, and Mary, a woman of wealth. Several of the males dressed as mountain men with fake rifles and fur hats. Pier and Ryan were gunslingers. Most of the ladies were in barroom attire of varying degrees of décolletage. I wore an old-fashion wedding dress with wide-brimmed hat decorated with flowers.

The evening was hot and the photographer took a long time taking 20 different pictures with an antique camera. While we stood posed, the boys behind Debby, who wore a skimpy red dance-hall dress, kept slipping the straps off her shoulders or partially unzipping her dress. This was all in fun as everyone was clothed in his or her regular clothes underneath. They were just teasing her. The photos were awesome and surprisingly authentic looking.

Dustin stayed through the photo session, enjoying the banter and chiding going on. He knew most of Rimrock males and some of the females. When everyone finally had their own photograph, he said, "I'm really hungry, Pat, do you want to walk up to The Irma for dinner?"

"Yes, I'm hungry too. I've never eaten there but I've heard it's beautiful inside."

The Irma Restaurant and Hotel called, "The Grand Old Lady of Cody", was built in 1902 by Buffalo Bill for his daughter, Irma. The hotel renovated its fifteen original suites, blending Victorian furnishings and western memorabilia with the modernism of TV and AC.

After Dustin and I filled out plates from the restaurant's fabulous hot and cold buffet, I looked around and noticed the ornate, cherry-wood bar that ran the length of the restaurant. "Look at that gorgeous bar with the mirrors running behind it. It's magnificent. Is it original?"

"Yes, historians claim it was built in France and gifted to Buffalo Bill from Queen Victoria."

I envisioned myself transported back in time, surrounded by gamblers and gunslingers and dancing saloon ladies. I felt right at home.

"I've got to shake down some of this scrumptious dinner. What say we check out the street dance up to the Eastgate Shopping Center? The feature band is Chris LeDoux's Saddle Boogie Band. I kinda fancy his music and would like to do a little two-stepping to it. How about you?" Dustin asked.

"Lead on, you're the guide."

I hoped Scott and Pier were here somewhere to see and hear their mentor play at the street dance. I didn't know if they'd stayed in town or had gone back to the ranch. I'd lost track of the other employees. I was on my own now.

I felt relatively safe. I reasoned Glenn wouldn't have kept Dustin on as a guide for three years if he wasn't of reputable character. I'd also learned more about him during our conversations today, like he'd been engaged once, but never married. He said he had more things to do before he settled down. He intended to run his own pack trips a few more years, then take over his parents' horse ranch to breed, raise and train Quarter horses. Seemed like a good plan to me.

* * * *

The shopping center's street dance was packed. Chris LeDoux and the Saddle Boogie Band had just come on stage to rousing cheers and applause. Although he was a major country music star, he was also a down-home country boy and a household name in Wyoming.

Chris began by playing his song, *She's Tough* and was soon singing his recent hit, *Haywire*. When the band started playing the song I was most familiar with—his duet with Garth Brooks—*Whatcha' Gonna Do With A Cowboy*, I was dancing in Dustin's arms in seventh heaven. I began to wonder: *What am I going to do with* this *cowboy?*

Dustin, also charmed by the music, held me close, and as if reading my mind said, "Do you want to leave here and find someplace we can be alone?"

The time had come for me 'to do or not to do'. I decided I was a big girl, could handle most situation, and I'd go as far as this would lead.

I said simply, "Yes."

"If you have in mind the same thing I have in mind, we could go back to my cabin in Pahaska. But, a better idea might be to stay here in town at the Big Bear, or nearer your ranch at the Wapiti Lodge. What do you think?"

"I don't have to be back to work until tomorrow night, so let's stay right here in town."

While Dustin checked us into the motel, I was quiet. I hoped I was making the right decision. I soon realized I had.

He kissed me as we stepped inside the door, cupping his hand around the back of my neck to pull my mouth against his. His lips, his tongue—were everything I wanted them to be.

I broke away gasping, "I, I need to use the ladies room . . . uh, do you have protection?"

He smiled and said, "Definitely."

We lay down on the bed; his body touching mine like a breeze bringing to life the surface of still water. Every place his warm hands touched me brought excitement. I thought, *It's been way too long since I felt alive like this.*

We kissed and groped and made love every which way.

Fatigue set in and we lay contentedly curled next to one another until morning.

* * * *

"So what would you like to do today?" Dustin asked as we finished eating a hearty breakfast at the Irma.

"You know, I haven't had time enough to sightsee much besides the inner loop of Yellowstone. Do you have any 'must see' suggestions for a lady from Maine?"

"Well, we can drive up Chief Joseph's Highway into the Sunlight Basin-Crandall area. It's about an hour northwest of here. Then we could come back through Beartooth Pass, Red Lodge and Belfry, Montana. We'd only be a few minutes from my parents' ranch. If we have time, we could stop for a visit. It's up to you."

"Let's start now and see how it goes. I need to be back to the ranch by suppertime."

I found the Chief Joseph Highway unforgettably scenic. It must be one of Cody Country's best kept secrets. I couldn't stop taking pictures. Luckily, I still had plenty of film with me.

Dustin told me the highway was named for the Indian Nez Percè Chief Joseph, who, in 1877, led his band out of Oregon after the U.S. government broke a treaty with his tribe to gain their gold-rich grounds. Their trek wound through Yellowstone Park, out to Clarks Fork Canyon, then north through Montana where the band was stopped near the Canadian border. "I will fight no more forever," Chief Joseph proclaimed.

Part of the road was still unpaved. Having to slow our speed created opportunities to photograph the many fields of wildflowers and red chug-water rock formations from the car window rolled down. We drove through Painter Canyon and continued up the highway to Dead Indian Pass. At an elevation of 8000 feet, the pass provided a dramatic view west to Sunlight Basin and north to Clarks Fork Canyon.

We descended a series of switchbacks into the basin and crossed Sunlight Creek Bridge, the highest in Wyoming. We stopped at the overlook, taking in the enormous depth of the gorge.

Dustin told me that when he was first out of college, he worked as a wrangler for an outfitter that did pack and hunting trips out of the nearby Cranall area. He said the abundance of wildlife was unprecedented, outside of Yellowstone, and Cranall's Swamp Lake area was home to the beautiful trumpeter swans and rarely seen moose.

We turned right at an intersection, choosing to go east up the Beartooth Highway to Red Lodge, instead of west through Cooke City and into the North Entrance of Yellowstone.

Beartooth Pass reached an elevation of 11,000 feet, providing stunning views of mountain scenery stretching over the Shoshone and Custer National Forests before dipping down into Red Lodge. We ate a late lunch at a small diner, filled the truck up with gas, took pictures at the town's monument of Chief Plenty Coup, and started driving back to Cody.

Upon reaching Belfry, Dustin said, "My folks' ranch is only fifteen miles from here, do you want to pay them a visit?"

"I'd love to—sometime—but it's 3:30 now and I really need to be back to the ranch before supper at 5:30. What do you think?"

"I think you're just about going to get back there in time."

"I would really like to meet your parents and see their ranch and horses. Maybe we can visit another day when we have more time. I don't want to say 'Hi' and then drive away."

"Agreed, and I'll hold you to it."

The drive back to Cody took too long to make it back to the ranch in time, and yet, it seemed too short as Dustin and I would have to separate. As the saying goes, "All good things must come to an end," and I thought, *This sure did feel like a good thing.*

We stopped at the Big Bear Motel where my car was

still parked, bringing back fleeting memories of the night before. Dustin kissed me tenderly on my mouth, eyelids, forehead, and held me tightly.

"I know you're really busy these days out at Rimrock, and I've got pack trips every week for the next few weeks, but I definitely want to see you again. I've really enjoyed your company."

"Same here," I replied. "If you get time, you can call me in between trips and maybe we'll come up with something or some *time* that will work out for both our schedules. The evening is the best time to catch me at the ranch.

"Keep in touch, cowboy." I smiled, traced his lips with my fingertips, kissed him lightly, and left.

Driving to the ranch from Cody, my mind and body were suspended in time. All too soon, I would have to get organized and become a wrangler again.

Until then I couldn't stop myself from thinking: *What if. . .?*

Chapter 17

I needed to stop thinking about the last two days with Dustin and get into the present. Vengeance was about to rear its ugly head.

I hadn't thought any more about the prospect of Ryan being vindictive because of my playing the 'short-stirrup' trick on him. I figured maybe all was forgiven—until I went to saddle Razan Saturday morning and: no saddle. My saddle was missing. I could easily have used a ranch saddle; there were at least a hundred in the saddle shed. There were kids' little dude saddles, ladies saddles with padded seats and narrow trees, and large-seated saddles for men. However, being a bit stubborn, I wanted to use my own.

I looked everywhere, in every shed, building, truck and corral. I asked the other wranglers, but only got a smirk for an answer. Finally running out of time, I said, "Okay, I give up. Where is it?"

Ryan innocuously pointed to the very top of the wrangle shed. I went inside and looked up. There in the rafters was my saddle, sitting on the highest crossbeam. There was no way I could climb up there and lift my saddle down. I had to 'eat crow' and ask for help. After that, I decided to call it quits on getting even, declaring a truce with Ryan.

On Saturdays, the guests had their choice of three very different rides: The Holy City Lope Ride, the Ranch Ride for novices or those who only wanted to walk, and Down-the-Rim Ride for daredevils. I had opted to go with Ryan, Cort and twelve guests on the Lope Ride as I had never ridden on the other side of the Shoshone River. The boys had assured me it was easy going so I'd decided to ride Razan. Scott and Grady led eight guests on the Rim Ride, and Pier guided ten guests at a walk, sightseeing around the ranch land.

After riding down the mile-long driveway, Ryan said, "Cort and Pat, you flag traffic. I'll lead the guests and wait for you at the bridge."

I stood my horse in the middle of the highway and stopped traffic heading into Cody, while Cort stopped traffic heading toward Yellowstone. Tourist usually enjoyed seeing the West in action and didn't seem to mind waiting.

The wooden planked bridge over the Shoshone was long, with no side rails. It could be dangerous if horses spooked, so we all crossed in a line. Ryan was in front guiding, I was in the middle of the pack, and Cortney brought up the rear.

The ride was going well until the trail narrowed along the side of a bluff. First, the horses had to cross a narrow wooden footbridge over a stream that had washed away the trail. Immediately after, they had to climb a steep thirty-foot bank up to some cliffs. Razan crossed the bridge okay and *scrambled* up the bank, as was his usual method of climbing. Unfortunately, a mare named Dixie was ahead of him, taking her own casual time walking up the bank, and Razan bumped into her. She switched her tail to warn him to back off before she kicked. He did, and went off-trail. He hadn't realized that *off-trail* could result in a fifty-foot slide into the Shoshone below.

Razan struggled back up onto the trail and finished climbing the bank. I could feel his heart pounding, as was mine. I gave him a reassuring pat and took some deep breaths to calm my horse and myself. We continued walking around the side of the cliff, then the trail headed down an overhang, that looked to horse and rider as if we were going to end up dropping eighty feet into the river. Just at the edge, the trail took a ninety-degree turn along the bank and finally ended up in open terrain.

Cortney said, "Pat, didn't you train your horse to stay on a trail? I thought you two were going to end up falling into the river back there."

"For a couple of seconds, I thought so too. What happened to the easy-going trail you told me about?"

"It was easy for these horses; maybe not for an Arab," he teased. Cort was familiar with Arabian horses, and on the surface, he was like the rest of the westerners in that he professed to dislike the breed. However, I'd seen him talking and patting my horse when he thought no one was looking. He later admitted to me that Razan was a good horse, ". . . for an Arab," he qualified, intending humor.

Ryan split the group into thirds, taking turns loping over the trail that wound around sagebrush, cacti and rocks. When we reached a cleared area to rest the horses, Ryan said, "If you look to your right, that's what's called Holy City. Use your imagination and you will see church steeples and temple domes on the crest of those bluffs."

The boys walked off the trail a ways to relieve themselves. I also thought it would be a good place for a pee break and found a large boulder to hide behind on the other side of the trail. Just as I was pulling back up my jeans, I heard a car horn beep. I turned around and there was the highway, just on the other side of the river, no more than a couple hundred feet away. People were waving and horns were tooting, at me.

"I wonder if Chief would approve of you 'mooning' traffic like that." Cort joked when I returned to the group.

"I can only hope no one knows where I work," I responded a little embarrassed.

On the return trip, we crossed the river instead of taking the narrow cliff trail. "The water's mostly belly deep," Ryan told the guests. "If you follow me, swimming will be minimal. If you do not follow me, you and your horse may get caught in the current and be swept down the Shoshone."

I didn't improvise and had my horse follow Ryan's horse

exactly where he stepped. We climbed the bank on the other side without incident. "Good boy," I said as I breathed a sigh of relief and patted Razan.

* * * *

Everyone participated in the afternoon's Guest Rodeo in the ranch's rodeo arena. Chief began the rodeo with an Equitation Class, judging guests' riding ability and improvement. There were an Eleven Years and Under Class and an Over Twelve Class. The fun competitive game events were next. Some required riding horses, like barrel racing and musical chairs (hay bales), while others were done on foot, i.e. roping a fake-steer head. Winners were acknowledged during the evening's talent show.

A guest and longtime friend of Glenn's, named Dave, suggested a wrangler race called an Egg-in-the-Mouth Race. I'd entered in gymkhanas (game shows on horseback) as a kid in Maine and thought I knew of every horse game or race invented, but I'd never heard of that race. I wondered what it was! Chief selected six older, non-competitive horses, wrote each name on a piece of paper, and the wranglers drew names. I drew, Guy, an aging Arabian/Appaloosa mix.

Wranglers had to ride in the saddle that was already on the horse we'd drawn—as is, no adjusting stirrups. Facing the gate, on the word "Go" we had to turn and race to the other end of the rodeo arena with a raw egg held in our mouth. Whoever got to the other end first, with their egg still in their mouth— unbroken— won.

Cort won, riding Chance, Ryan came in second on Happy, Scott got third with Jaws, I came in fourth. Grady dropped his egg on the ground, and Pier's egg broke in his mouth. The guests cheered and loved it. All the wranglers, except Grady, laughed also. He was so angry that later, during a fit of cursing and swearing, he put his fist through the glass in the door window of the saddle shed. I could only hope that he would clean up his language and learn to control his temper before becoming a Mormon minister.

* * * *

After the usual and scrumptious Saturday night prime-rib dinner with mashed potatoes, gravy, string beans, carrots, homemade rolls, and hot fudge sundaes for dessert, everyone adjourned to the lodge living room for the talent show.

Whenever forty guests plus twenty employees get together, there is bound to be unlimited talent. Sometimes I folded paper, origami style, into novelty items to entertain the guests. Other times, I was the Mistress of Ceremonies, announcing each act. The wrangler boys put on funny skits. The kitchen and cabin staff dressed up like cowgirls and sang country music. Scott, Pier and Frank played guitars and sang western songs. Grady blew up balloons, twisted them into animal shapes and gave them to the kids. Guests sang, recited poems they'd written, did skits and told jokes. Guests that had won rodeo events, received awards, and Glenn congratulated all for their participation and sportsmanship. It was a wonderful last evening and end of a great week for the guests.

Chapter 18

After a Sunday breakfast of homemade Danish sweet rolls, juice and coffee, Debby, Ann and I saddled up to go for a horse ride before the heat of the day descended. It was July and mid-day to evening was sometimes too hot to ride comfortably, or thundershowers popped up unexpectedly. The air was cool this morning, and the horses were feeling fine. Debby was astride Fiddler, and Ann was on her favorite mare, Mary Jane.

Ann liked Razan and looked at him with interest, commenting, "I understand you rode Razan up to Table Mountain. How was his breathing at that altitude?"

"Pretty good," I replied. "His lungs are conditioned by now. He got a little nervous on the way up, riding behind the other horses but did fine leading the group coming back."

Debby joined in, "He looks like he's adjusted well."

"It helps that he has a friend now, a horse he can boss around so he's not the lowest horse in the pecking order. His friend is Boots. Glenn bought him last week. He's old and has some arthritic stiffness going on in his front knees, but Razan doesn't care. He likes him anyway. Every time I get through riding Razan, he first does a complete rollover in the small corral to scratch and clean his sweaty skin. Then he hunts for his friend from among the other horses and chases him around a bit. Satisfied with his dominance, he drinks from the creek then hangs out with Boots until they are fed or run out to pasture. It's funny to watch his routine. He's a happy horse."

We had decided to explore the area where Glenn had indicated Jeremiah Johnson's cabin stood. The trail was only slightly inclined and easy to cover at a brisk trot for the first few miles. Even when the trail got steeper, it was no longer intimidating to me. Everything being relative, I'd already ridden steep and dangerous, so this seemed effortless. The forest was quiet this morning. All big game animals had long gone to the high country to find refuge from the heat. Only coyotes stayed, feasting on the still plentiful hare and rodent population.

Coming to the fork in the trail, we followed the west branch for another mile then dismounted at a clearing where the fir and pine trees looked smaller. We led our horses around until finding the remains of a cabin. Its roof was gone and only two log sides were still standing, but it definitely had been someone's cabin. Whether it was Jeremiah Johnson's or not, who knows. Glenn swears that it was.

As we descended the forest trail back toward the ranch, I noticed thunderclouds coming in. We hurried the best we could down the rough trail. About a mile from the ranch, in open terrain, it started pouring. Lightning burst from the skies and thunderclaps followed.

I said, "Riding out in the open like this is risky, but I don't know any better trail to take and there is no cover that I can see."

I donned my rain slicker, which I always tied on back of my saddle, and we kept plodding on toward the ranch amidst the rain, thunder and lightning. We returned to the corrals safely, although Ann and Debby were rain-soaked and cold.

* * * *

We must have been destined for adventure as we planned to go tubing down a creek the next Tuesday afternoon. Ann and Debby had tried tubing down Green Creek, but it was too shallow and their butts hit too many rocks. Debby had jogged in the area of a creek about ten miles west of the ranch, and it looked to her like it would be deep enough to be great tubing. I was game. I'd never tried tubing and it sounded fun to me.

Debby got truck tubes from a garage in Cody, inflated them, and tied them down in the bed of her Chevy S-10. We had to take two vehicles, so I drove my car, following Ann and Debby. We stopped at the first bridge over the creek and I parked my car. This way we would have a ride back up stream to Debby's truck once we had 'tubed' down the creek. That turned out to be a very good plan as it eliminated our walking—unknowingly—in grizzly country.

We put our tubes in the creek about 3-4 miles up from my car, figuring that was far enough to tube for our first time there. Luckily, we had worn shorts, T-shirts and sneakers because at times we scraped against bushes and tree branches hanging over the water's edge and had to push away with our feet. But what fun we had floating downstream on such a lovely warm day, no noise, only us and our tubes—we thought.

About a half hour had passed when Debby said, "I think the next bridge is where your car is parked, Pat."

I glanced her way and said, "Holy Crap! There's a bear over there on the bank behind you—and I think it's a grizzly!"

"What do we do, now?" Ann, always the calm one, said in a whisper. As if the bear cared how loud we spoke.

"I don't know about you, but I'm not stopping to say 'Howdy'," Debby replied as she began paddling furiously with her hands and kicking her feet to make the tube go faster.

I said, "Let's just keep going downstream and maybe the bear will stay where it is." Luckily we were in pretty swift current and we swept right by. Was I scared? You bet—I was petrified! I kept looking behind me to see if the bear was coming after us. I hoped it was hungrier for fish than for females.

In complete silence, we continued tubing until we came to the bridge where I'd parked my car. We stopped at the edge of the creek and elected Debby, the runner, to scout out the road to see if Mr. or Mrs. Bear was around.

"All clear," Debby hollered. We ran to my car and jumped in, leaving the tubes behind.

"Okay, now I hope we don't meet up with that bear on this dirt road because I don't know what it will do, and there is not room to turn my car around if it charges," I said.

We weren't exactly city girls and we knew about bears. However, this was a grizzly, and none of us knew anything about grizzly behavior. We only hoped we would not see it again. As luck would have it, we did see the bear again about half way to Debby's truck. However, it was on the other side of the creek moving away. The bear was gone by the time we drove both vehicles back to the main road. We returned to the ranch safe, but still shaken.

We hadn't asked anyone about tubing at that creek as it didn't seem necessary at the time. Later, we learned the name of the creek was *Grizzly* Creek, and it was a prime location for grizzly bears. Our ignorance and brashness could have cost us our lives. As it turned out, we got a well-deserved dressing down by Alice when she found out.

"Don't ever take off on your own again without telling me where you're going," Alice scolded. "You girls don't know this area, and we're responsible for you while you live here and work for us."

Her point was well taken, and remembered.

Chapter 19

I was ready for a good night's sleep, hoping I wouldn't dream of being chased by grizzly bears. Entering my cabin, I flicked on the lights, started undressing and got a weird feeling of being watched. I slowly looked around . . . then screamed.

There was a cowboy boot sticking out from someone (or something) sitting on my toilet. After careful investigation, with my flashlight in hand for protection, I found the intruder to be the ranch's stuffed, cowboy-mannequin mascot. About that time, I heard peals of laughing outside and knew I'd been the brunt of another joke.

I couldn't blame Ryan this time as he was gone on a pack trip until Friday. I stormed out the door and saw Frank rolling around on the ground in a fit of laughter. I went over and kicked him in the butt, saying a few choice cuss words to him. Pier, Ann, Mary, and Scott sat on the ladies' bunkhouse steps chuckling. I brought the cowboy mannequin outside with me to sit where we all had a good laugh and a beer.

Chief told each wrangler that he or she would get a chance to work on a pack trip at least once during the summer. This week was Ryan's turn. To make up for the one missing wrangler each week for the next few weeks, Chief hired a new wrangler— *new* being the operative word.

Mike was the son of longtime guests and friends of Glenn and Alice. He was from the Midwest and had the desire to become a mountain wrangler during fall hunting pack trips.

He was to apprentice at the ranch for the rest of the summer. However, he had *never* been around horses.

Chief said to teach Mike everything he'd have to know about being a wrangler. So we began. I found it difficult training someone who knew nothing about basic horsemanship, saddling, riding, or guiding. The first day I inspected his horse after he'd tacked it up and found he'd put the bridle on the horse—with the bit *outside* the mouth, under the jaw. Mike was a real nice young man but he had a lot to learn.

He claimed Ace as his wrangle horse and learned how to saddle and bridle him correctly. As the newest wrangler, he had to wrangle every day until Ryan returned. By the end of the summer, I had to give him his due; he'd persevered and eventually made a fine wrangler.

* * * *

Over the weeks several guests suggested some hands-on lessons in horsemanship. The ranch schedule was full, and all wranglers were usually busy so there never seemed to be time enough. Now with an extra wrangler around, Chief asked us about teaching an hour-long class. No one volunteered.

He said, "How about you, Pat. You can teach them, can't you?"

"I can do something after lunch on Mondays if another wrangler will help me and demonstrate while I talk." It would cut into my free time, but I reckoned it was only an hour and doable. The other wranglers agreed to take turns helping me. We'd give guests the option of trail riding or horse lessons in the rodeo corral.

I planned to teach guests useful horse knowledge rather than concentrate on riding 'heels down,' 'elbows in,' etc. I began by describing the use of the bridle and bit, stressing that the bit was not a brake mechanism; it was a communication tool, and to use it gently. Scott demonstrated how to saddle a horse while I explained the use of breast collars, stirrups, saddle blankets, and cinching—not too tight, not too loose.

I said to the guests, "You can help us by observing a few things yourself. For instance, if you find yourself riding on your horse's neck, or your saddle is slipping to one side, please bring it to a wrangler's attention. It may be that your saddle cinch needs to be tightened—and please let us decide that, not you— or your saddle may not fit your horse properly and we'll change it as soon as we can.

"Another thing to notice is: saddle blankets. They sometimes slip. If this happens to you or you see it happening to someone riding in front of you, please tell the nearest wrangler. It's simple to correct, but dangerous if they slip out from under the saddle."

I told the guests about horse language, how to tell what horses were thinking. "This comes in very handy preventing accidents or mishaps, like being kicked, bitten or bucked off. "Watch their ears. They are signaling devices. If they lay them *flat* back, look out. They are planning to bite the horse in front of them or kick the horse behind. Either way, take up your reins, nudge him in his sides with your heels and move him out of the way.

"If a horse is happy, his ears will be forward. If he's questioning something, one ear will be forward, the other halfway back or almost pointing at what he is asking about. If they are both partway back, he may be nervous if his body is also tense, or he may be lazy if his body and ears are relaxed. Don't worry about halfway back, only *flat* back.

"Any questions?"

"Yes," said one female guest. "Why did Glenn tell us not to let our horses eat grass while we're riding?"

"Good question," I replied. "It's a matter of dominance. With a horse, there is never an equal, not between horses, not between horse and rider. One is always the boss. We would rather *you* be the boss; things will go better for you and the rest of the riders.

"That doesn't mean you tell your horse where he/she should step. You don't have to guide them as they know these trails and how to best negotiate them much better than you. So let your horses do their jobs. What I'm talking about is getting their respect so they will pay attention to your commands, for instance—if you need your horse to move out of the way quickly.

"And you don't have to beat him or abuse him to get his attention.

"If you have let him graze anytime he wants or poke along as slow he wants, he will not respect your commands. He will think he's the boss, and he intends to stay that way.

"The simplest way for you to show your horse that you are the boss, right from the start—today, Monday—is to *not* let them eat grass while you are riding. You can easily control that by keeping the reins short enough so that he can't put his head down to graze. That simple act alone will show him that *you* are the boss and *you* decide what he is to do, not him. And don't give in, even once, or you'll lose your dominance.

"Another reason for not letting your horse graze is safety. If a horse stops to eat, all horses behind him in line have to stop, and they might be at a place on the trail where it's dangerous to stop. So try not to have this happen. Keep them moving, not eating."

I wound down my talk by having Scott name and show the major parts of a horse's body and explain what their functions were.

Glenn had walked down to the rodeo arena, where I was giving my talk. When I'd finished and we were heading back to the corrals, he said, "Good job, I think that's what they wanted to learn. We'll do that again next week."

Chapter 20

Guests came and went weekly, their names disappearing when the next group arrived. However, some left an impression. Amanda was such a guest. She came from Connecticut with her sister to ride not raft down the Shoshone or sightsee in Yellowstone. She rode every day, morning and afternoon. On Friday she and I did the Eagle Cliffs Ride. I rode Crystal again, and Amanda was astride long-legged Rowdy.

We had a lot in common and chatted as we rode. We both skied and were businesswomen in our real, other lives. We neared the halfway point up the ledges when I suddenly realized that she had become quiet.

I looked over my shoulder to make sure she was still behind me and said, "Are you okay? You're awfully quiet all of a sudden."

"I have a problem with vertigo, but I'm trying to live with it and I'm alright," she replied.

"Let me know if you get sick, dizzy, or need to stop," knowing that there was no real good place to stop on these ledges.

I wished Amanda had said something about her phobia earlier, I could have found an easier trail to test her fortitude. Although I greatly respected her desire to overcome her phobia, Eagle Cliffs Trail was definitely not the trail one should ride if one has vertigo.

* * * *

Judge J was another memorable guest. He was a retired New York Supreme Court Judge in his late 70's and had been a guest at Rimrock for the past 25 years. He sometimes repeated questions when meeting people, but he always remembered everyone's name. I was impressed. That was more than I could do at my younger age.

Alice asked me to guide him on a solo ride around the ranch, advising me that the judge couldn't see too well.

"You'll need to tell him if he should duck under limbs or any other problem that he might find it necessary to prepare for while riding. He always rides Hugo, who is the best trail horse here on the ranch, but Hugo won't necessarily look out for the judge. You'll have to do that."

Whereas Judge J was getting frail, four male wranglers helped him mount, but once astride, he was fairly well-balanced. I guided him across Canyon Creek and immediately Judge J asked me to turn left and take a trail through the cottonwoods that followed north along the creek. This was a new one to me, and I gladly guided him on the newly discovered trail. We rode around the Introductory Loop, with a few new variations, as requested by Judge J. We returned to the ranch with no mishaps. He was a wise and delightful gentleman.

* * * *

A guest had been observing two of the wranglers trying, unsuccessfully for a half-hour, to put shoes on Nemo's hind feet. They couldn't even get near his hind quarters without the horse kicking out. The guest asked Glenn if he could show them a training technique new to the West but growing in popularity around the country. The method was called 'round penning.' He said that his demonstration might be of interest to some of the other guests and wranglers, and he'd do it after lunch.

I had heard of round-pen training and was anxious to see it demonstrated. I was very interested in any kind of horse training, hoping to have some time to work with the ranch's wild mustang colts and fillies purchased from the Bureau of Land Management last spring.

Chief also showed up at the small corral. All cowboys used to, and most still did, train a horse by 'breaking' it. They'd rope the horse, force a halter onto it, as well as hog-tie it if it moved too much. This meant snubbing its nose close to a post and tying up one leg so it couldn't move. They'd throw on a blanket, a saddle, and mount, then someone else would untie the horse and throw the lead rope to the rider and away they'd go. The scared horse bucked around the corral until it got so tired it couldn't buck any more. That may have shown the horse that the cowboy was dominant, but it sure didn't teach the horse to trust or respect humans. Therefore, horses were not safe for novices to ride until they were nearing seven years old. This new technique would be interesting.

The guest, Rodney, first took Nemo's halter off and then made him move around the pen by stepping toward him every time he stopped and making a clicking sound with his mouth. Then Rodney stepped it up a notch and forced Nemo to trot round the pen, making the clicking sound and tossing the end of a lariat close to the horse's rear if he slowed. At times Rodney would step toward the front of the horse, facing it, holding his near-arm out straight shaking the rope, while pointing with his other arm to the opposite direction. The horse would turn and trot in the other direction.

After about ten minutes, Nemo stopped and faced Rodney, making a chewing movement with his mouth, looking him right in the eye. Rodney walked up to the horse, patted him on the forehead, neck and front quarters, then walked toward the center of the pen clicking as he went. Nemo followed. Rodney patted him all over this time, including his hindquarters and his hind legs. The horse fidgeted a bit, and Rodney sent him off at a trot again.

A few more times around and Nemo stopped and faced Rodney again. Once more he went through his patting routine then reached for Nemo's hind leg. Nemo stood still. Rodney picked it up, and Nemo's ears flicked back but he didn't move. Rodney crossed to the other side, patted the horse and reached to pick up the off rear leg. Nemo kicked out and got sent around the pen a few times more at a canter.

The next time Nemo stopped, Rodney picked up his hooves one at a time, cleaned them out then set them back down. The horse stood at ease and never moved.

The guests clapped. Chief and the boys were impressed. After putting Nemo back in the shoeing area, they went to talk to Rodney and find out more about this method. I understood: It was all about dominance. Young and unruly horses were safer to work with from the ground. This was a safe and effective way of using the horse's natural herd instinct of acquiescing to the dominant animal—in this case, Rodney.

Good job, Rodney.

I figured I would try this method on the young wild horses. They were still in a pasture just off the driveway and not turned out with the main herd. I could work with them evenings, right after supper.

I worked with each of the three yearling fillies, first. I got them to the round pen with the assistance of another wrangler. Usually Pier was willing to help. At first I just made them move at a walk, then pushed them to a trot, changing directions periodically. These fillies were used to acquiescing, as youngsters always acknowledge older horses as dominant. They quickly accepted me as their alpha leader.

All I could do to these yearlings was teach them to lead and stand tied while I brushed, groomed and picked up their feet. I accomplished this with alacrity.

Next, I wanted to work with Shiloh, a two and a half-year-old pinto. His disposition was friendly and he showed no fear of humans. He accepted my dominance with surprising speed. I led him everywhere within walking distance of the corrals.

Over the next few weeks, I proceeded to put a bridle on him and got him to accept a bit in his mouth. I sacked him out with a blanket, rain slicker, and anything else I could find that might spook him. Shiloh was unfazed.

I found a lightweight ladies' saddle, strapped it on him, and let him run and buck in the round pen. When he'd gotten used to it, I stepped up to him, quietly got on him, sat there a minute patting him, and dismounted. For the next couple of times that was all I did, sitting on his back longer each time. Soon I was riding him around the pen at a walk. He was not old enough or big enough yet to train on the trail. I hoped whoever worked with him in the next year(s) would be as gentle with him. Shiloh would never need to be *broken*, just trained.

* * * *

Glenn said he soon had an unusually large pack trip going over Eagle Pass into Yellowstone National Park with a group from New York City. He asked me to go along as an extra wrangler and public relations person. Apparently the group leader, Sandy, was apt to be finicky and fussy, and Glenn seemed to think I could handle her attitude! I had my doubts, but agreed to go along as I'd heard the trip over Eagle Pass was spectacular. I'd also be interested in seeing Yellowstone Park's new forest growth after burning in the big fires a few years past.

I hoped to hear from Dustin before I left on a pack trip for a week or more, or our paths might not cross again all summer.

Chapter 21

Friday evening Glenn told me that my pack trip would be leaving on Sunday. Luckily, Dustin called Saturday evening. He chuckled when I told him I was leaving tomorrow to pack over Eagle Pass into Yellowstone.

"I've just returned from that area and I'm going back out Monday. We'll follow Clear Creek to Yellowstone Lake, down the Yellowstone River to Mountain Creek then back through Eagle Pass. We'll be camped at Eagle Creek Meadow Thursday night and pack out Friday."

"I don't know our exact route or timing," I replied, "only that we're staying at Eagle Creek Meadow the first and the last nights out. We leave Sunday and are supposed to be back Friday. Wow, that puts us at the meadow on Thursday night, also. Can we all camp there at the same time?"

"No problem, the meadow is at least three miles long, and there are three different camping spots spread throughout the valley."

"It would be cool if we spent the night in the same valley. I'd really like to see you again." I said wishfully.

"It wouldn't be cool if we spent the night together, hon; it would be more like hot. Maybe we can take a pack trip together at the end of the season."

"I'd like that. Guess we'll just have to wait and see what happens." We said our goodbyes, hoping to meet up on the trail.

I made ready for tomorrow's trek, packing a duffel

bag with warm clothes: heavy sweater, wool socks, and long underwear. I'd wear chaps, light jacket, and gloves, tie a heavy jacket and slicker onto my saddle, and put a scarf, extra socks and another pair of gloves in my saddlebag. I'd ridden over the Continental Divide twice before and knew that it could rain or snow at any time in high elevation, and I wanted to be neither wet nor cold.

Glenn had told me to put my horse in the local pasture with the young mustangs while I was gone.

"Raisin doesn't have a brand on him like the rest of our horses, and he looks real nice down in the highway pastures. But he's also too friendly and a traveler might be tempted to load him up and take him away."

At least I knew my horse would be safe near the ranch. I also asked Cort to check on Razan occasionally.

* * * *

There were seven guests from New York City, all friends or relatives, and one lady, Anne, from Rhode Island going on the pack trip. Glenn had given Anne a free trip because she'd broken her wrist while walking down Rampart Pass on a previous pack trip and never complained or asked for special treatment. She was a good sport and Glenn appreciated her 'cowgirl' attitude. I had met her on my first pack trip. We were two of eight guests riding to Jackson Hole. It would be nice to see her again.

Five black packhorses, Gerald's guide horse Cowtown, and four riding horses were already in corrals at the Eagle Creek trailhead. They could stay there from one trek to another as long as there were only a couple of days in between treks. It was up to the trail guides to make sure the horses were watered and fed daily.

Early Sunday morning, Gerald and Trampus loaded the dark bays, Nemo, Earl, Beauty, Dixie, Sankey, Brownie, Bomber, Badger, Cassie, Cub, and Jubilee into the horse van and took them to the trailhead. The truck carried horse tack, chairs, guest tents and tarps. As soon as they arrived at the trailhead they fed and watered all the animals and then started sorting and packing. It would take three to four hours to get it all done.

Liz and I followed with a truck filled with the food panniers and cooking equipment. Liz was the ranch breakfast cook and substitute pack-trip cook. She was replacing Frank, who had a family wedding to attend in Montana. I was to ride Stubby, Frank's usual mountain horse, and Liz would ride Dixie.

Packing horses was very precise and difficult work. Fortunately, Gerald and Trampus had a lot of previous experience and began strapping the packsaddles onto the pack horses. Liz was busy filling panniers with foodstuffs. One would be filled and placed on each side of the pack animal. Cook gear, bedrolls, duffels, and tents were then placed on top of the panniers and covered by tarps tied down with rope.

My job was to saddle the riding horses. That meant I had to groom, blanket, saddle and bridle twelve horses, every day. I wanted to be a cowgirl and this was part of it—*So enjoy it*, I told myself.

The van carrying the guests arrived, and their duffels were prepared for packing. The guests stood around socializing until all packhorses were packed and riding horses, saddled. Anne had immediately come to my aid, helping me tack up the last of the riding horses. I appreciated her help and thanked her profusely.

Gerald assigned a riding horse to each guest. Trampus and I fitted their stirrups, giving them a few basic instructions, i.e. do not lag behind, and do not crowd each other on the trail.

"Mount up, let's move out," Gerald said.

Chapter 22

From the trailhead, the pack trippers immediately crossed Eagle Creek with Gerald leading a string of five packhorses and Trampus leading a string of four. Liz followed next, then the New York City guests, then Anne. I bought up the rear.

Eagle Creek proved too deep for Sankey, a small but sturdy packhorse, and he lost his footing. He would have been swept down river except that he was tied to the other packhorses and they pulled him across. His pack kept him afloat. Some bedding got wet, however Sankey wasn't upset; he ate grass on the other side while waiting for the rest of us to cross.

That was too much excitement already for Cindy, one of the city guests. She refused to cross the river riding Earl.

Gerald yelled, "Pat, grab Earl's reins and lead him across. Cindy, you stay in the saddle and do not move. It's either ride or swim."

Once we were on the trail, things settled down. The trail wound smoothly through the tranquil forest. I even spotted a moose hiding in some swamp brush watching us. The trail gradually ascended hills once parched by fire, then descended toward the creek again. At noon, Liz, the guests and I stopped alongside the creek and ate cold bag lunches while the guides and packhorses kept traveling toward the campsite.

Late afternoon we arrived at Eagle Creek Meadow, also known as Three Mile Meadow. The camp was set up at the third and farthest away campsite. The guests' tents were erected and the cook's tent assembled. Gerald was chopping wood for the fire; Trampus was tethering two of the mares, Cassie and Brownie, and the packhorses were grazing unrestrained nearby.

I turned the remaining horses loose to graze after I'd unsaddled them. I placed each saddle, with blankets and bridle, on a long log and covered them all with a tarp in case of rain. Next I collected my duffel and set about putting up my own tent. I was the last one to claim a bedroll and pillow. Unfortunately, the remaining bedroll was— the one that got wet when Sankey fell in the creek. I strung a line near the fire to dry the bedding. It was only partly dry when I put it in my tent that night. I found I was so tired, I slept soundly, wet bedding and all.

Morning brought fog and two young moose playing behind my tent in the tall grasses. I watched them for a while before getting up and telling the others. I found the fire roaring and coffee hot. Pack-trip coffee is not brewed, and definitely not instant. A metal coffeepot filled with water is put onto the open fire. Once boiling, loose coffee grounds are dumped in and the pot set aside to simmer. After a few minutes, an eggshell is dropped into the coffee to collect the grounds to the bottom of the pot, and the coffee is ready to drink—strong but good.

I had retired to my tent early last evening and missed some of the guests' requests and complaints. Gerald said that Sandy and her sister, Cindy, complained because they found pine needles in their tent. He said, "I think they expected a five-star hotel with a chocolate on their pillow. I handed them a dustpan and asked if there was anything else I could help them with.

"They also wanted to know where the bathroom was . . . I showed them the spade and toilet paper and said, 'Anywhere you want.' They huffed and went back into their tent. They may start turning brown with constipation if they don't learn how to poop in the woods before we get back on Friday."

The men guests complained about the ground being hard; the ladies were late for breakfast. Liz held off throwing breakfast in the fire as long as she could, but the outfit was moving over

Eagle Pass and everyone needed to get started. The city ladies were roused out of their tent at nine. Breakfast time had been at seven.

Before continuing up the pass, Gerald decided he had better get a few things straight with the guests: "I heard a lot of complaining last night and this morning, about too dirty, too cold, too hard, etc. The brochures that were sent you said, 'This trip is a progressive trek for six days and five nights, covering fifteen miles each day on horseback over mountains and sleeping in two-person tents on the ground at night.' It was never billed as a plush, easy ride, with hot showers and a feather bed at the end of each day.

"Now, we can turn around and go back to the ranch if that's what you want. But if we continue on over the pass to Yellowstone Park, I don't want to hear any more complaining or bellyaching. *You* decide, and tell me in the next ten minutes which way we go."

Everyone was silent.

Finally, the guests held a whispered conference. The consensus was to continue over the pass and stop complaining.

The Eagle Pass Trail climbed steeply through forested switchbacks until just before reaching the summit of near 9600 feet. There the trail crossed open ledges. Looking over the trailside at the terrain dropping a few hundred feet caused most first timers to become anxious. Cindy was petrified. Earl was as cautious and surefooted as a horse could be, but Cindy wasn't mollified. She wanted to get off her horse and walk. Unfortunately there was no place for her to dismount; the trail was only a couple of feet wide and the slope dangerously steep.

Gerald had reached the summit and upon hearing Cindy's crying tantrum, tied Cowtown and his pack string to stubby trees. He walked back, urging the others to find a tree limb or shrub and tie up at the summit near his horses. I was behind Cindy and unable to pass or dismount to help. Gerald appeared and, just short of threatening Cindy with bodily harm, told her to stop crying, keep her mouth shut, and he'd lead her and Earl the rest of the way to the summit.

We all took a badly needed break before descending to Howell Creek and easier riding. Gerald placed Cindy between his pack team and Trampus's so they could keep track of her. I was thankful. Putting up with Cindy's hysterical tantrums was more than I'd bargained for. Riding at the rear, behind the trekkers, was again peaceful and quiet.

We were now in Yellowstone National Park.

Gerald had planned to camp on the Yellowstone River and fish for the legendary Yellowstone cutthroat trout. However, the guests were only interested in reaching a campsite. Therefore, we stopped to camp a few miles before the river, along Mountain Creek, in an area previously burned in the Yellowstone fires. Fresh green grasses and growths of new pine trees surrounded charred tree trunks on still burnt ground. One life gone, another life begins.

For supper Liz prepared Italian spaghetti and meatballs, tossed salad and garlic bread. Tom, Sandy's brother, opened two bottles of merlot wine and shared it with everyone. Tasty blueberry tarts cooked over hot embers were dessert.

Anne and I shared a tent that night, as it meant one less tent to put up and take down. Early the next morning we heard rustling outside. Something was nuzzling our tent. We'd all been warned that this was 'grizzly country' and we should never have any food or gum in our tent—we didn't—but the rustling continued. Neither of us dared unzip the tent flap to look outside. We waited silently until we heard Gerald and Liz talking in the cook tent. The rustling turned out to be our horses grazing around our tent. Whew!

However, later that morning, while following the Yellowstone River, Gerald pointed out a female grizzly and her cub climbing the hillside across the river. When we stopped for lunch, Trampus noticed fresh grizzly prints in the sand, and nearby were large grizzly scat piles that were almost the size of horse manure piles. These were constant reminders of the presence of grizzlies. Gerald told us the grizzly numbers had increased substantially and were now under consideration to be removed from the Endangered Species List. Every night our food supplies were hoisted ten feet high and hung between trees—out of grizzly reach.

We followed the river valley to a point near the confluence of the Thorofare and Yellowstone Rivers, then rode east to the Thorofare Ranger Station. The log cabin, barn and corrals were historic structures nestled next to a hillside. No one was there. Such peace, quiet and solitude are hard to find nowadays. I immediately fell in love with the area.

Gerald said, "This territory around the ranger station is considered the most remote place in the continental United States. The region is called the Thorofare because it's wide and easy to travel. For centuries, Indians and fur trappers used this route. Mountain man Jim Bridger named the nearby Bridger Lake. This valley is approximately fourteen miles long and three miles wide and remains just as wild and free as it was two hundred years ago. We Americans are fortunate to have such a designated wilderness area as this."

I wondered if the city slickers appreciated being here.

We set up early camp along the Thorofare River, just beyond the ranger station. *What a spectacular place to camp*, I thought. *If Dustin and I ever get to go packing, this is where I would like to pitch our tent.*

Camp was all set up by mid-afternoon. The sun was shining brightly and blue skies were abundant. There was plenty of time to take a hike and explore, or take a swim in the peaceful, sublime river. The guests chose to relax in the folding camp chairs and read. Gerald intended to replace shoes on a couple of his horses. Trampus, with spade in hand, prepared to dig a pit for Liz to cook a roast in the ground for tonight's supper. I wanted to test the water to feel how cold it was, as I'd like to swim and wash my hair if it wasn't too cold.

Anne joined me at the water's edge; both of us wore shorts and had towels draped over our shoulders. I stepped in first, knee deep off a rock, and immediately stepped out. "I can't believe it's that cold!" I tried it again in a shallow place by the edge of the river. "This water is colder than the Atlantic Ocean along the Maine coast."

We finally asked Liz for a cooking pan, which we used to pour the river water over our hair before and after lathering with shampoo. "Brrrrrr," said Anne between chattering teeth. "This is as far as I'm getting into this ice water."

"Me too, I'll just wash strategic places with a soapy cloth and call it good until I get back to the ranch to shower."

We met Trampus on our way back to our tent, and he laughed at our tale of woe. "Of course the river's cold. It's snowmelt directly from those mountain tops over there." He pointed northeast to snowcapped peaks no more than five miles away. "Heat water over the fire and use a wash pan like us mountain wranglers do. It's a lot more comfortable, and we don't have to prove how tough we are to anyone." He smiled and continued digging the fire-pit. *What a smart-ass*, I thought. *Good thing he's easy to look at.*

Anne and I felt a little foolish at our naiveté, but we were cleaner anyway.

Twenty horses, eighty hooves thundering down the valley, woke me the next morning. Trampus was driving them to the river to drink before being packed and tacked up for the day's ride. I slipped into my jeans and boots, strapped on my chaps and donned my jacket, gloves and hat. Mornings were beautiful but chilly here in the valley. I gathered the horses' grain cubes from the cook tent and emptied them into two large ground-buckets. This would entice the horses to stay around until I slipped halters onto them and tied them to trees.

The aroma of hotcakes, eggs and bacon frying permeated the air, drawing guests, both men and women, from their tents. Gerald had told them that today's trek would be easy, and they were actually looking forward to riding. The group rode south and west around Bridger Lake then followed the Yellowstone River north to Mountain Creek. The ride up the valley was quiet and effortless. The guests enjoyed it, and pleasing them was important. *I* looked forward to climbing Eagle Pass again.

We camped at the confluence of Mountain and Howell Creek, not far from where we had camped two nights ago. Apparently, it had just dawned on the guests that we had been riding back on the same trail that we had ridden in on coming down off from Eagle Pass.

In a state of panic, Cindy asked Gerald, "Do we have to go over that same pass again?"

"Yep."

"Can't we go home another way?"

"Nope."

"Is there any way I can get home without riding Earl?"

"Yep, you can walk; we'll lead Earl."

"Can you call a helicopter to come get me?"

"Nope, not unless you break an arm or leg, or have a heart attack. You'd be wasting their valuable time, and I won't do it."

"I think I'm going to be sick."

"We'll help you the best we can. Have a little faith in us. We've been packing over mountain passes for quite a few years, and we've never lost a guest yet.

"Horses, yes—guests, no," he muttered, mostly to himself.

* * * *

Just before dawn the next morning, the camp awoke suddenly to—rattle, bang, clatter, clang.

"Oh, no. I don't even want to think about what that noise is," I whispered to Anne. "I'm staying inside this tent until sunup or until I hear familiar voices outside."

When the sun surfaced, Gerald told us that there had been a bear rummaging around in the cook's tent. "Ordinarily I would have shot over its head to scare it off, but guns are illegal in Yellowstone Park. They want us to use pepper spray," he said rolling his eyes.

"I carry a 44-magnum in my pack, but I'd use it only if it was a life-threatening situation. I think it was a black bear not a grizzly, and it was just being nosey not threatening, so I rattled a few pans to scare it off."

Well now, this day had started out exhilarating. I wondered what excitement Eagle Pass would bring!

Gerald had—somewhat—convinced Cindy that it was safer to ride Earl across the open ledges of Eagle Pass and down the switchbacks, than for her to try to walk it herself. While everyone stopped at the top for a breather, he took me aside.

"Pat, will you lead Cindy and Earl from your horse? Keep her close and talk to her constantly to keep her mind off the steep terrain. Are you comfortable doing this?"

"Sure, I'll turn around and talk her through it. I'm riding Stubby, and he's negotiated steep trails for the past five years, according to Frank, so I shouldn't have to pay attention to him. We'll be okay."

And we were okay. I asked Cindy to look to my left—up the mountain—instead of ahead or down the fall line. When we reached the meadows below, she said to me, "Thank you so much, I owe you, big-time."

We rode the length of the Eagle Creek Meadow, stopping at the furthest and last campsite, as was customary among packers. This was done as a courtesy so if another outfitter used the valley to camp at the same time, they would not have to pass through a herd of horses grazing free on the lush, meadow grasses.

Gerald knew that Dustin might be camping in the same meadow that night so he told Trampus to tether three mares instead of two. If our horses happened to stray throughout the long meadow—and they might, smelling another herd around—

he, Trampus and I might have a difficult time rounding them up. Generally, with one or two mares staked near the campsite, at least one mare would be in heat. That meant some of the geldings would be sure to stay close, and where a group of horses remained, the whole herd would likely stay nearby. He also tied a bell around the necks of the hard-to-catch horses, Nemo and Bomber.

I erected my tent on the far outskirts of camp and asked Anne if she'd mind sleeping in her own tent that night, "Just in case I have company," I tried to say nonchalantly.

With a sly grin, Anne said, "I don't mind as long as you help me put it up and take it down in the morning. And, keep the noise to a minimum if you and Dustin get together!"

To my delight, Dustin came walking into our campsite that evening. He already knew Gerald and Trampus; I introduced him to Anne and to Sandy's city group. We all sat around the campfire and chatted for a while then drifted off to our tents.

There was not much chatter between Dustin and I once we got to my tent. For one, there was little to no privacy, and two, we had more urgent matters that needed taking care of.

Dustin awoke before dawn. "Listen."

"I don't hear anything," I replied.

"That's the problem, no noise. No snorting, blowing, whinnying, no bells tinkling, no hooves stamping, or rustling of grasses—too quiet. I'm going to awaken Gerald and see what's up."

Unfortunately, Rimrock's horses did *not* stay close that night.

At daybreak Dustin, Gerald and Trampus saddled the three lone mares and set off to find the others. Soon Trampus came back with a few of the blacks. "Pat, you need to saddle a horse and come help. Our horses are all intermixed with Dustin's, and we need to separate them and bring ours back."

"I don't have my horse," I reminded him, "He was turned out with the rest."

"Ebony is saddle-broke, although he hasn't been ridden for a long time. Throw a saddle on him and come with me.

"Liz and Anne, can you halter and tie the other four I brought back so they don't follow us? Thanks."

I saddled Ebony. He was full of nervous energy and wanted to go. I had to lead him to a tree stump to mount up; he was half Percheron and seventeen hands. Ebony crow-hopped across the campsite before finally settling down to a consistent trot. I followed a grinning Trampus.

"Hey, cowgirl, I didn't know you could ride that well. Good job staying on." Trampus said as we rode up the meadow looking for any stray horses along the way.

"I didn't just come off the city streets, you know. I can ride. But, it's a good thing he stopped bucking when he did because I don't think I could have stayed on much longer."

We spotted Gerald and Dustin each attempting to cut out their own horses from the combined group of nearly thirty horses. Dustin's wrangler joined him, and with Trampus and my help, the cutting was more successful. Trampus roped Elvira, who was a half-sister to Ebony, handed the lariat to me and said, "Why don't you lead her back to the campsite. Start slowly. Gerald is roping Cowtown, who's another dominant horse, and will lead him back too. I'll round up the rest and hopefully they'll follow you guys."

They did.

Crisis over.

Even with the extra ride down the meadow, it was still early, so Gerald sent me to bring back Brownie, the Rimrock mare Dustin had been riding during the roundup. I saddled Stubby this time and really enjoyed the morning ride alone. I spotted a bull moose at the far edge of the meadow and jumped two mule deer out of a thicket of brush.

Dustin greeted me as I approached his camp.

"Would you like some breakfast before you ride back across the meadow, again? It's all ready."

"Love some."

I was hungry and quickly devoured scrambled eggs with sausage and some homefries. "I'd better be heading back or Gerald will be wondering if I got ambushed by moose or something."

Dustin held Stubby while I mounted and handed Brownie's reins to me. He put his hand on my leg and reached up to kiss me. "Well cowgirl, it was a lovely night but morning came way too soon. I'll call you in between trips, okay?

"Take care."

"You too, glad we could meet up here in the meadow, nice place. See ya . . . soon I hope."

Back at my campsite, the blacks had their packtrees strapped on, waiting the panniers and camp gear. I caught the remaining saddle horses and started grooming. Anne came over to help. "Nice guy, this Dustin cowboy, huh?"

"Yeah, I think so. Wish I could pack with him for a while."

"Maybe next summer," Anne said with a wink.

"Maybe, we'll see."

The return trek was quiet and uneventful. Sankey managed to stay upright traversing Eagle Creek, and even the guests were serene and seemed melancholy upon reaching the trailhead. Sandy actually told me, "We've had the experience of our lifetime." She didn't clarify if it was good or bad—I didn't ask.

Rimrock's van was waiting to take the guests back to their motel in Cody. Anne and I said our good-byes to each other and promised to keep in touch.

While I piled the saddles, breast collars, blankets and bridles into the back of the waiting pickup Pier had driven to the trailhead, Liz and Pier loaded the panniers and the five extra tents. Liz and I rode back to the ranch with Pier. Gerald and Trampus would follow with five of the horses loaded in the horse van, once they fed and watered the horses that were to remain at the corrals.

They had a small pack trip leaving Sunday, a group of five guests. Pier would replace Trampus as wrangler, as he had to get ready to go back to college. Frank would return as pack cook.

Chapter 23

At the ranch, I returned each saddle to its numbered spot in the saddle shed then ran to take a shower. I couldn't remember when I'd been this dirty, for this long. *Ah, hot running water at last,* I thought as I soaked, standing at least five minutes under the shower.

My second duty was to see how my horse had fared while I'd been gone. Razan trotted over to me in response to my whistle; so did the young mustangs. Razan was bigger, older and in charge. He'd gained a little weight from lack of exercise and grazing on irrigated pasture grass. I thought he looked good. I left him there until I talked with Chief about where to put him next.

When I checked into the lodge for mail, I found a message from the Horsin' Around Transport Company. They would be in the Cody area this Thursday and could pick my horse up to take him back to Maine. I was to call them immediately. That meant I'd have to schedule a vet check before Thursday.

Returning to ranch life, after packing out for a week, was like having jet lag and culture shock all at once. I found it difficult to get back up to speed. To make matters worse, things were changing at the ranch—much to my chagrin. Trampus and Cortney left Wednesday to find a house to rent for the four of them—Trampus, Scott, Cort, and Ryan—in Bozeman while they attended Montana State University. Grady had gone back to Utah.

There was a new wrangler, Bill, an older cowboy who would help take up the slack of the boys leaving early. He would remain, as would Mike, to work as wrangler through hunting season. Pier and I would stay through the end of August.

After I sent Razan back to Maine with the horse transport company, I spent time working evenings with the mustangs, but I missed having my own horse to ride on my days off. I also missed Dustin. He was still packing and wouldn't have any free time until Labor Day Weekend. We'd made plans to get together then. However, this Sunday I was off, with nothing to do.

Pier and I had previously talked about making a *sojourn* through Yellowstone Park to Jackson Hole, and this Sunday would be our last chance to go. I had never been into the town of Jackson, and Pier wanted to continue south to Big Piney to visit a cattle ranch where he'd worked the previous summer.

We didn't realize what a long trip we were making in just one day. We left before breakfast and encountered snow squalls as I drove through the East Entrance of the Park and carefully over Sylvan Pass. On the other side of the pass, a herd of buffalo crowded the highway along Yellowstone Lake, disrupting traffic. At West Thumb, we switched drivers and Pier drove south past Lewis Lake and out Yellowstone's South Entrance into the Grand Teton National Park.

There were no foothills here, which accentuated the Teton Range's dramatic rise from the plains to mountain tops. Jackson Lake reflected their rocky cliffs, glaciers, aspen groves and pine forests. I found something mesmerizing about looking at the majestic snow-capped peaks, hypnotic, like gazing into a fire. The view from the smaller Jenny Lake, nestled at the foot of the Grand Teton, was spectacular. I decided I'd also like to pack through this valley sometime. At this rate, I'd have to spend every summer packing, in order to see and experience all I wanted of the west.

Downtown Jackson was inundated with gift shops and art galleries catering to tourists. I decided I preferred the more relaxed atmosphere of Cody. Pier and I snapped pictures of each other under the Elkhorn Archways of Jackson's Town Square then ate lunch at Bubba's BBQ on West Broadway before proceeding to Big Piney.

Pier hadn't mentioned to me that Big Piney was *ninety* miles south of Jackson—no one was at the ranch—and *another ninety* miles to Farson, which was only mid-way through our trip! It was already two o'clock and we'd been traveling six hours. If we didn't get back by seven, in time for introductions, Alice would be very angry.

There was little traffic through Riverton and the Wind River Canyon, and we made good time. Through the flat land from Thermopolis to Cody, we exceeded the speed limit by at least twenty-five mph. We pulled into the ranch parking lot at 6:55 pm. Pier jumped out to get his guitar, while I quickly ran for the lodge.

We made it to the lodge just in time to sing Rimrock's welcoming song with the rest of the employees, still puffing and out of breath. We'd been gone twelve hours and the others chided us about eloping or thinking we had runaway together. We took the teasing in good humor; we were just glad to be back.

* * * *

Debby left to apprentice polo in Argentina the next week; I wished her the best. Scott and Ryan left for college. I had really liked working with the boys: Ryan, Scott, Cortney, and Trampus. I would miss them. They treated me as their equal and with respect.

On the other hand, Bill, the older cowboy, treated me as if I didn't know one end of a horse from the other. He was obnoxious, patronizing and chauvinistic. When Chief promoted me to head wrangler after Ryan left for college, things just got worse. He spat and said, "I'm not taking orders from any woman."

Chief replied, "You will, or you'll find another job."

Bill stayed, but his attitude didn't change. Thankfully, the other wranglers worked hard to make up for Bill's disrespect.

I did the best job I could, given the circumstances. I figured I only had two more weeks here anyway, so I just ignored Bill and his rude, sarcastic comments. I knew it was time to leave while I still had mostly good memories.

* * * *

Dustin called the Friday before Labor Day, and he and I made plans to meet at his cabin early the next Sunday morning.

Until then I had my gear to gather and pack, and good-byes to say. I hugged Glenn and Alice, wished them the best and hoped to see them again sometime. Glenn told me to take good care of *that Arab*. Alice smiled, thinking of her own Arabian. Pier and I agreed to keep in touch via letters.

I would miss the tranquil beauty of Wapiti Valley.

Chapter 24

I drove slowly toward Pahaska, reflecting on my summer experiences. Spending the next two days with Dustin would likely be my last adventure here in Wyoming.

I had never been to Dustin's cabin, but he'd given me driving directions from the Pahaska Tepee Resort, located just outside Yellowstone's East Entrance. I took the next left and drove about a half mile on a dirt road then spotted an A-frame cabin on my right.

Dustin came to meet me from his horse shed and corral area. It looked like he had only three horses in the corral.

"Hey, cowgirl, glad you found my place okay."

"Hey, yourself." I reached up and gave him a kiss on his cheek. "Where are the rest of your horses?"

"I took all but these three to my parents ranch to rest and fatten up before they have to endure hunting trips later this month and next. I kept this young paint mare here just for you. I think you'll like her; she's a five year old, half Arab/half Quarter horse. Name's Reena."

She stood about 14.3 hands and was nicely built, with good legs, soft intelligent eyes, wide forehead and small ears—very Arab looking. She also had a strong chest and rump—very Quarter-horse like. Her color was deep sorrel with a white strip down her face, four white stockings, and a large white patch on her left shoulder and right rump. Her mane, forelock and tail were black, brown and white. I liked the looks of her. "Is she trained for pack trips?"

"She's trained, but has never done a pack trip. I didn't want to take her out packing for the first time with guests on board. This will be good experience for her. Her dam is my mom's mare; we raised her."

"What about climbing the pass, will she be okay?"

"Well, we need to talk about that, hon. You said you'd like to ride up Eagle Pass and camp near the Thorofare, but that's not possible now. It snowed there last week, and the trail isn't safe for horses. So if it's okay with you, we'll just stay camped at Three Mile Meadow and explore."

"Fine by me."

"If you want to throw your gear in the truck bed and park your car over there by the cabin, I think we're about ready to go."

* * * *

We unloaded Dustin's truck and horse trailer at the trailhead and set to work getting the horses ready. He saddled my horse for me. It was nice being waited on for a change.

"Reena has a very soft mouth so I've been riding her with just a headstall and no bit. If you want, I'll put a snaffle on her," he said.

"No, that's fine. I frequently ride my horses with no bit when I'm on the trail."

Dustin's horse was a seasoned gelding that'd been lame most of the summer but was sound again now. He was a big bay Quarter-horse type with a white blaze and one white sock, named Cochise,

I helped Dustin finish packing the third horse, Runner. He showed me how to tie the pack with a double diamond hitch. I hoped I didn't have to remember that one.

We crossed the river without incident, and wound our way along the trail at a nice steady trot. Reena and I got along just fine, being an Arab (at least part), the mare responded well to my soft hands and a gentle touch. We arrived at the meadow early afternoon.

"Let's take the trail on the right and camp at the further end. I want to show you something."

About a mile down the meadow, Dustin pointed out a wrecked airplane in amongst some brush and trees. He said, "A few years ago someone crashed this plane, and for some reason, there it stays. No one ever claimed it or hauled it out of here. Looks a little out of place, don't you think?"

"That's weird. What, were they poaching and didn't want to get caught?"

"Probably, it's a large wilderness area for wardens to patrol, mostly by horseback. If they have a suspect they're hunting, then they might use a helicopter or small plane, otherwise they're on horseback."

We did an easy lope to the end of the meadow, had cold sandwiches for lunch and set up camp. After the horses were watered and staked out, Dustin asked, "Did you bring some foot gear you can hike in?"

"I've got sneakers with good tread."

"Let's hike part way up that mountain. There's an old mine we can explore." We both changed out of our cowboy boots into something we could wear hiking.

The afternoon was a pleasant fifty-five degrees and just right for hiking, although I was a little out of breath from the altitude. Once we reached the mine, we surveyed the entire length of the meadow settled in-between nine-thousand-foot peaks. All that remained to observe of the old mine was a decrepit shaft, but we did find two obsidian arrowhead tips and a flaking stone left behind from the arrowhead-carving process.

"Removing antique items is prohibited by the Antiquities Act," Dustin told me, so we stuck the arrowheads and stone back into the ground. The hike proved interesting and exhilarating.

After working up an appetite hiking, Dustin started

supper. I led the horses to a nearby stream to drink then fed them a container of grain cubes. Supper was steak, roasted potatoes, peas and carrots. We giggled and laughed while making smores over the coals, for dessert.

We stored the remaining food in a bear-resistant container chained to trees that had been left there by the warden service for just that purpose. The night was peaceful if you call being serenaded by wolves howling in the distance, peaceful. I snuggled close to Dustin.

* * * *

There was frost on the ground when I awoke in the morning. I could smell breakfast cooking and heard Dustin yell, "Come and get it, cowgirl." He had scrambled eggs, biscuits, bacon and coffee ready. *I could get used to this treatment*, I thought.

It was a chilly morning packing up. My fingers and toes kept getting cold and I had to warm them by the fire frequently.

"Boy, is it cold, or what?" I said between chattering teeth as we rode side by side down the meadow.

"And that, my dear, is why we do not pack into the mountains after August. It snows in the higher elevation anywhere from mid-August on, and it's too dangerous to try to take guests over the passes."

"So what'll you do for the next few months?"

"I have a couple of weeks off to prepare for hunting trips. We use base camps not progressive moves, and we do not go to the high peaks or overpasses. Even then, we frequently encounter snow where we have to walk, not ride, the horses. It's not fun, but the hunters all know this can happen."

"You don't guide hunting trips all winter, do you?"

"No, no, the law and the imposing amount of snowfall both prohibit it. I work at the Sleeping Giant Ski Area; you passed it on your left about four miles before my cabin. I used to supervise their ski school, but now I work independently, giving horse-drawn sleigh rides December through March. And skiing free is a great perk—providing I have time.

"After that, I have about a three-month break and go back home to help out during foaling season. I also train a few of the youngsters before I begin packing again the last of June."

"I didn't know you skied. I've skied downhill for the past fifteen years on local mountains in Maine."

"I didn't know you skied either. Guess there's a lot we still don't know about each other. I'd like to find out more. I've never known a lady like you."

"You mean one who doesn't mind getting down and dirty in horse dust and manure?"

"Yeah, that and other things. How about coming to work for me, with me, next summer? I really like you."

"I really like you too, but I'll have to wait and see what happens over the winter. Unfortunately I live many miles away."

We rode for a while in silence, then Dustin said, "How many miles between Wyoming and Maine?"

"About 2500 too many."

However, I was already thinking and scheming how I could make his offer materialize and return to Wyoming again the next summer.

PART TWO

Chapter 25

Dustin and I kept in touch over the winter. He called often, which managed to increase my need to return to Wyoming as soon as April arrived in Maine bringing spring fever. I got restless and called Glenn Fales at Rimrock. He said he would welcome me back to work as wrangler and guide, and that Pier, Ryan, Scott, Cortney and Trampus would be returning also. I looked forward to working with 'the boys' again. They were like younger brothers to me.

This year my horse, Razan, was not accompanying me. He had been injured inside the commercial horse carrier on his return trip to Maine last fall. It was 2500 miles to travel between Maine and Wyoming and I decided he could stay home. After all, I would already have 125 Rimrock horses to help take care of and my choice of the ranch's wrangle and guide horses to ride. Razan and his stable mate, Shasta, would be fine for the summer with my son taking care of them, and I would not have to worry about transporting him back and forth.

I had told Glenn that I would be arriving at Rimrock by the last week of June. Glenn, or Chief, had said this was okay since I already knew my job routine and most of the guests did not arrive until the last of June anyway. Dustin and I had agreed that I would go to his family's ranch in Montana to work with him and his parents May through mid-June.

But first, I was going to meet Dustin in Cody. I was really looking forward to hooking up with him again and seeing where our relationship would go this summer. We would stay the night at the Big Bear Motel—where we had spent our first night together—before going on to Montana.

I had arrived in Buffalo late the previous evening and stayed at a Motel 6. This morning, I drove over the Bighorns in frozen mist and on a slippery highway, but my car still had studded tires on, and I knew it could handle the road conditions safely. There had been gorgeous spidery ice-formations on branches overhanging the highway, and as the sun ascended, I had stopped at an overlook and took—what I hoped would be—some beautiful pictures. I attached the camera to my tripod to ensure clarity—I was attempting to catch the pale morning sunlight shooting beams through the mist and fog onto the glittery tree-branch configurations. Over the past winter I'd enrolled in a couple of photography classes and hoped to use some of what I learned taking pictures of Wyoming and Montana's exquisite scenery.

Arriving at the intersection of Route 120 and Cody's main street, Sheridan Avenue, I looked west down Cody's extra-wide main street toward Rattlesnake Mountain. It felt like I was coming home. I was thrilled to be back and excited by the anticipation of meeting Dustin again after seven months.

The city of Cody, the largest in Park County, has a population of approximately 8,000. Sheridan Avenue's eight-block length ended with a sharp left 90-degree turn. Cody's West Park Hospital was on the right beside the fantastic Buffalo Bill Historic Center, a complex of five internationally acclaimed museums. The late author James Michener called The Center, "The Smithsonian of the West"—with good reason.

The Center encompassed more than 300,000 square feet on three levels and entertained/educated nearly 250,000 visitors annually. Its cultural attractions included thousands of priceless treasures related to the art, history, ethnology, natural history and technology of the American West. On rainy-day excursions, I had driven guests from Rimrock to The Center several times last summer and enjoyed touring the various museums myself. I especially relished visiting the Plains Indian Museum—perhaps satisfying some past karmic experience—and the Whitney Gallery of Western Art appeased my present appreciation of the arts.

Sheridan Avenue then became West Yellowstone Highway. The Big Bear Motel and Dustin were less than a half-mile away.

Then I saw *it* and could not believe my eyes . . . a new *Wal-Mart*, right there in my beloved, proverbial western town of Cody. My heart sank as I realized that modern day civilization was imminently invading Cody's small-town, hometown atmosphere. Thank goodness, Wyoming has protected national parks, forests and wilderness areas where corporate America was prohibited from assaulting and destroying the land for profit. Pristine places like the Thorofare, near the Ranger Station in the Teton Wilderness where we pack-trip camped last summer, would thankfully remain unsullied, just as it was 200 years ago.

Happy thoughts replaced my melancholy ones as the Big Bear came into view. I parked my car beside Dustin's blue Dodge 4x4 just as he sauntered out of the same room where we had stayed last year. He sure was a welcome sight . . . tall, lean, and ruggedly handsome in his jeans and cowboy boots. His dark eyes twinkled under his Stetson, smiling mouth now kissing me, arms holding me. Wow, I had missed him and wanted him—right then, right there!

"I have missed you, cowgirl. For two hundred and fourteen nights I've thought about this moment," he said as he drew me into the room and closed the door.

"And I have missed you, cowboy," I replied, pulling his mouth hard against mine. His tongue and hands filled me with excitement and desire. We undressed in a hurried state of anticipation; clothes were tossed or dropped anywhere without concern. We made love every way we could imagine, sleeping for a few hours then awakening to renewed passion.

We slept spooned together until morning sunlight shown through the blinds. "Wake up sleeping beauty, and let's get some breakfast at the Irma. I'm famished."

"Me too, but I want to shower first. If you can find your jeans—it looks like a tornado struck here—can you please bring my suitcase inside so I can have a change of clothes? Then join me in the shower, if you'd like?" I added, winking.

* * * *

The Irma Restaurant and Hotel, known as The Grand Old Lady of Cody, was built in 1902 and named for Buffalo Bill's daughter, Irma. After a buffet breakfast 'to die for', our appetites were finally satiated. Sipping his third cup of coffee, Dustin said, "Do you want to leave for the ranch right away? Or is there something in town you want to do? My parents aren't expecting us until suppertime."

"You know this may be a little hokey, but I've noticed the Old Trail Town exhibit beside the Big Bear and I've never been there, have you? And is it worth seeing?"

"I've never been there. I figured it was a tourist attraction, but it might be interesting. I'm game to see it if *you* want to."

The Old Trail Town's collection of historic buildings and western artifacts sat on the area Buffalo Bill Cody and his associates had surveyed for the first town site of Cody City in 1895. Most buildings were dismantled at their original location, some as far away as 150 miles, then moved to Cody and reassembled. The collection included a cabin used by Kid Curry and the Sundance Kid, a cabin from the Crow Agency in Montana—once belonging to Curly, a scout for George Armstrong—and the Coffin School cabin where a rancher died of gangrene after he cut his leg while hewing logs.

Dustin and I liked the Rivers Saloon, built in 1888 west of Meeteetse. It is the oldest remaining saloon in northwest Wyoming; the door had original bullet holes in it from barroom brawls.

Old Trail Town also had an original livery stable and more than 100 horse-drawn vehicles. And of course, there was the *graveyard*, where mountain man Jeremiah 'Liver Eatin' Johnson is buried, along with Buffalo Bill's last surviving grandchild, Bill Garlow Cody, and rodeo champion Floyd Stillings, who was an inductee to the Cowboy Hall of Fame.

Reaching the far end of the graveyard, I noticed the Cody Nite Rodeo grounds nearby. "They don't open 'til June, do they? I had such fun there last summer I can't wait to go this year. I hope they are going to host the Wild Horse Race during Cody's Stampede Days once again."

"They're not going to," Dustin replied. "It was deemed inhumane treatment to the horses so last year was the last wild horse race in Cody. I understand Cheyenne still holds wild horse races during their Frontier Days, though.

"It's getting near noon, want to head to Montana? I'm anxious to show you the D & L Ranch."

"I never heard you say the name of the ranch before. What does the D & L stand for?"

"My parents are Dan and Leena."

Chapter 26

Since I had just driven 2500 miles across country, I left my car in the motel parking lot, and as Dustin transferred my gear I hopped into his truck. I was anxious to settle in a place where I could finally stretch my legs and *veg-out* for a few days. We drove about 65 miles north of Cody then turned east toward the Pryor Mountains. As much as I would like to have taken the roundabout route to Dustin's family ranch via Beartooth Pass, sightseeing would have to wait.

Dustin stopped his truck just outside the entrance gate to the D & L Ranch, and I admired the vista of mountains keeping watch protectively over the Crow Indian Reservation. This was the territory of Custer's demise. Dustin explained that the ranch bordered the Custer National Forest and was close enough to horseback ride into the Bighorn Canyon National Recreation Area as well as the Pryor Mountain National Wild Horse Range.

"My parents adopt mustangs whenever BLM hosts a wild horse roundup," he said. "They've had great success taming and green-breaking them to resell for trail horses. I'd guess they've adopted at least twenty over the past few years. My mom crossed her Arab mare with a young mustang stallion a few years back to experiment in raising potential endurance horses. Endurance racing seems to be the up-and-coming thing around here . . . but she'll want to tell you about that herself and maybe get an easterner's point-of-view."

"Endurance racing is real big in the east; I have many

friends who've raced for years. I look forward to chatting with your mom about this—it'll give us another common interest to talk about except you." I gently nudged him in the ribs.

"My mom and dad will want to tell you about the ranch themselves, so let's get going, okay . . . I'll bet supper is about ready.

"Oh, one more thing, my parents are from the old school and may put us in separate rooms. I hope not, but I don't want you to be surprised if this happens. Just go with the flow for now and I'll have a chat with my dad in a couple of days.

"If worse comes to worse, we can always tiptoe between rooms at night." Dustin smiled and winked.

During the three-mile drive to the ranch house, I observed the terrain changing from semi-arid flatland to a rolling grass valley between sloping foothills. Thick clusters of pines grew on the hilltops while horses grazed contentedly in the greening valley pastures, each with a creek running through it.

And there was the J & L Ranch sitting near the end of the valley sprawled out like a miniature village with: hay and horse barns, saddle, feed and maintenance sheds, bunkhouses, garages, and other sundry buildings. The main ranch house was built of hand-hewn logs and looked roomy with a relaxed atmosphere. Large cottonwoods that grew along a creek behind the house and a couple of old Douglas fir trees provided shade. A few low shrubs lined the stone walkway, and some perennials would soon bloom in the small garden surrounding the house.

Activity was everywhere as Dustin pulled up and parked his truck. Paddock horses contentedly chomped on hay, three dogs of various sizes and shapes came running toward someone carrying filled dog-food dishes, and work hands appeared from all directions headed to the ranch house.

"I do believe we're just in time for supper. Let's find the folks then settle down for some super delicious chow. Our cook, Henry, is the finest in these parts; we're lucky to have him . . . and he knows it."

Dustin introduced me to his mom and dad and to at least a dozen more people whose names I was sure to forget. Leena was a petite, fine-looking woman, with twinkling eyes like Dustin's and a beautiful smile. Dan was a handsome, aging gentleman with graying blond hair and sun-born wrinkles. He was more ruggedly built than Dustin but he had the same gracious manner and welcoming handshake. I knew I was going to like this family.

We all sat down around a long rectangle table, and without formalities, homemade biscuits were passed (or thrown) around, and platters of beefsteak, dishes of mashed potato, gravy, carrots and coleslaw were soon gone. Dessert consisted of apple pie and ice cream accompanied by more coffee. When we were all pleasantly full, Dan and Leena suggested Dustin and I join them in the living room for a glass of after-dinner wine. *Uh-oh,* I thought, *here comes the inquisition.*

Large hand-carved beams spanned the living room's high ceiling, and long windows ran down one wall facing the mountains. On the walls were paintings of ranching scenes, horses, and western panoramas. In the center of the room, oversize leather chairs and couches grouped around a massive coffee table. On the back wall, above a stone fireplace, hung a portrait of Dan and Leena in their younger years.

Actually, they were very intuitive and sensed that I was near exhaustion and needed some rest. After a few minutes of polite conversation, Leena said, "Pat, you look weary. I'll show you to your room if you'd like. I've already had your bags put in our daughter Laura's old room. It has an attached bathroom. I hope you'll be comfortable there."

"Yes, that would be great. I'm looking forward to seeing the ranch and getting acquainted, but I am *really* tired right now."

Not daring to look at Dustin for fear of seeing him smirk and of me bursting out in giggles, I uttered a generic, "Goodnight; see you all in the morning." Sleep settled upon me somewhere between shutting the bedroom door and climbing into bed.

Chapter 27

Morning brought rays of sunshine through my bedroom windows, unshielded by curtains that I had been too tired to close the previous evening. Hmmm, so this was Laura's room . . . nice. She must have been quite a horsewoman as I noticed many pictures of her at various stages of her childhood on horseback and in rodeos. A least a dozen trophies lined a shelf on one wall. Dustin never talked much about his sister—*a little sibling jealousy going on there*, I wondered? I would have to ask him about that later. Already I could hear activity in the yard and barn and hoped I wasn't too late for breakfast. As I climbed out of bed, I smiled to myself wondering what adventures would be in store for me today.

Suddenly I heard a bell clanging, just like at the ranch where I had worked last summer. *Must be breakfast is ready,* I thought as I hurriedly showered and dressed in jeans, boots, cotton shirt and bandana. I carried my leather work/riding gloves inside my Akubra Aussie-style hat and set off for the dining room.

Leena, Dan, Dustin, and Jeff, the head wrangler and resident vet, along with John and Jim, who were both wranglers, were just sitting down.

"Howdy, cowgirl." Dustin's familiar greeting was music to my ears. "Sleep good?"

"Wonderful, and I must have slept soundly; I don't think I stirred all night."

"Would you like juice, coffee, hotcakes, eggs, bacon,

toast, or the works this morning?" a smiling Henry asked.

"Juice, coffee, a couple hotcakes and bacon would be fine thanks, Henry. So what's on the agenda today?"

Leena answered, "Well, after breakfast I thought Dan would show you around the premises while I do some office work, like paying bills. Then later I'll introduce you to the horses; we have ten new foals and two more due any day. We're putting Dustin to work rounding up the yearlings for branding along with bringing in the two-year-olds for their shots and worming, and helping to castrate three colts. Messy work, but necessary, can't have any unplanned foals on a breeding ranch."

Therefore, off I went following Dan as he told me the history and present operations of the ranch.

"We bought most of the ranch land thirty-one years ago this spring when Dustin was five and Leena was pregnant with Laura. We decided the kids would need space to grow, explore and develop. The log house was finished by fall; Laura was born there in November. We built a small barn and the corrals, and started buying and selling horses. We'd keep the prime stock for ourselves and eventually started our own quarter-horse breeding program. We began adopting wild mustangs about ten years ago—Leena can tell you more about that; it was her idea."

We talked and walked from the bunkhouses to the maintenance building, then to the grain and tack sheds adjacent to the horse and hay barn. The barn contained six large box stalls complete with 50-foot outdoor runs, storage for five hundred bales of hay, and a small room across from the stalls containing a bed, toilet, fridge and an array of vet supplies.

Dan explained, "The barn stalls are mainly for our stallions, foaling mares, and sick or injured horses. The local pastures all have three sided shelters to protect the horses against severe weather. During the winter if the weather is extreme for a period, we bunch the younger stock together in the stalls and adjoining runs. Of course, the mustangs prefer to stay outside, and they're okay as long as they have shelter."

"How many acres do you own and how many horses?"

"D & L Ranch now owns about 1000 acres and nearly 80 horses including 15 of Dustin's. We don't have enough grazing land for *all* our horses *all* year long. We, like most ranchers, pay approximately $1.50 per animal, per month to graze on federal land during the winter. Mid-November we drive our horses about fifty miles from here and bring them back mid-April.

"For obvious reasons, we keep our two stallions, the youngsters under two, any sick, injured, or older horses and the mustangs here at the ranch all year. That amounts to keeping 20-30 horses here all year and another 50 most of the year. That's enough."

"How many people work here?"

"Besides Leena and me, we employ 10-12 people at peak season, which is spring due to foaling, breeding and training. I oversee the logistical operation, and Leena is the financial manager in addition to collaborating with me on the horse breeding and training. We have a barn manager, two maintenance men, and three wranglers, whose talents include basic farrier skills and veterinary knowledge, a cook and kitchen helper, and a cleaning person.

"Growing up, our daughter Laura used to help around the kitchen and cabins; she loved to cook and clean. However, she's married now with two youngsters of her own and a husband to tend to so she only works here in an emergency.

"Dustin is multi-talented and helps wherever he's needed when he's here, which isn't often enough as far as I'm concerned. His specialty is training the mustangs, colts and fillies. He has a gentle manner and seems to converse with them in their own language—some different from when we used to "break" horses.

"At the end of the year we somehow manage to make enough money to support the ranch and love every minute of it."

"Wow, what a way to live! I was born and brought up in Maine, but I have known in my heart that I wanted to be in the west since I first traveled to Cody five years ago. I feel a real connection to the mountains and the wide-open spaces, as if I've lived here in a past life."

To my surprise, Dan replied, "You just might have, you know."

My belief in reincarnation and karma was not always an accepted philosophy. I looked forward to discussing this topic with him in the future. Right now however, it was time to eat again, as I heard the lunch bell clanging.

* * * *

Dustin had a problem getting the yearlings and two-year-olds back to the ranch by himself. Usually, all he had to do was rope one of the older colts and the others would follow—but not today.

First, he had roped a small paint colt that came right up to him when he rode out to the grazing pasture. This was going to be easy, he figured, as he began leading the spotted colt back toward the corrals. Then he noticed the beautiful bay colt acting as herd leader, rounding up the rest and keeping them from following him. So he took the rope from the spotted colt's neck and decided to rope the bay troublemaker instead. That was easier said than done. The colt would first run, then zigzag back and through the herd getting the rest of the young fillies and colts all excited. Finally, after a few passes, Dustin got his rope around the colt and pulled him up short.

"What a beauty you are," Dustin said to no one in particular. "You're one nice piece of horse flesh . . . why haven't I noticed you before?"

The colt gave Dustin a hard time on the way to the corrals; he'd first nip at Dustin's mare, then hang back and try to mount her. When the lariat pulled too tight around his neck, he would attempt to bolt ahead.

Dustin began a soothing talk to calm the colt.

"You are just full of yourself, aren't you young fella? Guess I'll have to be talking to Mom about maybe keeping you a stallion instead of gelding you. You are a prize! Bet you're the half mustang/half Arab all the hands have been raving about. Let's see, they named you . . . *Jaalam Akeem*, the "wild prince", right? They got that one correct; you're sure a prince by the looks of you. Don't know about the wild part . . . you can settle down if you have to, huh? Good boy."

He continued talking to the colt until they reached the corrals where Jim and Jeff shut the youngsters inside with access to water and hay. Dustin put Jaalam in a separate pen beside the others.

The branding irons were already hot in the fire. One at a time, Jim and Jeff roped and hog-tied each of the dozen yearlings, gave each a quick dose of worming medicine and a tetanus shot, then Dustin applied the hot iron to their rump with the DL brand. They were quickly untied and sent to an adjoining pen, still scared, but they would get over the pain shortly and be healthier and safer.

The two-year-olds were separated into two groups. The fillies received their worming shots, got their hooves trimmed, and were given a quick health checkup.

The two colts also had their hooves trimmed and a worming shot. Jeff would castrate them with Jim and John's help. After first checking to ensure that both testicles had dropped, Jeff gave each colt a mild sedative before castrating them. He liked to do the castrating while the colt was standing because it was better for the colt that way—not as much local anesthesia was necessary and the blood would drain better. However, if a colt was a "kicker," like the second one, then he was thrown to the ground. Jim sat or leaned on its head to keep the colt down; John helped keep its hind legs apart while Jeff did the cutting.

Dustin tended to the colts after they were cut, washing the dirt and blood off them with warm water, praising and patting gently as he turned them into one of the 50-foot runs with plenty of water and feed.

Then he went to find his mom.

Chapter 28

Leena, Dustin and I stood observing Jaalam at one of the horse corrals. My heart skipped a beat or two as I watched him run, spin and reverse directions periodically, living up to his name by prancing like a proud prince. He had fine black-tipped ears that were alert to every nuance around him; intelligent eyes set in a nice wide forehead that narrowed to a delicate muzzle. His wide jowl and neck were typical mustang; his black mane and tail were long and thick. His high tail carriage and short body were definitely Arab. His long legs, set nice and square under his body, were sturdier than most Arabians at his age, his hooves a bit larger, his extended pasterns would ensure smooth gaits. His coat was a rich brown with black leggings and a black dorsal strip—I was definitely in love.

"So what do you think, Mom? Do we geld him or keep him a stallion?"

"I'm not sure," she answered. "He has some wonderful blood in his heritage. His dam is Reba, my desert-bred Arab mare, whose lineage goes back to Raffles and Skowronek. His sire was that handsome grullo Pryor-Mountain mustang we adopted three years ago. We intended to keep him a stud, but as a four year old, he became feisty and just too rowdy and untamed to handle as a breeding stallion. We bred him just that once then gelded him, trained him to trail, and sold him last spring—nice horse—once he was gelded.

"Jaalam would sire some handsome foals that's for sure.

Let's keep him here in the corral and work with him to see if he's inherited his dam's disposition and is cooperative enough to be a breeding stud. We could breed him back to his dam's offspring in a couple of years. It would be a little unusual to breed him back to his dam, but first generation inbreeding is not unheard of. His mustang tendency for soundness, strength and sturdiness combined with the Arabian's courage, speed and stamina should make for good endurance stock.

"Endurance seems to be the *hot* thing around here these days. Do you know much about endurance riding or racing, Pat?"

"Excuse me for interrupting," Dustin cut in, "but I think I'll go check on the colts and yearlings to make sure they are all doing okay and leave you ladies to discuss horses in general and endurance racing in particular. I'll see you later, babe." He gave me a kiss on the cheek and left.

"I know little about endurance," I replied. "Some of my close friends back in Maine have raced endurance for the past ten years. I have ridden my Arabian horse, Razan, with them, but it has never appealed to me to race a hundred miles in twenty-four hours. To be competitive and place among the winners, you actually need to finish the race in ten hours or so—that's faster than I want to go for that many miles."

"Janey, a friend of Laura's, has asked me about the possibility of her entering my Quarter/Arab mare, Reena, in the Fort Howes Endurance Race over around Ashland. You rode her last year, do you think she'd be a good endurance horse?" Leena asked.

"Reena's athletic with nice gaits and a willing spirit; she's what, six now? She could do a 50-miler if she had some good conditioning. It would be excellent advertising for your ranch and a good way to get your foot in the door with the endurance crowd.

"Has Janey started putting some miles on her?"

"She's been working with Reena since January to build

her up slowly and not stress her muscles or tendons. The race is June 15th. Maybe you could ride her tomorrow and tell me how you think she's coming along."

"I'd be glad to. Dustin and I talked about taking a ride across your land on into the mountains; I'll plan on riding *her*."

"Good, now let's go on to the barn," Leena suggested, "and I'll introduce you to a couple of nice looking stallions and the rest of the horses."

Leena led the way to the stallions' stalls. "This is our older stud, Pepper Doc; AQHA (American Quarter Horse Association) registered, son of the famous Doc Bar. Pepper is 18 now and has sired nearly 400 live foals since we bought him 14 years ago. His stud fee is a healthy $1750 and he breeds 25-30 mares each year, plus half of our mares."

Pepper was a chestnut with white socks and face blaze. He stood about 15.3 hands. I am not much into quarter horses but he had a gentle eye and was personable as he came over to greet us. Obviously, he had good breeding and was worth *beaucoup* bucks.

"And this is Casey Dee who's a ten-year-old sorrel/tobiano, APHA (American Paint Horse Association) registered, grandson of Sonny Dee Bar. He throws tobiano marked foals 98% of the time and his stud fee is also $1750 including the mare's boarding fee.

"Not long after the American Paint Stock Horse Association combined with the American Paint Quarter Horse Association, we applied to the newly established APHA for a breeding grant and received $50,000 to specialize in our present Tobiano breeding program. That was a real financial boost back in the early 1970's."

I did not even know what a *Tobiano* was; he looked like a sorrel/paint or pinto to me. I soon learned that a Tobiano *was* a type of paint or pinto horse, but one that has special markings. These are: white legs, dark head, and oval white spots that cross the top line and have clean, crisp edges. Generally, the dark color will extend down the neck giving the appearance of a shield and will cover at least one of the flank areas.

The major difference between the paint and pinto registry is their breed. The APHA, or paint registry, requires that both sire and dam are registered Tobiano, Quarter Horse, or Thoroughbred. The PHA, or pinto registry, accepts a broader range including pony, Arabian and American Saddlebred, along with a provision for non-pedigreed lineage.

"Registration does not guarantee a good horse," Leena added, "but most people love to flaunt their horse's pedigree, therefore a sire and dam's registration *is* important in selling foals."

We moved on to the pasture containing mares with foals either nursing, lying down sleeping, or bouncing around chasing each other. A dozen mares and ten new foals—chestnuts, bays, sorrels, paints, and pintos, dotted the meadow.

As we walked among the mares and skittish foals, Leena said, "Two of my mares haven't foaled yet; they are due any day. Look at this one, her teats have a bit of wax on them and her bag is getting so full she waddles like a cow when she walks . . . won't be long now."

The foals interested me more than the mares. I squatted down to their level and waited to see which one, if any, would be curious enough to come over. Soon a pinto filly, perhaps a month old, walked up to my hand hesitantly and stretched out her tiny nose to sniff me. After a few minutes I stood up and she moved away.

"She's the daughter of my Arabian mare, Reba. She's that beautiful bay over there watching you." Leena smiled. "Bey Sharreba is her AHA (Arabian Horse Association) registered name, sired by Bey Arrogance."

"It figures the filly's Arab," I chuckled. "What other new foal would be so friendly to a stranger. Is her sire Casey, the Tobiano?"

"Yes, you're learning fast, and she's a full sister to Reena."

We walked back to the corrals where the yearlings and two-year-olds were recovering from their morning ordeal. I noticed Dustin was on his way to Jaalam's corral.

"We'll keep these youngsters here in the corrals for the next couple of weeks," Leena said, "putting halters on, tying them to posts a few minutes at a time, and grooming them so they get used to being handled. We show and sell a few of them before they are green broke at three. Yearlings sell for $2000; at two, they sell for $3000; after they're trained and broke to trail, they sell for $5000. You might like to help with the youngsters. They are willing, intelligent and fun to work with at that age."

"I'd like that. Where *are* the three-year-olds?"

"We'll bring them in and work with them after the youngsters are turned back out.

"Now, on to the mustangs. They're my special project."

Chapter 29

Leena's adopted mustangs came from the Pryor Mountain herd of about 180 wild horses. They roamed in small bands of 3-15 head usually comprised of a stallion with his mares and foals, but there are also bands of young stallions exclusively. The Pryor Mountain Wild Horse Refuge encompasses some 38,000 acres located southeast of the D & L Ranch near the Wyoming border. The land is extremely rugged with elevations from 3900 feet to 8000 feet. The contrasting landscape is high grass meadow, timber and arid desert. The climate is very cold in winter and hot in the summer.

These tough little horses of Spanish ancestry have been present in this mountain area for nearly 200 years and cannot be genetically reconstructed. Although their biological viability, together with their history, must be preserved, it has been a tough battle for these mustangs to survive.

In 1851 when the Pryor Mountains became part of the Crow reservations, it was estimated that the Crows had as many as 40,000 horses on this range.

In 1913, the Supervisor of Farming for the Crow Reservation recommended reducing the thousands of horses and they were gathered off the Pryors for the government.

From 1924 to 1931, the government allowed grazing lessees to shoot the horses for $4.00 a head, which reduced the count to about 150 by the 1960's.

In September 1968, Secretary of State Stewart Udall

announced the creation of the Pryor Mountain National Wild Horse Refuge to help preserve this unique breed.

In 1971, President Nixon signed the Free Roaming Wild Horse and Burro Act, which effectively protected all wild equines inhabiting federal lands. This new law was well intended but had no population control provision in it and within a short period, there was too many horses for the land to support.

The U.S. Department of the Interior's Bureau of Land Management, commonly referred to as BLM, administers the wild horse refuge. For many years, through annual roundups (or 'gathers' as they are called) they made young wild horses available for adoption in order to control the herd population. The cost was $100 per head and the purchaser had to keep the horse for at least a year before becoming its legal owner.

Unfortunately, in the past, motorized vehicles were used and presently helicopters are utilized to gather the horses. Most deem the practice of gathers inhumane.

Thanks to research headed by the director of The Science and Conservation Center in Billings, Montana, there is a recent trend toward immuno-contraception, or vaccine-based fertility control to stop reproduction and curb herd population.

The vaccine called PZP is 95% effective. Mares can be treated with darts without capture; its reversible, doesn't cause pathologies or affect behavior, has no long term debilitating health effects, is reasonably inexpensive, can alter entire populations, and enables the mares to live several years longer than before treatment.

The vaccine is working and although BLM still has gathers, they have fewer of them and remove fewer animals.

The current issues that the Pryor Mountain mustangs are trying to live within are three-fold:

(1) A nine-year drought brought the range conditions and lack of water to a point where the designated horse refuge can hold no more than 50 horses in a healthy manner. The horses respond by "trespassing" on National Forest Land outside their

designated refuge, thereby angering many groups.

(2) A small population of bighorn sheep lives on the horse refuge and various wildlife departments have created pressure to reduce the number of horses thinking to increase the number of sheep. They do this despite the fact that recent federal studies show there is minimal competition between horses and bighorn sheep, and that a combination of predators and disease is causing the sheep population to decline.

(3) A bizarre third issue has arisen with the arrival of a campaign to ignore range conditions and lobby for legal actions to stop gathers, adoptions, and all use of contraception.

The plight of these plucky horses is an ongoing saga.

* * * *

As we walked over to visit the three newly adopted mustangs, Leena said, "They are still getting used to human voices and touch. See what gorgeous coloring they have! The girls are the red dun with striped legs and the light buckskin; the beautiful blue roan is a colt."

"Do you mind if I come see them whenever I have time? I'd like to help gentle them."

"Feel free to visit and talk to them any time as they'll need human attention and companionship until they can be turned out with the other yearlings. Just make sure someone else is always around if or when you enter the corrals with them."

"Where are the other mustangs? You said you had six total."

"We kept the three fillies, adopted two years ago, in the corrals for the first year, handling them regularly. They are pastured with the three-year-olds and will be brought in and trained soon with the others.

"Mustangs make wonderful loyal companions if they are gentled and treated kindly at the onset, rough them up or scare them and someone will have their hands full of wild fury. Over the past fifteen years we've successfully adopted, trained, and sold twenty mustangs to good homes."

I don't think Leena realized that I had trained young mustangs at Rimrock Ranch last year. I looked forward to working with all of them: the yearlings, two-year-olds, three-year-olds, and especially *Jaalam Akeem*. My heart was happy.

Chapter 30

At supper that evening, we discussed the day's events. Jeff reported that all the branded yearlings were doing okay as were the two castrated colts—now geldings.

"Jaalam is pretty restless," Dustin said. "I think I'll put my big pack-gelding, Runner, in with him to keep him company and settle him down. Runner will also teach the kid some respect without hurting him."

Leena added, "The young mare, Roda, will foal within the next couple of days, and seeing as her foal was a breech last year, I'd like to bring her in and put her in one of the box stalls. Jeff, can you make sure someone bunks in the barn nights to keep an eye on her 'til she foals? She may need help delivering again, and I want someone right there at the onset."

"I can bring her in after supper, Ma'am, and I'll sleep there tonight," Jeff replied.

"Pat and I intend to take a ride tomorrow," Dustin said. "I'll check the north fences as we head up into Bear Canyon. We'll circle down the other side of Gypsum Creek and back via the south pastures. I've asked Henry to fix us some bag lunches because we may not be back until late afternoon.

"Everybody all set here for the day? I'll check on Jaalam and the new mustangs when I get back."

"We'll try to manage without you, son," Dan chided. "Would you remember to check to see how well-4960 is doing this spring? The situation over in that area has been pretty dry for a while, and I need to know how much to rely on our well for the summer."

"Sure, I'll check it out tomorrow on our way back."

As I said my "good nights" and walked down the hallway, Dustin followed me into my room.

"Are we going to get in trouble with your mom if you stay here awhile?"

"I had a talk with my dad earlier and told him we were consenting adults in a responsible relationship and that we ought to be able to sleep together. He agreed, but said we should still respect Mom's wishes and to ease into the all night sleepovers a little at a time. But Dad also added that sneaking from my bedroom across the hall to yours once in a while was probably okay, as long as we didn't get caught."

"I'm beginning to feel like a sneaky teenager."

"*Sneaky's* good as long as you're sneaking with me," Dustin replied, pulling me down onto my bed with him.

* * * *

The morning was crisp and cloudless; it looked to be a marvelous day for riding. After crossing the creek behind the ranch, we rode the north fence line as it followed up and down the sloping hills. Reena was in great shape and feeling fine. We loped the next couple of miles then climbed the juniper-covered foothills at an easy trot. Cochise, Dustin's favorite big bay gelding, seemed to be in pretty good condition also, but then, Dustin had ridden him regularly since March. We exited the ranch land and walked the horses in silence for a while, enjoying the early morning stillness. As we rode across the top of a thick wooded ridge, elk and mule deer scat was everywhere.

We climbed high into forests of Douglas fir and timber pine. Halting on an exposed craggy overlook, Dustin pointed out Bear Canyon with its colorful ravines surrounded by the Pryor Mountains. It was a stunning view of Custer National Forest.

"Look," he said, "there's two bighorn sheep over on that side of the ravine. They are a beautiful sight to behold, aren't they?"

"Gorgeous creatures. Time to get out my camera. What other wildlife do you find in this area?" I asked as I snapped a half-dozen shots.

"Well, let me see. The Pryors are home to black bear, bobcats, mountains lions, golden eagles and peregrine falcons, as well as the elk, mule deer, bighorn sheep, and wild horses."

As we stood quietly watching the sheep, they seemed not to notice or care we were around. Unfortunately, that may not be true in the future as this region was being threatened by industry proposals to expand and develop new limestone quarries.

We rode northeast passing the Red Pryor Ice Cave then followed a trail south, finally stopped for lunch atop a high pine ridge between the Old Glory Mine and the Sandra Mine. Looking west, we could see the historic grassy mesa called Demijohn Flat.

"Is that a small band of wild horses in that gully down there?" I asked excitedly while digging out my camera from my saddlebag.

"Sure is. Looks like a stallion, three mares and two foals. They'll be making their way up to the tall grasses of the high meadows soon. Mares usually drop their foals in May then they start their trek to the high country to avoid the summer heat."

Dustin hobbled our horses so they could feed on mountain grasses as we ate our bagged lunch of sliced beef, tomato and lettuce sandwiches, pickles, and granola bars. We rested an hour or so, enjoying the view and the company and taking more pictures before descending south toward the badlands that bordered the green grasses of Crooked Creek Valley. We picked up the pace following a rough 4 x 4 or ATV (all-terrain vehicle) trail until crossing Gypsum Creek again.

Turning east away from the badlands, we rode over rolling hills and arid lands. We loped and trotted for four or five miles before coming to what Dan referred to as well-4960. Dustin dismounted and checked the contents as his dad had asked. He said it looked almost dry and probably would not be reliable for ranch use, come summer.

We set off again toward the ranch at a ground-covering trot. I had wanted to approach the subject of Laura before this, but not wanting to break the magical spell of the ride if it was going to bring up negativity with Dustin, I put it off.

We were only a few miles from the ranch when I unceremoniously blurted out, "So why didn't you ever tell me you had a sister? Is there bad blood or some sibling thing going on?"

Silence ensued; Dustin continued trotting without answering.

"Hey, what's up? I'm a good listener you know."

Dustin slowed to a walk. "Well . . . I was engaged to be married to a friend of Laura's a couple years back and, put it this way, I figure my sister was the main cause of our breakup. Things between Laura and I have been strained ever since.

"Guess I should get over it, huh? I wouldn't have met you had it not happened. I'll tell you more about it later tonight. Let's end a perfectly wonderful ride on a positive note, okay?"

With that, and the ranch in sight, he challenged, "Race you to the barn."

* * * *

"And how did Reena do on your ride today?" Leena asked at supper that evening.

"Dustin said we rode about 25 miles today, at various paces and over very mixed terrain. She did real well. After working hard climbing a high ridge, she was breathing well, taking long deep breaths. When we stopped for lunch on top of the ridge, I took her pulse rate after five minutes and it was down to 60, which is within the limits for a well-conditioned horse. Her normal resting pulse is 36, which also indicates she's in good condition. She showed no signs of fatigue, her PR (pulse and respiratory) remained stable throughout our ride, and she didn't get nervous when crossing a swift running creek or navigating narrow switchbacks. If you still want to enter her in a 50-mile endurance race, I'd say, 'go ahead'. Just don't race her to win; she's still young. Coming in fourth or fifth place would be excellent for her first time competing. It would give her some racing experience and still provide your ranch with some good exposure for breeding and raising endurance stock."

"Good, then I'll talk to Laura's friend about entering her.

"Dustin, how's Jaalam doing?" Leena asked, changing the subject. "I see you put Runner in with him when you got back."

"They're sparring to see who's going to be boss right now, but the kid will acquiesce before morning. Runner's ordinarily pretty mellow, but he's older and will demand respect, and besides, he's a *lot* bigger."

"Has Roda had her foal yet?" I asked.

"No, but my bet is she'll deliver tonight," Dan replied. "Leena and I will take turns staying in the barn—just in case. Have you ever watched a foal being born, Pat?"

"Not actually 'being born,' no. All my mares seemed to wait until my back was turned and then they'd drop the foal."

"That's not unusual; mares don't like to be watched foaling. A mare often appears to stop in the middle of the birth process when someone walks in, just relaxing and waiting. They seem to have some degree of conscious control over when they foal, with the result that a majority of foals are born at night. We use peepholes to observe our mares unless they need our help. If you want, we can call you when she starts serious labor."

"That would be great," I replied with enthusiasm. "Guess I'd better get my beauty-sleep while I can, then. Good night all." Dustin knocked softly on my door just as I was climbing into bed. He said, "I just wanted to tell you what a great day I had, babe, and what a wonderful riding companion you are."

"Back at you. Want to stay and talk a few minutes? You promised to tell me 'the rest of the story' tonight, remember?"

Settling on top of the covers, head propped up on pillows, Dustin began, "I won't get into sordid details, but over the summer two years ago, I didn't see much of my fiancée, Laura's friend. We'd been engaged a year and a half, waiting until she got her law degree before we married. She usually spent some weekends with me when I was in camp at Pahaska. That summer I saw very little of her.

"I think my sister was always a bit jealous of our friendship, and that summer Laura fixed my fiancée up with her husband's cousin—although Laura says it was her husband Fred's idea. They double dated frequently and went camping together several times.

"Anyway, when the truth came out, I broke the engagement. She wanted to date both of us; I loved her and wanted an exclusive relationship or no relationship. I haven't seen her since.

"That's kinda the end of the story. It's been a while since I've seen Laura; maybe we could go visit and make amends. What do you think?"

"Okay, let's call first though, to warn her we're coming. By the way, does her friend, your ex-fiancée have a name?"

"Yes, it's Janey."

Chapter 31

Janey? Janey, the friend of Laura's who wants to race Reena! I wondered if Dustin knew this. And should I be worried? Deciding to take the path of trust instead of suspicion, I let it go—for now.

Sometime in the wee morning hours before the sun made its appearance, I had a call saying that Roda was about to drop her foal. I dressed hurriedly and ran out to the barn where Dustin and Leena were quietly standing around. Dan was in the stall with the mare.

"I'm going to need some help here," Dan said suddenly. "It looks like the back hoofs are protruding, not the front. Dustin we've got about five minutes to get this little one out before it suffocates. If you'll come in and talk to Roda to keep her calm and the contractions coming, I'll help her deliver."

With Dustin talked in soothing tones while stroking the mare's forehead and neck, Dan grasped the foal's two hind feet and pulled in a downward motion, working with the mare's labor contractions. The small hooves were very slippery and Leena had to keep handing him towels to use to help grasp them. Soon, there *he* was—a little chestnut stud colt. Dan removed the membranes from its muzzle and reached into the colt's mouth to scoop out any mucus. The foal stated breathing on its own.

Whew, I felt as if I had done the delivery myself. But it was not over yet . . . after a few minutes, the colt tried to struggle to his feet, staggering like a drunk, and the umbilical cord separated from the mare. Dan dipped what was left of the cord into a cup of strong iodine, letting it soak thoroughly, including the navel, to prevent infection. Roda licked the colt to dry him, and soon he was trying to find her teats. He nuzzled her chest and her belly, then Dan guided him to her udder and he started sucking.

Dustin removed the afterbirth and soiled bedding and gave Roda some warm bran mash, some hay to nibble off the floor, and a bucket of water with the chill off it. Come morning light, he would wash her with warm water, as some of the blood from the afterbirth still clung to her tail and hindquarters. He would also check the foal's stall feces to make sure it had passed the *me conium*, which is the dark feces present in a foal's gut.

All this happened within 45 minutes, but it seemed like hours. On the walk back to the house, and to bed, I noticed daylight coming up in the eastern sky. The smell of coffee permeated the house so I decided to grab a cup then go shower and get ready for another day at the ranch.

Dustin remained with Roda and her colt. When I took him out a cup of 'joe' after showering, I found the mare washed, cleaned and resting comfortably, as was her sleeping foal, and Dustin.

"Hey cowboy, wake up and have some coffee. Smells like you could use a shower and a change of clothes too. I'll stay with these guys a while if you want to clean up."

"Thanks, guess I dozed off. I'll take you up on that offer. See ya at breakfast, babe." Dustin gave me a kiss on the cheek and left.

At breakfast everyone was a little groggy from interrupted sleep but perked up when Dan announced, "Bella dropped *her* foal out in the pasture last evening. Both are up and about this morning. Jeff and I moved them into a barn stall so we can keep an eye on them for the next couple of days. I checked both and there doesn't appear to be any problems. Of course, this is Bella's ninth foal so she's a seasoned pro. The foal's a chestnut colt and half brother to Roda's colt. They look identical except one has a wider white strip on its face."

"That's the twelfth and last foal this spring," Leena said, "so now we can concentrate on training the rest of the young stock."

Dustin said, "Why don't we make it an easy day today and we'll start training heavy tomorrow. Pat, I'll give you a lift into Cody if you want to pick up your car and then I'll go on over to Powell to their livestock supply outlet and pick up more halters for the yearlings. I also want a special training halter with attached rope for Jaalam, and Jeff said he's short of tetanus vaccine since we used most of it on the yearlings. Anything else we need while I'm there?"

"Yes, I need another pair of hand-held wire snips," said Dan.

"And I need groceries," Leena added, "so I'm going to tag along if you don't mind. Maybe Pat and I can do some girl-stuff and check out the Plush Pony or the Custom Cowboy Shop while we're in town. Is that okay?"

"Fine by me; any place but *Wal-Mart*," I replied.

* * * *

And what a fun day it turned out to be! After giving Dustin a see-ya kiss and he looking a little dubious about leaving us alone for the day, Leena and I got into my car and drove off. She guided while I drove, first to browse for girly things in the clothing shops. I bought a couple of long-sleeved, cotton cowgirl-shirts, and Leena exchanged a gift certificate for a new belt with a fancy cowgirl buckle. She said it was a gift from Dan for her birthday last month.

"I'm going to wear it home; I wonder if he'll notice."

Next, we stopped into the Big Horn Galleries where I found some stunning, western, realist paintings on display. Local artist John Davis, who used to guide pack trips for Rimrock, had his beautiful scenic Wyoming oils displayed there, which was a pleasant surprise. I really loved the western sculptures but figured now was not the time to buy things that I had no place to display and couldn't use. We also perused the nearby Simpson Gallagher Gallery, a fine art gallery featuring some of America's leading representational artists.

Leena suggested lunch at Bubba's BBQ where we feasted on their scrumptious ribs and accompanying salad. Then we re-joined the real world—grocery shopping at Albertsons at the Eastgate Center.

We had laughed and giggled like a couple of schoolgirls while in Cody; however, on the way back to the ranch we both got serious. I asked more about Janey, and her riding ability, etc. to see if Leena would volunteer any information about Janey's being Dustin's ex-fiancée. She did, saying only that they had once been engaged but they no longer saw each other. Apparently, Janey had boarded Reena over the winter and the mare was returned to the ranch the day before I arrived.

Laura's name never entered the conversation.

I also learned that Janey was an accomplished equestrienne who had won national recognition in both western pleasure and quarter-horse jumping competitions. I was impressed and looked forward to meeting her, if for no other reason than to size up my (former) rival.

Leena, not so subtly, asked about my family background, business, riding ability, and horse knowledge in general, as well as indirectly inquiring about Dustin and my relationship.

Honesty has always been a good policy. Therefore, without revealing confidential details between Dustin and me, I told her how we had met, about our dating last summer, which she already knew, and what a caring and wonderfully thoughtful person and partner he was. Also, how much I appreciated and admired his gentleness, horse sense, and determination to do his best, whatever the situation. "And that's besides his being handsome and a good dancer," I added with a smile.

"Wow!" she exclaimed. "Finally someone sees the same fine qualities in him that I have seen all his life. Thank you for your frankness; now please forgive mine . . . I know you and Dustin have been sneaking between rooms at night. If it's more convenient and to your liking, you can choose whichever room is the largest and bunk together."

"It *is* to my liking," I said, more than a little embarrassed, my face flushed a bright pink. "I'll talk it over with Dustin and see what he says. Thank you for your understanding, and sorry if we disrespected you in any way." I was grateful to be back to the ranch by then where I helped carry the groceries inside then hurried off to find Dustin.

I found Dustin in with the new foals, talking softly and handling them all over including their ears, mouth, feet, and between their legs. Giving foals lots of human touching and handling early in their lives enables them to trust, thus they would be easier to train later. If he showed up at the same time every day, they would eventually look forward to seeing him, and come to him on their own.

"Hey cowboy, I could use some of that touching right now. I missed you today. And, I have some interesting news to tell you."

After I told Dustin briefly, about his mom's and my conversation regarding our sneaking and sleeping together, he said, "I can't believe she said that! You mean she actually gave her permission for us to 'bunk' together, as she calls it. Boy you must have done some real sweet talking, or she really likes you."

"Maybe both," I said coyly. "She's more understanding than you (we) gave her credit for. So whose room is larger, yours or mine?"

"My room is small and probably too mannish for you. Your room is too girly and small, although it does have a private bath.

"Maybe there is another alternative. You know, there's a separate room with bed, bureau, toilet and shower at the end of one of the bunkhouses. It used to be for the barn manager when he was married. Now he's divorced, he bunks with the other guys. I think it's big enough for both of us. Why don't we go check it out and maybe move in there? Mom might be more comfortable with that arrangement and it would give us a little privacy."

* * * *

The first comment made at the dinner table that night was: "Nice belt! I take it you gals had a good day doing downtown Cody," Dan said nonchalantly.

"Yep, it was fun and sure took the drudgery out of grocery shopping."

The remainder of supper conversation centered on working with the yearlings, the mustangs, and two-year-olds, including Jaalam.

Dustin said they would all get halters put on every morning beginning tomorrow, and taken off evenings. It was unusual to keep halters on horses in corrals; however these youngsters needed the experience, and if they should get in trouble, i.e. a hoof caught in their halter, someone was always around during the day to handle the situation.

During the family's after-dinner wine and private talk in the living room, Dustin said, "Mom, Pat and I have looked over the vacant room at the end of bunkhouse number two. We think it would be big enough for both of us to move into, if that's okay with you and Dad."

Dan coughed and feigned surprise. Leena said, "Of course. When are you moving?"

"We're going to move some of our things this evening and the rest after it's cleaned. No one has stayed there recently, have they?"

"No, not since last fall. I'll get the cleaning person to give it a good going over tomorrow. You're going to need towels, linens and a bedspread, and I'll hunt up some curtains for the windows. Anything else you need just let me know."

As we left the room, I saw Dan slyly give Dustin a thumbs-up.

Chapter 32

Dustin decided he and I would work together and handle each of the ten yearlings for twenty minutes every morning. Handling included putting halters on, teaching them to lead, and to stand quietly while tied to a post and being groomed and having each of their feet picked up and cleaned out.

While we were working the yearlings, Jeff would halter the two-year-olds. They had been through their basic training the season before and should accept their halters without any problems. Dustin and I would work with them after the yearlings, reviewing their basics while adding sacking out, crossing obstacles, accepting the bit and bridle, blanketing and saddling. This would prepare them for being mounted and ridden as three-year-olds.

While I kept the remaining yearlings together, Dustin isolated one yearling at a time and herded it into an adjacent 40-foot round corral. I was glad to learn that he also used the round-pen method of training for all horses at any level. The round-pen method is designed to help gain control of the horse's mind and body, using its natural understanding of body language and herd dominance.

Using a lariat, Dustin moved a stocky spotted colt in both directions around the pen at a walk then a trot, teaching the colt to keep an eye on him, the alpha male. Used to being subservient to older horses, it did not take long for the colt to turn and face Dustin, looking at him with both eyes as if to ask, "Okay, I get it—you're boss. Now what do you want me to do?"

At that point, Dustin stood quietly; the colt relaxed and did not move. He slowly approached the colt, who then walked toward him, receiving a pat on his forehead and praise, "Good Boy".

Next, I worked the colt to get him used to being submissive to another person. Within a few times around the pen the colt turned and faced me, accepting his praise and pat on his forehead.

Dustin brought in a halter and gradually slipped it over his nose; the colt tensed up but did not move away. Dustin removed the halter then slowly tried again. He slid the halter off and on the colt's nose a few more times before pulling the crownpiece over his poll and buckling it. The colt stood relaxed a few minutes then Dustin slowly removed the halter. He received a pat and praise then he was returned to the corral containing his peers; his lessons ended for today.

I worked with a frisky, liver-chestnut filly next, sending her around the pen in different directions until she faced me, relaxed. She did not take to the halter so readily and moved away, therefore I signaled her to stop and look at me, and I tried again. This time she not only accepted the halter, she moved her nose toward it and I slipped it on. I decided she had just demonstrated a little independence—she wanted things done at her convenience. I chuckled to myself as I could relate. I knew the filly would eventually find it more rewarding to act on cue.

"She's an independent one, isn't she? What's her name and breeding?"

"Name's Pepi Fire," Dustin replied, "by Pepper Doc, our old Quarter-horse stud, and out of Fire Maiden, a young mare with racing quarter horse bloodlines. Might be a good prospect to mate with Jaalam in the future. Pretty filly. She's got spunk, too."

"Pepi has a special quality. I predict great things from her."

Dustin and I finished working with eight of the yearlings then took an hour lunch break. We still had five more, including the mustangs, to round-pen and halter. I was also anxious to begin working with Jaalam to see how much he remembered of his yearling training from last year.

The three mustangs proved more of a challenge, especially the blue roan colt. He took the longest to 'turn and face', but none of the three became submissive as readily as the ranch-born yearlings. Knowing that trust and respect would come in time, we moved slowly, stroked gently, and praised often, in soft voices. We figured our teaching was successful when they finally relaxed enough for us to touch them all over without their moving off. Not wanting to mess with success, we put off haltering until tomorrow's lessons.

Dustin moved his gelding Runner into another corral as I began ground-working Jaalam to review what he had been taught as a yearling. He had a fine head carriage and wonderful extended trot. I moved him both directions easily then relaxed and he came to a halt along the fence. I encouraged him to face me by making a kissing noise. He responded by walking toward me, seeming to enjoy the interaction and attention he was getting. Pats and praises followed as I ran my hands over his sturdy legs and maturing body. He still needed to grow into his long legs, and his muscles were still developing, but he sure was a handsome boy. I continued talking to him as I showed him his halter and lead rope. Memories of past lessons must have returned as Jaalam lowered his head so I could slip it on and buckle it. So far so good.

Next I backed up and made the kissing sound—he followed, so I took the lead rope with just light contact and led him forward in both directions, stopping periodically to give him practice in responding to pressure. All was going well until Dustin entered the pen. Jaalam suddenly jumped sideways pulling the lead rope out of my hand and galloped around the pen in frenzy.

"What happened?" Dustin asked as he came up beside me. "It looked like he was doing good."

"I don't know, maybe you spooked him when you came in. Why don't you work with him and get him calmed down again while I watch from outside?"

Dustin tried to control Jaalam's movements around the pen. The colt remained anxious and dripping with sweat. After a few minutes, Dustin said, "Pat, *you* come back in here and let *me* leave and see what happens."

When Dustin left the corral Jaalam settled down, and though he snorted and was still breathing hard, he faced me, and on cue walked toward me in the center. "What's up with the bad behavior, Jaalam Akeem?" I asked him softly. "Has someone abused or hurt you? Or do you just like the ladies?" I walked him until he cooled off and relaxed, took his halter off, and gave him more pats and praises. Dustin brought Runner back into the corral and we left.

"So what do you think that was all about? I've never had a horse react like that toward me," Dustin said, feeling confused and disappointed. He had looked forward to befriending the good-looking colt, now it seemed that it might be a challenge just to get Jaalam to tolerate him.

"I sure don't know. Who worked with him last year? Maybe they have a clue."

"I'll ask Jeff. I don't remember seeing the colt when I was here last spring. He must have been ground-worked after I left for Pahaska."

* * * *

During the evening supper, Dan and Leena asked how the yearlings' first lessons had gone. Dustin told them, "Fine, no problems. That blue roan mustang colt has plenty of spirit but he'll come around okay."

I told them I especially liked Pepi Fire and I thought she might make a great horse someday.

Leena responded, "You've got a good eye for horses.

I've already planned to keep her—she's not for sale at any price. Very special, that one.

"And how did Jaalam do, Dustin?"

"Well he and Pat were doing just fine 'til I busted in on them. He spooked something fierce when I showed up. Maybe he's just a ladies man, or Pat has a magic touch, because he was nothing but scared and anxious with me around.

"Jeff, do you know who worked with him last year?"

"No one did. He'd gotten an infection after we branded him and was feeling poorly, so we left him be. Guess he got turned back out without ever being handled properly."

Well now, that put a different spin on things, I thought. Dustin and I agreed that for a two-year-old colt who had never had any ground-work lessons, he had done just fine. Scared and mistrust were his only faults. That could be overcome with gentle handling.

Chapter 33

It was mid-May and the endurance ride was only a month away. Leena suggested we launch a racing plan. She had already sent in the entry form, fee, and signed release form to enter the 50-Mile Race over in Ashland, located near the northeast corner of the Crow Indian Reservation. I called Janey, introduced myself, and asked if she could come to the ranch the next morning to discuss a game plan with Leena and me for racing Reena.

Janey's attitude and demeanor toward me was probably the same as mine was toward her—apprehensive. We had heard of each other, we were Dustin's past and present significant other, and we both rode Reena. At best . . . a touchy situation. Physically, she was the antithesis of me: tall, medium-build, long dark hair, young and pretty. Figuring what goes around comes around, I decided to put my natural inclination toward selfishness aside, for now, and get along the best I could.

Endurance races are normally 50 to 100 miles per day in which all horses are under strict veterinary control. The first horse to finish in 'acceptable condition' is the winner. In addition, out of the top finishers, one horse—not necessarily the first horse over the finish line—is judged to be in 'best condition.' This is based on vet scores, weight carried and riding time. All horses that finish in acceptable condition are given completion awards.

Ride veterinarians have preset recovery criteria and set maximum pulse and respiration limits, known as parameters, eliminating any horse that may be in danger if allowed to continue.

The Ashland Ride's parameters were a pulse requirement of 60, with the respiration rate being equal to or lower than the pulse rate. The vet also checks each horse's vital signs—gut sounds, dehydration, and CRT—and will ask that the horse trot-out to check for soundness, coordination, and impulsion. The vet has the right to say, "You may complete the ride only if you lead him all the way to the finish."

Vet checks are done at mandatory holds, requiring all horses to stop for either a gate- or stop-and-go-check, or a meet-criteria-and-hold-check. A gate-check has no time limit—instead, the horses come in and as soon as they meet recovery criteria, they can resume the ride. At a meet-criteria-and-hold-check, horses come in and meet the criteria for that checkpoint then must wait a mandatory timed period before proceeding, giving the horse an opportunity to rest and eat for a while. All this is to protect horses against overzealous, competitive riders.

Horses must be at least five years old—calculated from their actual date of birth—in order to compete in 50-mile rides. The age limitation is set because horses seldom reach physical maturity before then. Reena turned six years old this spring so she would qualify.

Before lending my limited expertise on the matter, I had several questions for Janey. "Have you ridden in an endurance race before?"

"No, but I have a close girlfriend who has ridden in three races. That's what got me interested in racing."

"How have you been conditioning Reena?"

"I started last January with 15-20 miles of walking and trotting at least three times a week."

"That's called "long, slow distance" or LSD," I told her, "and it's a great foundation for strength. Have you increased her speed any?"

"I've been trotting her more and walking less for the past month."

"I noticed that she's in terrific condition. The only

suggestion I have would be to concentrate on *anaerobic* exercise now, doing speed work and sprints. She will use more oxygen than she takes in and will be forced to huff and puff to get enough air to continue. Ride her at least every other day up and down hills. Alternate: one day do 12-15 miles per hour speed for 10 miles, including at least two half-mile gallops; the next day, do 10-12 mph for 12 miles, including at least one half-mile gallop. I'd like to take her out on long 25-30 mile rides into the mountains on weekends."

Since this would be Reena's *first* race, I proposed that Janey pace herself and not try to win, but strive for Best Condition as her goal. Coming in fourth or fifth place would be an excellent showing for Janey, Reena, *and* the D & L Ranch.

"I'd like to add a half-pound of high fat grain to Reena's daily feed, if that's okay with you, Leena. In addition, she'll need electrolytes to help keep her hydrated and probiotics to aid her digestion before, during, and after the race. Do we have any on hand?" I asked.

"No, but I can have some picked some up at the feed store tomorrow. Will you need anything else special for the race?"

"Her hooves and feet are fine now, but she should be shod again a week before the race, and we'll need extras to take with us in case she throws or loses any. Do you keep her size on hand?"

"Yes, usually. I think she takes a size one. But I'll check with Dan to make sure we have enough. If not, we'll get more."

"What kind of tack do you use on Reena?" I asked Janey.

"I've been using a lightweight Sharon Saare saddle with a wool saddle pad. The saddle has a fleece-lined, nylon-web cinch with an elastic end."

"Sounds good. And you use her regular hackamore?"

"Yep. And my friend suggested that I carry stuff like: a stethoscope, sponge, string, hoofpick, an Easyboot, a pocketknife, and a folding bucket. Is there anything else I should have with me?"

"A water bottle for you and maybe some health or granola bars. And you're going to need a pit crew.

"Leena, are you game to learn about endurance racing by pit crewing with me?" I asked. "You'd meet many potential buyers for your horses at the race."

"Sure, although I don't know anything about it. But, you tell me what to do and I can do it."

"First we'd need to trailer Reena to Ashland a couple days before the race to get her acclimated, and Janey can check out the trails. We'll need hay, a hay net, regular grain, mash, a feed bucket, blankets, cooler, brushes, a couple of water buckets, sponges, extra horse shoes and maybe an additional saddle pad and cinch if you have them."

"Anything more I should know or be prepared for?" Janey asked.

"I'm sure there's a lot, but I can't think of anything right now. How about you Leena?"

"Let's break for today and think on it," she replied.

We all agreed that Janey would keep Reena Mondays through Fridays to speed train and bring her back weekends so I could take her on long rides.

* * * *

The rest of the day, Dustin and I worked the yearlings again, reviewing and reinforcing yesterday's lessons before adding touching and grooming without restraint. The spotted colt— we named him Scooter—had it down perfect and acted like it was yesterday's news. *He must have some Arab intelligence in him*, I thought. Pepi, on the other hand, still demonstrated some independence when I added touching. She tensed and walked off, so I moved her around the pen again until she faced me. I asked her to come to me and slowly stroked her neck, withers and rump while talking softly to her. She decided she liked the attention this time and did not move a muscle while being groomed. What a character!

The mustangs were attentive and eager to please. Even the blue-roan colt we named Blue Jeans was more cooperative today. That was encouraging; he was a nice colt.

Our game plan for Jaalam today was to treat him the same as an untrained young mustang and expect that same type of behavior from him, because as a two-year-old without ground lessons or handling, that's what he was. After removing Runner, Dustin immediately returned to stand beside me in the center of the pen. Only *I* did the talking and moving; Dustin stood quiet. Jaalam eyed him but paid attention to me as I reviewed yesterday's lessons including leading him in both directions. I added backing up by first stopping and facing him, and then I applied pressure to his noseband until he took a step backward.

"Good boy," I praised him. "You sure are smart, aren't you?" Before long, he would walk when I walked, stop when I stopped, and back several steps when I cued him with pressure on his nose.

"Okay, he's doing real good now; let's add *me* to his lesson," Dustin said. "Take his halter off and let him roam around, I'm just going to sit here quietly for a while."

"You want me to leave?"

"Yep, I'd like just the two of us in here for now."

As Dustin knew would happen, curiosity soon got the best of the colt, and he came sniffing around. Dustin paid no attention at first; he ignored him. Soon he stood quietly and moved toward the colt taking up his space. He did this several times until he had to use arm motion to move the colt from place to place. From there he graduated into moving Jaalam around the pen as I had done, until the colt turned and faced him, indicating by his chewing mouth and calm manner that he was willing to submit to Dustin.

"Well I think we made progress, young fella. See, we can get along; we just have to learn to trust and respect each other. Now off with you," Dustin said as the colt followed him to the gate. "We have other horses to tend to, you know."

Once outside the pen, I said, "I think you won him over, cowboy," as I gave him a hug.

"You can tell he's still leery of me, but he's much better than yesterday. He responds to you so well that I think you ought to be the one that works with him the most. I'll show up once in a while to reinforce the trust factor toward another person. Okay with you?"

"You bet. I really love that young guy. He's so smart I could probably start the regular two-year-old training program with him, don't you think?"

"I think he's ready and he needs the attention—just make sure he minds his manners. After all, he's still a stud colt and can do unpredictable things like nip or strike at any time his hormones happen to override his brain."

"I'll be careful, I promise."

Chapter 34

For the next couple of days, we worked teaching each yearling to lead, stand quiet, and relax while being groomed, and to allow us to pick up each hoof for inspection. They did not need tie-training at this point as they were standing at ease and unrestrained when we worked with them. Jeff, John, or Jim would continue these basic lessons while Dustin and I ground-worked the two-year-olds.

There were ten, including Jaalam, and we worked a half to three-quarters of an hour with each for the next week. "Let's work with the two colts first," Dustin suggested. "They're still sore from being gelded, and the exercise will do them good."

We used the large 60-foot round-pen for their training. We needed to 'sack out' each of them before we went any further with their lessons. By building the youngsters' confidence with sacking, we would teach them to control their natural flight-or-fight instincts in response to something new. This would also develop their trust in us and help prevent such annoying—and potentially dangerous—problems as head-shyness, kicking, and spookiness.

We had gathered various barn items ranging in size, texture, and degree of intimidation—a rag, towel, grooming brush, lariat, a blanket, saddle pad, garbage bag, slicker and saddle cover. Dustin had picked out a tall bay gelding named Bomber to sack-out first.

Dustin moved Bomber around the pen a few times to

get his eye and attention. When he turned and faced him, Dustin approached with an outstretched hand and touched Bomber's forehead then continued rubbing his ears, neck and down his body and legs. Bomber had experienced this as a yearling so he stood relaxed and unrestrained. Next Dustin rubbed the rag all over Bomber, building up to the towel, grooming brush and the coiled lariat. I brought the saddle pad over and let Bomber smell and look at it. He was still relaxed so I rubbed the pad along his head, neck, shoulders and legs just like the other objects, ending with the pad across his back—Bomber ignored the pad and rested his head on Dustin's shoulder. We continued rubbing him with the garbage bag and saddle cover, and ended the session by draping the slicker over Bomber's back and leading him around.

Although I loved the Arabian's intelligence and human bonding aptitude, I respected the warm-blooded quarter horse's serene demeanor compared to hot-blooded Arabian's—calm versus anxious.

This same sacking method, with different variations depending upon the horse's response, would be used on each two-year-old that day, including Jaalam. Dustin had two more fillies to work with when he suggested I start work with Jaalam.

"Just leave Runner there, he'll stay out of your way, and I think Jaalam wants your attention more than Runner's at this point. If that doesn't work, send Runner out through the gate, he won't go very far alone."

Jaalam seemed to think this was all a game when I began draping things across his back. I would put the blanket on; he would bite it and take it off. I would put the saddle pad on; he would take it off. "Okay, we need to get serious about this, young man," I said, chuckling to myself.

The lesson was to accustom him to the feel, sight, and sound of scary stimuli, not to teach him tricks. So, I put the saddle pad back on and as he reached around to bite it off, I firmly said, "No" and tugged his halter rope. He flinched at my reprimand, and his head went up, ears back. I waited for him to relax then put the saddle pad on again, and to give him something to think about besides biting the pad, I immediately led him around the pen. "Good boy," I praised him. I successfully did the same with the slicker.

Lessons completed for today, I took off his halter, stroked his neck and walked off, only to find that Dustin had been watching from outside the pen.

"How long have you been here?"

"Long enough to enjoy the show. For a while I thought you were teaching him to be a trick horse," he chided, "until I saw you reprimand him and give him something else to think about besides playing games. Good job."

"If his actions are due to his still being a stud, maybe I should practice tie-training him tomorrow. As a half-Arab stud, his behavior's never going to be as calm and serene as the others, and he's going to have to learn to be tied at times."

"I agree, just hone his relax-and-give-to-pressure responses a little more before you actually tie him to a post or rail."

"Yes, dear," I said sarcastically. I detected a pink blush of embarrassment on his tanned face as he realized I did not need to be told how to train horses.

* * * *

The next day we added crossing a series of obstacles such as poles, plywood, a tarp, and a wooden bridge to the two-year-olds' ground-work training. This lesson would build their confidence and develop their coordination as we *led* them across foreign obstacles before they were asked to negotiate them willingly under saddle and rider.

Again, I started with the easiest, which at this point was Bomber. With him by my side, I used the go-forward cue I had used throughout his train-along series to approach and walk across the series of poles—the least intimidating obstacle. Once he consistently crossed the poles without hesitation, I used the same approach to teach him to walk across the plywood and tarp from each direction. Bomber was curious, sniffing everything before he stepped over or onto it, obviously liking the new work. When he had crossed both obstacles without hesitation or concern, it was time to cross the flat bridge. This proved to be the most difficult, albeit the most important obstacle, and one that would lay the foundation for crossing bridges on a trail ride or trailer loading if or when it was necessary.

Bomber inspected the bridge, and I tapped his hip and asked him to 'walk on'. He willingly put one leg on, and with a bit more urging, he placed his other front leg on the bridge. I patted and praised then asked him to back off the bridge. He heaved a sigh of relief, and I allowed him to relax before I asked him to walk-on again. This time as he got all four feet on, I asked him to stop a moment to settle, then cued him to walk the rest of the way across the bridge. He confidently crossed from both directions before his lesson was over.

The lessons went well until we came to the filly, Fancy Dee, a bay part-Arabian granddaughter of Reba. Her sire was Casey Dee, the Tobiano. She had four white stockings and a wide blaze from mid-forehead to nose tip. She was strikingly beautiful, and intelligent, but flighty. She crossed the poles okay, but skittered sideways across the plywood and tarp as if saying: Oh no, it might bite me so I'll hurry across.

"Pat, maybe if you stand on Fancy's right side while I cue her from her left, she'll feel more secure and focus her direction forward not sideways."

With much more encouragement than Bomber had needed, Fancy finally settled and crossed the obstacles, including the wooden bridge, from both directions.

I worked the last filly while Dustin went to Jaalam's corral. We had agreed that he was not ready to deal with obstacles yet. Another day or two of reviewing his ground-work lessons would be good for his trust and self-confidence.

That evening after adjourning to the living room, Leena proposed that we all visit Laura on Saturday evening. "I can call her tomorrow to make sure she'll be home and warn her that we're coming over," she said, smiling.

Dustin and I exchanged looks and acknowledged it would be a good idea. Tomorrow was Friday and we were planning to go to the rodeo in Cody that evening. Saturday we would finish the first phase of the youngsters training, and they would all be turned back out to pasture. We could relax Saturday night with the family.

On Friday, Dustin and I introduced all the two-year-olds, except Fancy and Jaalam, to the bit, bridle and saddle. Fancy needed another day's training to deal calmly with obstacles, and we did not want to hurry Jaalam's training. Manners and respect were going to be an important part of his life as a stud, so his training was going in a little different direction. I opened his corral gate on Friday and led him around the working ranch area, which introduced him to a variety of new sights, smells and noises. We passed pens containing other horses and sheds sheltering scary machines. After his initial excitement of being outside his pen, his behavior was excellent, although he still remained curious and nosey. He received lots of praises and pats.

Dustin said, "Fancy needs to *focus*. Let's set up more obstacles for her to deal with."

We added a row of plastic strips for her to walk under, barrels to walk around, and poles raised at a variety of levels and angles to walk over. She did wonderfully. The secret apparently was to keep her busy moving.

"She might make a good endurance horse," I told Dustin, "or with her Arab lines, maybe cross her with Jaalam when she's three. They'd produce a beautiful foal."

By now, the two-year-olds had been handled until they were cooperative and responsive to our cues. Bitting, bridling and saddling should be accepted as a natural training progression. Dustin used a full-cheek snaffle for training, attached to a headstall with a browband.

We had already taught the youngsters to lower their heads when being haltered. We gave the same cue so we could gently insert the bit in their mouth and pull the headstall over their ears and crown. We led them around the pen a few times to ensure they were relaxed, then put the saddle pad in place and introduced the saddle. They were allowed to inspect the saddle as long as they did not lap or chew on it. When they were no longer interested, Dustin set the saddle on their back in one smooth motion. Once he fastened all the straps, I unhooked the lead rope and stepped away.

Most of the horses just stood quietly until asked to walk or jog-on in a circle around the pen. A couple of the fillies bucked and spooked when the stirrups hit their sides, but settled down when nothing more happened. It was a rewarding day's work. Dustin and I quit early and got ready to go into Cody for the evening.

Chapter 35

Dustin and I ate at Cassie's Steak House before heading to the Cody Nite Rodeo. It was opening night; the stands were full. We sat above the bucking chutes in the Buzzard's Roost, relishing the cowboy banter and frenzy of bucking broncs, calf roping, team roping, bulldogging and bull riding events. Dustin knew many of the local contenders as he used to do some saddle-bronc riding and team roping. The rodeo stock took on cowboys from all across the country, all vying for the purse as well as the glory of being top cowboy. I enjoyed the drama and excitement.

Cowgirls of all ages competed against each other and the clock, as they raced around barrels, horses turning so tightly that they looked like they were going to tip over.

Younger cowboys joined in the steer riding, a prelude to riding bulls when they grew older.

I knew Rimrock Ranch's guests must be here as they always treated them to the rodeo on opening night and once a week after that. At intermission, I looked around for any of the Rimrock wranglers and spotted Ryan, Scott, Cort and Trampus, talking to some cowboys over by the bullpens.

"Dustin, I'm going to go talk to the Rimrock boys, want to come with me?"

"I'll join you if you're not back soon, right now I need a cup of hot coffee. Do you want me to get you one too?"

"Yes, thanks. See you in a bit," I said, and went to find 'the boys.'

I met them on their way back to the stands and gave a hug to each. It was nice to see my young, good-looking work *compadres* again.

"So when are you coming to work at Rimrock?" Ryan asked.

"In a few weeks, I'll be there by the last of June anyway. Are there many guests at Rimrock yet?"

"No, not many. Scott is head wrangler and is guiding guests while Cortney and I hang around the ranch clearing trails and mending fences. Trampus has been bringing the horses back from wintering in Montana."

"So what are you doing?" Cort asked.

"I'm staying at Dustin's parents' ranch over next to the Pryor Mountains. We're busy training the young stock, and enjoying life." I winked.

"Well get your butt back to Rimrock. I'm going to need help with the new ranch wranglers and too many new horses to deal with," Scott added.

"See you guys soon." I waved and headed back to find Dustin, waiting for me with hot coffee and keeping our seats warm.

Rodeo clowns entertained at intermission and tonight they provided lifesaving assistance to one cowboy. They separated him from a Brahma bull when he was thrown and the bull turned on him, raking him with his horns in the last event of the evening.

It was cold when we left. Dustin wrapped me in a blanket and I fell asleep on the way back to the ranch. Being a cowgirl was exhausting, exciting and rewarding. I loved every minute of it.

* * * *

Saturday we worked the two-year-olds one more time, taking them through their ground lessons. We had managed to bridle and saddle Fancy without incident. The added obstacle course seemed to give her more confidence in herself and trust in us. They had all graduated and were ready to be turned out to pasture again until their fall lesson review.

"I've picked out another filly I like the looks of," I told Leena at supper. "She's a two-year-old, name's Fancy. She's beautiful and smart; too smart maybe, she needs a challenge to keep her interested."

"I know which one you mean, Reba's granddaughter. She has some different bloodlines through her dam's sire. We bred Reba to a half-Arab stallion we were going to lease. He was a gorgeous horse but too hot and hard to handle as a stud. I didn't want that characteristic mixed with our horses so we sent him back to his owner after only one breeding. We'll see how she matures as a three-year-old before deciding to keep her or not. Thanks for pointing her out to me though. I respect your opinion of horses.

"Dustin, what are you going to do with Jaalam and the young mustangs? Are you going to turn them back out?"

"They've trained very well and have done as much as could be expected at their age. Jaalam's come a long way; he's learned trust, respect and manners. The mustangs are not much different from the other yearlings now that we have handled them daily for the past few weeks. They're pretty well domesticated and *need* the companionship of the young herd, so I recommend turning them *all* out to pasture in the fall."

"Sounds like you and Pat have been busy and done some great work. So let's turn them out tomorrow." Leena said.

"Pat and I want to take another ride into the mountains tomorrow, but we can run the youngsters out before we leave. Jeff will help us round up the three-year-olds on Monday for their intensive training."

"Sounds like a plan. Let's head to Laura's, she's expecting us around 6 o'clock. Are you coming Dan?"

"You bet. I haven't seen them young'uns for a month

now. They'll be all grown up next thing I know."

* * * *

Fred and Laura lived in a medium-size log home in Bridger, Montana. There was a small barn behind the house with two corrals, on what looked to be about three acres of land.

Laura greeted her mom, dad, and Dustin with a hug. "Pleased to meet you," she said as she shook my hand.

"Same here," I answered a little awkwardly. Having heard Dustin's story of his engagement breakup, I had too many preconceived ideas about her to feel comfortable. She was warm and sincere, taking after her mom in looks with dark hair, pretty face and a slim build.

"Hope y'all are hungry for ribs," she said as she led us onto the open porch.

"Sounds wonderful! Henry sent over some of his special coleslaw and we brought some Merlot," replied Leena. "Where's Fred?"

"He's out back tending grill. He'll be around in a minute.

"Kenny, Kassie, take it easy on Grampa. You look like you're trying to bulldog him."

Much to his pleasure, Kenny age six and Kassie age four, were climbing all over Grampa Dan, chattering incessantly and competing for his attention. He was a fun-loving man and thoroughly enjoyed romping with his grandkids.

Fred, short, blond, with eyeglasses and a smile, appeared from around the corner, greeting everyone and shaking hands. "Welcome," he said to me, smiling and shaking my hand with a firm grasp.

"Ribs are ready; let's all go inside and eat."

Originally, from the mid-west, Fred was an ophthalmologist with a practice in nearby Billings, besides being a gentleman farmer with chickens, a cow and calf, one horse and one pony. He was also a good cook—the ribs were delicious.

Good food made for amiable conversation, and the evening went well. Dustin and Laura were not gushing over one another but neither did they argue. It was a good beginning toward patching up their distant relationship.

No one mentioned Janey.

Chapter 36

I had grown emotionally attached to the young mustangs, especially Jaalam. I stroked his sleek neck as he put his muzzle on my shoulder. He knew by my demeanor that something different was about to happen. I would miss him but I knew he would relish being herd leader of the youngsters again this summer. I was feeling sentimental and hoped I would see them all again.

"Ready, cowgirl?" Dustin asked as he came to the pen leading our horses, Reena and Cochise. Our saddlebags brimmed with cold fried chicken, biscuits, candy bars and my camera, canteens hung on the saddle horns and slickers tied on back. "Jeff and the boys will open the gates. I'll lead them out if you'll ride behind and push them along."

There was not any *push* to it. The twenty-three youngsters ran, kicking and bucking all the way to the upper pasture where they'd graze until fall. The early morning air was crisp, the horses obviously feeling good to be free of corrals and pens.

My happiness level rises whenever I get on a horse and ride into the western mountains, especially with a wonderful partner. Dustin suggested we ride to an area called Wild Horse Park on Pryor Mountain to check out the wild horses before they moved to higher grazing grounds.

As we climbed, we followed a rough dirt road, making good time with a constant trot over its ruts and bumps. The area was filled with lovely rock outcroppings, tree clusters, and meadows where we would break into a canter, stopping occasionally to enjoy the vista from one of many overlooks. We rode around a curve and, as the landscape opened up before us, we saw three bands of mustangs in the open meadows.

"Some small bands of wild horses roam these juniper foothills year round," Dustin said, "but many prefer this part of Sykes Ridge only seasonally, from February through May."

"Where do they go after May? Any particular area?"

"Most migrate over the South Ridge of East Pryor to graze its high summer pastures."

We ate an early lunch atop the grassy ridge near the rustic Penn's cabin. Dustin explained that the cabin was open for public use on a first-come, first-serve basis. It conveniently provided shelter from inclement weather and contained wood board bunks for sleeping bags and a wood stove.

As we rested, we let our horses graze, restrained by tether lines so they would not be tempted to join the wild ones. We watched a nearby gorgeous black stallion seemingly keep his eye on Reena as a possible new addition to his herd. "No way, big boy," I told him. "Go back to your four other beautiful mares and new foals. She's mine, not yours." He must have been an older stallion because his glossy black coat showed scars from head to hoof from fighting to protect his ladies and babies. His herd was a mix of colors: duns, grullos, roans, spotted and bays.

I took my camera and crept forward to catch a few close shots of the mares and foals. The black stallion kept grazing, always watching yet thoughtfully ignoring me as a guest on his range.

God could not have created a more perfect setting than this. I felt blessed to be a small part of it.

We had ridden at least 30 miles by the time we returned to the ranch mid-afternoon. It was good LSD endurance conditioning for Reena.

* * * *

Monday morning, Jeff, Dustin and I rounded up the three-year-olds from a far pasture west of the ranch, bordering the Bear River. I was astride a chestnut gelding, Shifty, usually ridden by one of the wranglers. He was a well-trained working quarter horse, quick as lightning. He knew what he was doing. I was just along for the ride.

There were eleven three-year-olds, including the three mustangs adopted two years ago now well integrated into the herd. Dustin and Jeff had worked with all the young horses as yearlings and two-year-olds and began reviewing their ground-work lessons in two separate round pens. After each had been bridled and saddled, Dustin began teaching a new lesson, 'giving from the ground,' to a buckskin filly named Lucy. This course would teach Lucy to relax her jaw, poll, neck and shoulders, and *yield* in response to direct-rein pressure from the ground.

I watched as Dustin stood on the young horse's left side with his hands just in front of her withers. He encouraged Lucy to deliver a 'baby give', a soft jaw and slightly tipped nose, when he lifted the inside rein up and back, making light bit contact with the corner of the horse's mouth. Dustin released the rein pressure as soon as Lucy responded. By increasing the amount of pull, Lucy would increase her bend and begin yielding to pressure with her poll and neck. Dustin worked the horse on both sides then began asking the horse to move in a circle with her head in flexed position.

Soon Lucy was ready to add lateral work as Dustin encouraged her to take a diagonal step away from the circle while maintaining flexion, thus beginning the movement of sidestepping. This lesson taught Lucy to 'give to the bit' and would enable the rider to control Lucy's forehand and hindquarters with rein cues.

Dustin asked me to take Lucy to her next lesson of 'snubbing up.' This would get her used to something being above her head, which is where the rider will be.

"Ride Shifty," Dustin said. "He used to be a rodeo

pickup horse and will tolerate being bumped in close quarters with another horse."

I used the other corral and began moving the two horses around the pen, reaching over and petting Lucy along her neck. This reassured her that having someone above her head was okay. I tugged on Lucy's saddle, bumped her in the shoulders and along her sides with my boot toe, and slapped my lariat against her saddle, letting the end dangle on her croup. The goal was not to torture Lucy, but to get her accustomed to the feelings and sounds that occur when she's being ridden. She seemed comfortable through all of this—tomorrow I would get on her back.

When a horse had as much ground training as these had, mounting Lucy or any of other the other three-year-olds and moving off at a walk was generally not a problem. They had been taught to walk on cue and to give to pressure to turn and stop. However, Dustin attached a lunge line when I trotted Lucy around the pen—just in case.

Working with these young horses and preparing them to be good trail horses took an hour with each horse each day. At that rate, it took us a couple of days to complete their walk and trot phase. Next, Jeff set up the obstacle course again, consisting of poles of various lengths, plywood, a tarp, wooden bridge, a blanket draped across the fence and a flapping towel hung on the gate.

The importance of groundwork could not be overstated. With a little curiosity of her own along with urging from me, Lucy walked over the obstacles in both directions on cue, stopped to look at the blanket and towel then moved on. She was ready to go out on the trail.

We planned to trail ride in pairs, a seasoned horse and a green-broke three-year-old. Sometimes Dustin rode the green-broke horses, sometimes I did. He had me ride the fillies and he rode the geldings—*Was there a little chauvinism going on here?* I wondered, *thinking that I couldn't handle male horses.*

I chuckled and let it pass. I might call him on it later in a joking manner. I was having too much fun to cause a controversy over such frivolity. He probably believed he was protecting me—and maybe he was—after all, he knew his horses better than I did.

There is a saying about: "The best laid plans . . ." Dustin and I were training on a preset trail that he had mapped out years ago. The trail went up and down forested hills and contained a muddy area before crossing a small creek and a narrow wooden bridge. Western horses had no problems crossing water as there was usually a creek running through each pasture for drinking—they were used to seeing and being in water. There was also a blow-down across the trail, which meant the horses had to negotiate their way around it through the forest, without a trail.

It was in this area of forest with no trail that a jackrabbit jumped just as we passed by. The young gelding, Buttons, that Dustin was riding, forgot his training and bolted through the brush then suddenly remembered about "facing his fear," and spun 180 degrees around, sending Dustin flying off into a hedge of juniper bushes. Dustin's ego was bruised, as was his right hip and arm, but nothing was broken. Buttons stood shaking, not knowing what to do—his training had not covered what to do when you throw your rider.

When dealing with young horses anything can happen at any time. The ranch had been lucky, besides Jeff getting his foot stepped on while trimming hooves last week; Dustin's was the only accident this spring.

We enjoyed riding and training the three-year-olds for the next couple of weeks. Five of the young horses would be sold at an upcoming auction in Lovell, Wyoming. They would bring a good price.

The three mustangs were already sold. Leena had decided to keep two of the fillies: one half-Arab filly for endurance training, and the other filly, who had an ugly scar on her shoulder but had excellent bloodlines, would make a good brood mare. Dustin wanted one of the larger geldings for his pack string.

Chapter 37

Race weekend was here. We had checked and double checked to make sure we hadn't forgotten anything we'd need. Leena had packed supplies for us; I packed for our horse. Dustin tended to the logistics of trailer, camping equipment and truck. Janey brought her riding and personal gear. I figured we had more than enough of everything.

Reena's last workout was Sunday when Dustin and I took a LSD ride of 30 miles into the Crow Indian Reservation. She had been turned out to pasture to graze and frolic until this morning when she was brought in and given grain, probiotics and electrolytes. She was now loaded in the trailer happily eating her hay.

Dustin had kept a low profile when Janey was around. However, at his mom's request, he had consented to drive us to Ashland and stay in case we needed additional help or a *go-fer*. I'd gotten used to his company, I trusted his judgment, and was glad he was coming with us. This would also give me a chance to observe him and Janey and see if I discerned any remaining romantic feelings between them.

The drive to Ashland took a little over four hours. We arrived at the ride camp a little before noon. The valley, where two-dozen horse trailers and campers were already parked, looked to be about 50 acres, nestled between hills with a creek running the length of one side. We set up camp near the creek, convenient to the water, cook tent, toilets and vetting area.

Figuring Reena needed to stretch her legs and might be thirsty, I led her to the creek. Dustin fashioned a picket line between his truck cab roof and the end of the horse trailer, giving her some wiggle room, then left to fill her water buckets.

I was grazing Reena on the backside of trailer, apparently unbeknownst to Leena and Janey who were in the tack room, and happened to overhear their conversation.

"Janey, is it uncomfortable for you to be around Dustin and Pat when they are together? I didn't give your past relationship a thought when I asked him if he'd drive us here. I'm sorry if I was thoughtless."

"I have to admit it's a little awkward. Pat's okay, but I wish he and I had never broken up. I still care about him very much. They seem to get along, so guess the best I can do is be his friend.

"I can live with that, for now," Janey added.

Knowing I should not have been listening in the first place, I was still shocked and alarmed by this revelation. It sounded like she wanted him back! Well, *too late honey*, I hoped.

Leena and Janey left to find the ride manager. They checked in at the registration desk and paid the additional AERC (American Endurance Ride Conference) non-member fee. The manager issued Janey number twenty-six and gave her a veterinary card to carry with her and present for signing at every vet check throughout the ride.

The pre-ride vet-check would be Friday afternoon at 1pm where the vet would examine horses for soundness and overall good health. If a horse was lame or ill, the vet would not allow it to start. The vet might ask to have a horse re-shod if the current shoes were in poor condition or might jeopardize the horse's chances for a safe completion.

Leena knew the ride manager and stayed at the office to chat a while. Janey met up with her riding friend and went to her camp to visit.

Once everything was settled in our camp, and Reena was

busy looking around and eating her hay, Dustin and I strolled the camp to see if we knew anyone. He knew cowboys and packers; he did not know endurance riders. I knew endurance riders from back in Maine but they were not racing here. I recognized the names of some top riders but I did not know them personally. Stone Rochenk and Vicky Kenvedy were top contenders and were entered in the FEI (Federation Equestrian International) 100-Mile Ride on Sunday.

Riders ate free; the rest paid to eat all we wanted at the cook's tent. Good deal, good food. We were hungry. The cook was slow-roasting a pig in the ground pit for dinner Saturday night after the 50-mile ride.

Reena stood tied in her trailer stall during the night to keep her out of potential trouble. Leena and Janey slept on mats in the truck bed under cover of a tarp. Dustin and I bedded down in a small dome tent he had erected that afternoon. We giggled at the thought of disturbing the campsite by bouncing and groaning, feigning lovemaking. Instead, we whispered.

"We haven't talked much about you and Janey. So, tell me, does it bother you or make you uncomfortable being around her—especially with me present?" I asked.

"I'm glad *you're* with me and don't forget that. Yes, I'm a little lost for words when she and I are alone. It seems like she wants to talk intimately. I just give short 'yes' or 'no' answers and don't start conversations in hopes she'll get the message and leave our past alone."

"You mean, like she's 'coming on' to you?" I said, getting a bit perturbed at the thought.

"Yeah, maybe."

"Well, *maybe* you two really ought to talk seriously sometime, to set things straight. I overheard her say that she wished you two had never broken up. Avoiding her obviously will not solve the problem forever."

"We'll see," he said as he conveniently pretended to go to sleep.

Janey and her friend rode the last few miles of the race trails in the morning. They had also decided they would ride together during the race. Reena vetted through the pre-ride check that afternoon in great condition. Dustin and I got a little bored with inactivity and went hiking while Leena took a nap. We hiked horse trails, meeting and being passed by a few riders exercising their horses and checking out the trails. As the paths ascended and descended steeply, I began to have difficulty breathing.

"I always knew I'd rather ride than walk," I said between taking puffs off my inhaler. "My asthma won't take much of this altitude."

"That sounds like an excuse for being out of condition if I ever heard one," Dustin chided.

"I'm in condition to ride, not walk," I informed him sharply.

At the pre-ride briefing that evening, the ride manager told about the trails, how they're marked, where the water sources are, vet criteria and types of checks. At this ride, all checks were in base camp. There would be three mandatory holds: a gate-check after traveling the first 12 miles, a timed meet-criteria-and-hold 30-minute check at mile 25, then another meet-criteria-and-hold 30-minute check at mile 37.

Horses had to reach a pulse rate of 60 or below within 30 minutes of completion or be disqualified. They were also required to present to the vet within one hour of reaching the required pulse rate to stand for completion.

* * * *

Race day was here! Morning mist shrouded the foothills. I was excited; Dustin was serious; Janey was 'oh well,' and Leena stood back watching the drama unfold. Reena enjoyed being fed early and seemed unperturbed by the camp activity as she stood quietly while being saddled. It was about 15 minutes before the start when I noticed that Janey was not wearing her number.

"Why don't you walk or jog Reena around to limber up and I'll go get your number bib?" I said.

In endurance, there is a *controlled* start or a *shotgun* start. This was to be a shotgun start. All competitors would start at once—in a mad dash. I called Janey over to give her some last unsolicited advice.

"Seeing as you and Reena have no experience at this, why don't you hang back until the front-runners' dust has settled? I know you're riding with your friend but *you* know your horse; set your *own* pace, and ride your *own* race. If your friend doesn't want to ride *your* race, then 'oh well', let her ride her own. You are racing for yourself and the ranch. Your goals should be to finish, and to keep Reena healthy and sound.

"Good luck and have a great ride," I said, and I meant it.

The shotgun turned all forty-five competitors loose promptly at 6am. Reena was excited now, and doing spins as Janey held her back from running with the front speedsters. They left riding with the last third of the pack—*good job, Janey.*

Reena was twenty-fifth coming into the first vet check. She drank some tepid water while Leena and I ran wet sponges over her head, neck and lower legs. Her pulse went quickly down to 60, and she was through the vet check in a couple of minutes. Janey had her back out on the trail ahead of some riders who had come in before her. Things were good for us so far. Janey's friend's horse was held due to an elevated pulse rate.

The next vet check was halfway the race and was a mandatory 30-minute hold. Janey was stripping off the saddle as she headed toward our spot; Leena was quick to put water to Reena's neck. Once the saddle was off, I sponged with one hand and used the sweat scraper with the other over her neck, shoulders, withers, rump and inside hind legs. After vetting in, we used cool water to finish cleaning and cooling her, brushing dirt from her legs and towel-drying her head.

We had time to replace the sweaty saddle pad and cinch.

She ate some wet mash with electrolytes and probiotics, nibbled at her hay, and drank some more tepid water before leaving. When she left, she was running in seventeenth place and doing well.

Between loops, we refilled the water pails, cleaned the sweat scraper and brushes, replaced wet towels, and had time to take some deep breaths to relax and socialize. Everyone else was doing the same things we were to get ready for their horse to come back in.

A man from the trailer next to ours came over and asked, "Howdy ma'am, do you have an extra sponge I could borrow? My son brought just one as he thought he'd be crewing alone. I came along at the last minute."

"Sure," I said. "We brought extra everything. Do you need another sweat scraper or brush?"

"Yes, that would be great, if you can spare them. Say, that mare of yours is a real looker . . . where're y'all from?"

"The D & L Quarter Horse Ranch, about 150 miles southwest of here, over on the other side of the reservation . . . name's Pat, this is Dustin and Leena. Where're you from?"

"Please to meet ya. I'm Robert, from Missouri. We love these mountain rides and are planning to do the Shamrock down in Wheatland, Wyoming the first of July. Will you be going there?"

"No, we do pack trips into the mountains during the summer," Dustin explained.

Leena added, "This is our mare's first ride. We'll see how she does in this one before we enter her in another."

"Well, good luck and nice meeting you, I'll return these after the race."

"Okay, and same to you," I replied as I spotted the first of the horses beginning to come in for their next mandatory 30-minute hold check. Reena was twelfth coming in. We went through the same cooling-out procedure as the last stop, only I vetted her in so Janey could rest. Reena vetted through still in great condition. Leena made sure she drank and ate her mash-mix and hay, and sponged more water over her neck, shoulders, and withers, under her belly and between her hind legs, while I massaged her muscles. Janey asked Dustin if he would massage *her* muscles. He looked at me, rolled his eyes, mumbled something and walked off. I let it pass; the race was more important, at the moment.

"Janey," I said, "during these last miles Reena needs you to get enthusiastic so she can feed off your energy. No more tired until after the race, okay. See ya at the finish line." Thirteen more miles to go.

Reena finished in fifth place, completing the 50-miles in five hours and twenty-two minutes, a half-hour behind the first place horse. Good showing for her first time out. Leena was beaming like a proud mother when they announced, ". . . and the half-Arab mare, Bey Shareena, from the D & L Ranch in Warren, Montana, is judged to be in Best Condition". She won a new horse blanket for the ranch and a Montana Silversmith Buckle for Janey.

Twelve out of the starting forty-five did not finish, including Janey's friend whose horse was pulled at the mile-25 vet check.

Robert's horse finished tenth.

Chapter 38

We were still floating on 'Cloud Nine' when we arrived back at the ranch. Many prospective buyers at the ride camp had queried Leena about her breeding programs and bloodlines—of special interest seemed to be her upcoming mustang/Arab line. She could see a potentially good market for her mixed-Arab horses in the endurance field.

They did not realize that a big part of Reena's extraordinary condition was because she had been used in the mountains as a light packhorse since she was four. "Oh well," she told Dan later at dinner, "those who think they know everything about 'conditioning' could find this out for themselves."

Janey had asked about entering Reena in more endurance rides over the summer. However, Dustin pointed out, "She's part of my summer pack-trip string and I'd like to take her with the rest of my horses to Pahaska this next week." Leena agreed. She might have been trying to keep Janey away from the ranch, and Dustin—which was okay by me.

That evening, Henry cooked a roast beef dinner with all the trimmings. Janey had gone home—hopefully forgotten—but *we* were still celebrating. Reena was being treated like a queen with all the hay, water and attention she could handle. Laura's family had come to dinner, which added to the festivities. It felt like a farewell dinner to me. It was nearly time I went back to work at Rimrock Ranch as I'd promised Glenn. I felt sad when I thought about leaving this beautiful horse ranch and these lovely people who were like family to me now. I would miss them. I would also miss Jaalam, Pepi, Blue Jeans, Fancy, and Reena. I did not know if I would see them again or not. I said my "good-byes" to Laura, Fred, Ken and Kassie; I was not yet ready to say farewell to the others.

Luckily, I had a week to make the transition between ranches. Dustin and I had his horses to move to Pahaska for the summer then I'd move on to Rimrock to work for the next two months.

The area of Pashaska was located 52-miles west of Cody, just before the East Entrance of Yellowstone Park. Dustin had corrals for his twelve horses, a tack and feed shed, and an A-frame cabin that he used as home base six to eight months a year. A small creek running through the far side of his horse corrals supplied water. My mood was melancholy as we pulled into Dustin's "mini-ranch" as he called it. The thought of spending most of the week alone with him was appealing; however Rimrock was ever on my mind.

Dustin suddenly woke me from my reverie. "Hey cowgirl, where are you? You look lost in thought. I'll get these horses unloaded and fed if you'll go open the cabin to get it aired out. The key's the third one on my truck key-ring."

We had brought just three horses on this run; hay bales took up the rest of the trailer space. Dustin had left no horse feed or groceries when he closed his mini-ranch last spring as hungry grizzlies roamed the Pahaska area, or any place in and around Yellowstone, for anything edible after coming out of winter hibernation. Dustin's feed shed had been broken into and there were deep scratches in his front cabin door. I was concerned.

Thoughts that grizzlies might be in the neighborhood brought chills down my spine. Last summer, while three of us ladies were foolishly tubing down a wilderness creek just east of Pahaska, we had suddenly floated passed a grizzly that was standing near the bank fishing. Luckily, the bear was more interested in catching fish than eating ladies that day. I did not care to be that close to a grizzly again.

"Would grizzlies come after the horses?" I asked apprehensively.

"Not usually this time of year. They should have satisfied their famished spring appetites by now. Yellowstone is full of natural bear food May through October."

"I'll take your word for it, but if there are any strange noises outside tonight, you know who's staying inside, behind a locked cabin door." I was very serious.

I had never stayed in Dustin's cabin. We had stayed together at the Big Bear Motel last summer and in tents while pack tripping. His cabin interior was more spacious than it looked from the outside. It contained a kitchen with counter space for eating, as well as a small stove and a large combination freezer/fridge, a moderate living room with stone fireplace, and a full bath, with a washer and dryer. We slept in the loft, which featured a floor to ceiling window. We could look up at the moon and stars. We could also look down upon the horse corrals— or spot a visiting grizzly. The creek added tinkling background music to the night sounds making sleep come easily.

Before going to bed, we'd made a 'must have' shopping list for cabin and pack trip supplies—frozen meats, canned foods and dry goods—that we'd purchase in Cody the next day. Dustin decided to keep the trailer hooked, and we brought back horse grain and a load of hay along with the stacks of grocery items.

We stayed three days in Pahaska, sorting and cleaning pack equipment, and oiling tack and harnesses before returning to D & L Ranch to finish personal packing and bring back the remaining nine horses. Dustin called Chad, his friend, pack cook and wrangler, to have him look after his cabin, supplies and horses while we were gone.

"How come I've never met Chad?" I asked as I cuddled up to Dustin in our bunkhouse "suite".

"He's newly married and doesn't hang around after pack trips any longer than necessary. His wife's expecting early fall.

Hope he continues to work for me . . . he's a trustworthy friend and worker. I'll introduce you to him this summer. You'll like him."

This was our last night at Dustin's parents' ranch. Leena pulled me aside after our evening meal and as a concerned mother, she asked, "Do you think you'll be back in the fall, Pat? You really fit in here and you do an excellent job of training horses. What's more, Dustin is happy."

"I hope to get done work at Rimrock the last of August, so if that happens I could come back—but we'll see. I can't say for sure right now." I replied as tears welled up in my eyes. She gave me a hug and said, "You know you're welcome anytime. Now let's join the men before we both start sobbing."

After breakfast, Henry the cook gave me a big bear hug; I shook hands with head wrangler Jeff, along with wranglers Jim and John; Dan embraced me with a kiss on the cheek. Leena hugged me gently and whispered, "You remember what I said now. And I hope we'll see you in the fall."

With tears flowing freely, I left, driving my car, followed by Dustin, his truck and trailer. No matter what happened in the future, these past six weeks had been some of the happiest in my life.

Dustin and I agreed to celebrate our last night in the quiet of his cabin. It had been a hectic week and quiet seemed appropriate. He cooked steaks and potatoes on the outside grill while I made a salad and biscuits. We sat on the porch watching the stars and pointing out constellations while sipping a second glass of Merlot. The creek's delightful sound added to the almost perfect scene. Perfect, except that I was leaving tomorrow.

"In a way, I've dreaded this evening, you know," he said. "We've had such fun together that I hate to part for the summer. We don't talk much about us. But I think it's time to state the obvious: You're a wonderful partner and I love you, cowgirl. *And*, I'd really like to extend what we have into the future to see where it goes. What do you think?"

"What do I *think* . . . I think I'm not very good at acknowledging my feelings, much less expressing them. I love the comradery we have working and playing together. I love the ranch, the horses, and yes, I love you too. However I carry a lot of hurt and past baggage with me, the same as you, so I want to proceed with caution. Let's see what the summer brings before we plan any further, okay?" I replied, hoping he was not too hurt by my evasive answer.

"Whatever you say, just always be honest with me—in every way."

"I will. I no longer play games in relationships."

"Maybe we can get together whenever I layover between pack trips. I'll call you."

"I hope so. No problem getting out nights as long as I am back by morning work-time. And there's always the weekend off during Cody's Fourth of July Stampede Days—great memories there, huh?" I said, trying to lighten the mood.

"Sooooo, last one to bed makes breakfast," he said as he dashed inside and scrambled up the ladder to the loft ahead of me.

Too soon—after I had made hotcakes and bacon for breakfast—the time had come to leave. Having already visited the corrals and petted my favorite horses, Reena, Cochise, Runner and the new three-year-old Zane, Dustin walked me to my car.

"I pick up five guests in Cody this afternoon for a short three-day trip, and then I'm back again. I'll give you a call this weekend, okay?" Dustin said, trying to act as if our parting was an everyday occurrence.

"I'll look forward it," I replied as we embraced.

"Remember, I love you, cowgirl."

"And I love you too, cowboy."

Chapter 39

On the way to Wapiti Valley I tried to make the transition to thinking pleasant thoughts of working at Rimrock Ranch again and seeing their horses and my fellow wranglers. However, my heart was heavy, and it wasn't until I turned onto the ranch's mile-long driveway that my mood changed. I took a deep breath and decided to make the best of my decision to work there for the next two months. After all I would still see Dustin whenever we had time.

Rimrock Ranch was located halfway between Cody and Yellowstone. Besides the main ranch house, bunkhouses and various sheds, nine guest cabins that held up to 48 guests were grouped around a couple acres of land shaded by cottonwoods with Canyon Creek running through. Its 600-acre horse pasture bordered the Shoshone National Forest on its south and west, which made it appear larger.

Being Sunday, most of the horses were resting and grazing in the roadside pasture. However, a half dozen were feeding in the big corral. I recognized two wrangle horses, Reno and Patrick. The ranch's personal horses, Ronnie, Casper, Crystal and Phyllis were there also—must be special friends were going riding today. Guests were in the process of moving out after their week's stay, making way for new ones checking in. Wranglers had the morning off.

As I entered the log ranch house lodge, Glenn and Alice's daughter was busy behind the desk checking guests in and out.

She looked up, gave me a smile and pointed to the dining room. Glenn was socializing with some guest-friends over coffee.

"Hi Chief," I said as extended my hand. "Long time, no see."

Glenn, respectfully called "Chief", was my mom's age and suffered some stiffness from being thrown too many times in his former bronc-riding days. However, he still ran a tight ship and he had likely forgotten more about cowboys, horse, and running a dude ranch than I would ever know.

"'Bout time you got here, girl," he replied with a smile. "This is Lon and Lonna, you remember them from last year. They're good friends who have been guests here for the past twenty years. They've offered to help on trail rides if we need them."

"Hi, nice to see you again." I recognized them as we shook hands.

"We were just discussing horses, trails and things you'll be involved in, so why don't you sit a spell?"

After getting myself a cup of coffee, I sat down— puzzled. "So what's up?"

"Well, Scott is head wrangler this year. Ryan does not want to do it anymore, said he would 'rather work on pack trips'. Cortney and Mike also want to be mountain wranglers like their buddies, so I've hired three new boys to work at the ranch, and Pier will be back. They'll all be here by next week and Scott will be busy. I'd like you to help out planning rides, taking care of horses and all. You two decide who does what. The ranch has a full house from this week through August so you'll both have plenty to do."

"Alright," I said, knowing he was telling me not asking me. "Is Scott here today? I didn't see him when I came up the drive."

"He fed the corral horses this morning so he's around somewhere."

"I haven't unpacked yet; do you know if I have the same

end-room of the bunkhouse as I had last year?"

"Yup. Why don't you find Alice and tell her you're here so the girls can get sheets and towels to your room? I think she's helping guests out of the artist's cabin."

"OK, I'll find Alice, get my gear stored and then go talk with Scott. See y'all later." I said, still somewhat puzzled.

I was lucky; everyone else had to share his or her space. Because of my different working hours, I roomed alone instead of sharing with another female. I liked it that way. My room contained a double bed with a small window over it, a dresser under a large picture window that overlooked the creek, a small closet, wall hooks for my jeans and jackets, and a wash sink and toilet. I plugged in my coffeepot and radio, unpacked and stored my suitcases under the bed.

I found Scott napping in his bunkhouse. I had worked with him last year. He was a nice guy with a good sense of humor who looked like Garth Brooks, played guitar and sang like Chris LeDoux.

"Hey, we need to talk. What's Chief mean when he says that you're head wrangler but that he wants *me* to help you?"

"And hello to you too," he said as he woke up. "How do *I* know what Chief means? He told me I would be head wrangler, but didn't say anything about *you* except that you'd be here the last of June. *But*, I'll be glad to have your help. Come on in and sit if you can find a place in our not-so-clean room. Ryan, Trampus, Cortney and I aren't exactly neat-freaks. They got up early to take Mike on his first rattlesnake hunt."

"And *why* would they hunt rattlesnakes?"

"There's a market for their rattles and cured skins. Guess they don't make enough as wranglers," he said as he laughed and shrugged.

"Back to wrangling—what I'd like to do is have a say over the horses: young ones, old ones, and injured. I'd like to make sure the young ones get enough training, the old ones get more feed and used less, and the injured receive care and put out to pasture until they're well. It would be nice to be able to help Chief assign horses to guests, too, as I would know their condition and if they were able to be ridden. What do you think?"

"I think Chief will always want final control over who rides which horse, but might like your input. If you want to be in charge of the horses, I'll be in charge of the wranglers—whoopee. We can share duties on trail rides and the rest. Sound good to you?"

"Sounds good to me. Now you can go back to sleep. I'll help you fit saddles later if you want."

"Thanks, now get out of here so I can catch some more zzzzz's before lunch," he said good-naturedly.

The outside dinner bell always rang promptly at twelve o'clock noon. Lunch at Rimrock was a buffet of cold meats, cheeses, sandwich veggies like tomatoes and lettuce, a hot dish casserole, and pudding or Jell-O with cookies, for dessert.

Chief asked Scott and I if we would catch and halter the four ranch horses so he, Alice, Lon and Lonna could take an afternoon ride. "We'll be at the corrals around one o'clock. Lon and I can saddle our own horses—he can ride Crystal—if you'll saddle Casper for Alice and Phyllis for Lonna."

"I can saddle my own horse," Alice piped up. "Just get my saddle down from the maintenance shed—and don't tie Casper. Just throw his lead rope over the rail; he'll stay."

It was a lovely afternoon to horseback ride. If Razan had been there I would have gone for a ride with them, but I didn't consider Reno or Patrick pleasure horses, so I didn't go. I'd known I would miss Razan not being here this summer, especially on Sunday afternoons like this, but I had plenty of other horses from which to choose to ride. My choice for best wrangle horse would be Navaho, a small spirited paint who had been my assigned wrangle and guide horse last summer. Fiddler was a quick-moving liver chestnut, good manners, and an excellent all round horse. Washakie was a leased, three-year-old gray, half Arab/half Appaloosa that I really liked. I managed to train him while I used him as a guide horse late last summer. Pecos was a bay mustang that I could not use for wrangling but I liked to guide with him—he had spunk. He shied too much to let guests ride him.

Before supper Scott and I fitted each guest to a saddle according to the size of their butt, lengthening or shortening stirrups as needed. I also used this time to subtly interview them as to their riding experience and ability so Chief and I could match them with a horse they'd enjoy and get along with for the next week.

Trampus joined us in time to charm the female guests and impress the males with his cowboy knowledge and gift of gab. He said he had left the other boys early to stop in to check on his mom who was recovering from a horse-kick to her ribs.

Ryan, Cort and Mike showed up later for the Sunday evening introductions and guest briefing. They had shot five rattlers that day while hiking Rattlesnake Mountain, just outside of Cody. Ryan with his welcoming smile gave me a hug, while Cort and Mike, being more reserved, simply shook hands. Ryan had been my boss as head wrangler my first year, but I also liked him as a friend. He had gotten engaged over the winter and gained some weight; being tall anyway, he carried it well and looked good.

Cort was as handsome as ever with his dark twinkling eyes and easy smile. He wanted to be a mountain wrangler in hopes of someday running his own outfit.

Quiet and serious, Mike, had become a good wrangler last year after arriving late summer and having never been around horses before. He'd worked wrangling at hunting camps into late fall while the other boys were at Montana State University in Bozeman. He was going to be a pack-trip wrangler this year. Pack trips didn't begin until July so they'd all be working as ranch wranglers with Scott and I until then.

"By the way Ryan," I said semi-seriously, "let's agree right now—no short-stirrups, no hiding saddles, and no putting mice in my bedroom, okay?"

"It wasn't just me . . . you instigated some of that."

"Yes, and I got the worst of it; that's why I'm saying 'No' this year."

"Okay, if you say so. I'll be in the mountains most of the summer anyway. Boy, you're grouchy already."

"No, I'm just not as naïve as last year." I added with a grin.

* * * *

Forty-five guests survived Monday morning's riding instructions on their newly assigned horses. Then everyone left on the Introductory Ride, skirting the wooded Shoshone National Forest and up over the mesa and down the other side to return to the ranch in time for lunch.

I was astride Fiddler today and found him very spirited after being laid off all spring from a bowed tendon. In the afternoon we were leading an intermediate group on a three-hour ride up the East Fork of Canyon Creek when he suddenly spooked at a coyote and took off bucking up the trail. I finally got him back under control just as Ryan, who had been riding behind, caught up to me with the guests.

"If you can't handle your horse, Chief would probably let you ride Ol' Buck or pokey Waldo," he said jokingly.

"I don't think I need to change horses, smarty, but I might swap places with you and ride drag the rest of the way—if you don't mind. Fiddler's needing some serious miles on him to take out his friskiness. I think I'll be riding him the rest of this week." I reined him in behind the line of riders.

Scott had stayed at the ranch corrals to give lessons to the beginners, while Cort and Mike took an advanced group up the West Fork of Canyon Creek for a scenic ride. Trampus had taken Lon and Lonna on a private ride on the other side of the Shoshone River.

After a lively evening of square dancing with guests and employees in the Ramuda Room, it was bedtime and lights out. This was my first night in seven weeks without having Dustin lying beside me. It would take getting used to.

Chapter 40

The ranch's schedule of events never change; we all got up early Tuesday morning and rode up Green Creek to Glenn's breakfast of blueberry hotcakes, bacon, eggs, sausage, coffee and juice. On the way back to the ranch, we split into three groups according to ability and rode accordingly. The novices and youngsters were content to walk; the intermediate riders could trot some when the trail was level; and the daredevils got to lope part of the way back.

The other boys drove all the guests into Cody for the river float trip Tuesday afternoon. Scott and I had the afternoon off. He went to Powell to visit his family, and I hung out in my room alternating between reading and napping. Later in the afternoon, I put on my sneakers and hiked up the rim-trail behind the ranch. I took my camera, as the view from the rim was spectacular. It overlooked all of Wapiti Valley; I could see east almost as far as the Buffalo Bill Reservoir, twenty miles away.

To break the routine, we wranglers often pulled pranks on one another—it was Mike's turn Wednesday. After wrangling all the horses into the corrals before breakfast, Ryan and Cort turned Mike's favorite horse, Ace, back out to pasture. Of course, Ace wasn't going to leave the herd by himself so they turned his half-brother Deuce, who wasn't being ridden this week, out with him—and off they ran—to who knows where.

The ranch guests and wranglers all played softball in a sagebrush and cactus covered picnic area a couple of miles from the ranch on Wednesday mornings. We wranglers usually saddled up for the afternoon's Lost Creek ride after the game. We had plenty of time, good thing. After looking all around the corrals, Mike said, "Did Ace come in with the herd this morning?"

Ryan replied, attempting to appear serious, "I assume so but I didn't do a head count. Why, are we missing some?" Cort was trying not to laugh as he nudged Trampus.

"Don't put me on," he said, getting a little perturbed. "Did you *shits* hide him somewhere, or turn him back out?"

"Who us? Would we do that to you?" Cort added with a grin.

"You *shitheads*. Just wait, I'll get you guys." And with that, Mike hopped on Stubby bareback and rode off to find Ace.

I was silently glad it was him not me they were playing tricks on. They weren't beyond putting a burr under another wrangler's saddle pad or loosening a previously tightened cinch so his saddle would roll when he mounted—all in the name of fun, called 'cowboy humor'. I was older than these boys, and I didn't see getting hurt as fun. I kept a low profile.

At lunch, trying to smooth over any remaining hostility, Scott said, "Mike, why don't you lead this afternoon's ride?"

"Sure, Ace and I can do anything you want," Mike responded—everything seemingly back to normal. I figured that he was just biding his time until Ryan and Cort were out on pack trips, then he'd *more* than get even with them. I could envision their horses turned loose at the South Fork trailhead or hidden somewhere in Three-Mile Meadow on Eagle Creek.

Next day, Mike helped Cort pack Allen-mule with food and drink for the all-day ride to Table Mountain. The ride climbed slowly via switchbacks up to 9500 feet above sea level. It was a long day, but riders of any ability could go if they wanted to. Ryan and Trampus cooked hamburgers and hot dogs for the guests, accompanied by pickles, tomatoes, and lettuce on the side. Marla, our cook, had made oatmeal cookies for dessert, served with coffee or hot chocolate, as it was windy and chilly at that elevation. We relaxed for a couple of hours, letting the horses graze. Kids hiked and climbed boulders; adults wandered around and took pictures looking down on Wapiti Valley; we wranglers got in a short snooze before leading the group up to the apex. The top of the mountain was not flat but rolling, similar to a golf course. At any given time deer, elk, or cattle could be seen grazing its high open pastures. It was great riding as long as we stayed near the wooded areas. Out in the open, the wind blew fiercely most of the year.

We descended riding a different trail on the other side of the mountain. We usually hurried at a fast walk on the trip down the mountain. Thursday was rodeo night and guests needed time to change and get ready.

Vans left promptly after supper. Chief would yell, "Let's go rodeo!" and guests and wranglers alike would pile into the vans dressed in cowboy and cowgirl attire. Cody Nite Rodeo here we come!

That night, one of our young guests, an eight-year-old named Jason, caught up with the calf during the kiddies' half-time calf-scramble and brought back the tail ribbon—and the new cowboy belt he'd won for a prize. He was grinning from ear to ear when he entered the van, having beat out seven other kids from the ranch and at least fifty other six- to ten-year-olds in the contest.

"Hey *partner*," Cortney said as he gave Jason a high-five, "nice job grabbing that tail ribbon."

"And I like that new belt you're wearing, can I have it?" Trampus joined in.

"No, it's too small for you," Jason said in all seriousness. "I'm going to wear it at our rodeo on Saturday and *beat* everyone."

The guests loved our rodeo. All ages participated. We had serious competitions i.e. age-appropriate equitation classes. Most couldn't wait to show off their horsemanship skills they'd learn during the week. Jason trotted and bounced on Waldo's back, winning first place in *his* age class. Afterwards he said, "See, my new belt was lucky for me."

We had fun games like the egg race, barrel race, and steer roping. It gave everyone a chance to 'cowboy- or cowgirl-up' and ride their horse as fast—or slow—as they wanted in the individual events. Most stayed on, some fell off, but no one got hurt, and everyone enjoyed himself or herself.

A ten-year-old boy named George had teased every day to race his horse, aptly named Shorty. Scott had told him that being only ten, he was too young and still too inexperienced at riding to go with the advanced group on rides like the Holy City trail where loping was allowed. So when it came George's turn to race around the barrels, he looked at the wranglers, smiled and said, "Watch *me*."

Now, Shorty might have been small and usually pretty docile, but he was not a horse to be handled roughly—and that's just what George did. He gave Shorty a big kick with both heels and the horse leaped up in the air as if a firecracker had gone off under him. George stayed on until Shorty hit the ground then flew over his head and landed in a heap. We weren't surprised and managed to stifle our laughter as we ran over to see if he was hurt. To George's credit, he stood up, raised his hands as a sign that he was all right, and walked off to cheers and applause . . . however he decided *not* to enter Shorty in any more races that day.

Even the wranglers had fun, which they demonstrated in a skit Saturday night at Rimrock's talent show. Cort pretended to be bucking-horse-Shorty, Mike pretended to be bronc-rider-George. Scott was the judge, announcing George the winner as he rode Shorty the full eight seconds and scored the most points. Guests clapped and cheered when Scott gave the *real* George a blue ribbon for Best Sportsman of the week.

* * * *

Pier arrived Sunday. I picked him up at the Yellowstone Regional Airport in Cody. Pier was from Northern Italy where he was a third-year college student, majoring in Veterinary Medicine. He was dark, handsome, had a beautiful smile and sexy eyes. We had been assigned as wrangle partners the year before. He said he had learned to speak English by mimicking American country and western singers. His forté was singing western ballads as he accompanied himself playing guitar. Females from age six to ninety-six were charmed by his naïveté and all were secretly in love with him—he loved Wyoming.

I liked the fact that he was gentle with animals, helping me vet the sick, lame and injured horses.

It was just like old times with Pier back. We all got together in his room that evening to watch movie videos, drink pop, eat chips and popcorn, getting crumbs all over his bunk bedroll. Two cabin girls, Staria and Diane joined us.

Although the girls' and boys' bunkhouses were next to each other, hanky-panky between employees was forbidden. I'm not saying it never happened, just that Glenn and Alice would fire anyone caught in a sexual relationship. So *platonic* was prevalent. We were like brothers and sisters, playing and joking, fighting and feuding. And God help anyone who got in a confrontation with *one* of us; they'd have to contend with *all* of us.

Chapter 41

All good things must come to an end, and our *wrangler reunion* ended abruptly as Trampus and Mike left to join Rimrock's guide, Gerald, on a pack trip into Deer Creek, and three new wranglers showed up to work. Ted, Tom and Brad, all fresh off ranches down on the South Fork, could ride, rope and handle a horse but were unfamiliar with *our* horses, trails, and Rimrock's way of doing things. Scott would have his hands full.

On Monday afternoon, I told Scott I'd like to stay back and vet a couple of injured horses in the hospital pasture. "Is it okay if Pier stays behind to help me? One of the mares is new to the ranch and has a severe injury to her shoulder from being kicked. It might take two of us to keep her quiet enough to clean the wound and stitch it if necessary."

"Sure, we've got enough wranglers going on the ride, and Cort will be in the corrals giving beginner lessons with Chief if you need more help. I checked that mare when she came in, and she's a spooky one. Who's the other mare with her?"

"It's Cassie who has a mildly swollen front tendon. I'm going to soak it with Epsom salts first, then stand her in the cold creek to see if I can get the inflammation out of it. I'd like to be able to use her next week as we're going to be really short of ranch horses. The second pack trip is leaving Friday taking fifteen head with them."

"That's right, we'll be losing Ryan and Cort to that trip . . . no more excess wranglers after they leave."

"Keep the faith, we'll be okay." I left to find Pier who was cinching up his favorite horse—a sorrel Appaloosa named Clyde.

"Hey Pier, Scott said you should stay behind this afternoon and help me vet the mares in the hospital pasture, okay?"

"What are their problems?"

As I explained the mares' injuries to him, we gathered grain cubes, halters, lead ropes, scarlet oil, antiseptic salve, fresh gauze, a curved needle and catgut for stitching, disinfectant, clean sponges, Epsom salts and buckets. We could use creek water that ran through their pasture for cleansing.

Observing the new mare, Bitterroot, from a distance, Pier commented, "Looks like her wound is still fresh so I may be able to suture. Otherwise, I'll trim the dried edges and treat it as an open wound." I nodded my head in agreement accepting that he knew what he was doing.

Deciding to vet the worst, first, we tried unsuccessfully for a half-hour to catch Bitterroot. She would have no part of being caught. Frustrated, I said, "Pier, why don't you go get Cortney and a lariat. The three of us should be able to run her into a corner where one of you can throw a rope around her. I'll start soaking Cassie's leg in the meantime."

Guess the boys decided they did not need me to help rope Bitterroot. I was bending over the bucket of Epsom salts soaking the mare's leg and heard them chasing the injured mare near me. I paid no attention. The next thing I knew, the mare had somehow run into me catapulting me into a front summersault. Her front feet clipped my head as she tried to jump over me; one hind hoof scraped my right leg while the other hoof landed full weight on top of my left foot—Man, that hurt!

Pier and Cort carried me to the ranch house. On the way, Cort said, "That mare must be part Arabian to be such a harebrain."

"I disagree," I said vehemently. "An Arabian might run

from people trying to catch her, but wouldn't run over someone in the process." His mother owned an Arabian. He didn't argue.

Alice cut off my boot then got ice to apply to my foot and ankle. Hoping nothing was broken and not wanting to create any more fuss, I asked not to go to the hospital. I wrapped my injury with an ace bandage, soaked it in ice every hour for the rest of the afternoon and hoped it would be better by morning— It wasn't.

My ankle and foot had turned deep purple and it hurt to step on it. *Great. Now what do I do and how do I pull my weight around here with a bum foot?* I thought.

Apparently, I wasn't the only employee to ever be injured, as a plan was quickly put in place. Alice brought me crutches, and I was designated 'driver' instead of 'wrangler' for the next few days. I *drove* the guests into Cody to their river float trip on Tuesday. I *drove* one of the vans to the softball field and kept score instead of playing. I *drove* four adults who did not wish to ride on Wednesday afternoon to the Buffalo Bill Historical Center. And on Thursday, while everyone else was enjoying the All-day Ride, I *drove* to Powell to pick up an order of supplies for the pack trips and ranch. Chief gave me a list of items, saying, "Just ask for Albert and explain that you're crippled. He's the manager and he'll have his guys fill the order and carry it to your car. Anything *you* need for horse supplies?"

"Yes, we need some new curb straps and a couple of cinches need replacing."

"Pick up a half-dozen of each and just sign the slip, they'll send a bill at the end of the month."

I also stopped into Wayne's Boot Shop and purchased a pair of Justin lace-up boots, figuring I could stretch the laces enough to get my bandaged foot inside the boot and tie them tight enough to give my ankle some additional support.

On Fridays all guests are transported to Yellowstone for a day-tour around the inner circle, and yes, I drove one of the vans. At least it was keeping me productive until I could safely wrangle again. Chief said that I would have to be able to *run*, without limping, *three* times around the ranch house before he would let me back to work as a wrangler. He was especially concerned about my being in the small corral with the horses, where being able to move out of their way—fast—at any given time, was a must.

Ryan and Cort left to wrangle for Rimrock's guide Griz, packing into Eagle Creek area, so I was needed as a wrangler again. Lucky for me, there were no long rides on Saturday. Scott told me to lead the one-hour walking-ride in the morning and to keep score—no riding involved—at the rodeo that afternoon.

Sunday was my day off. I walked down to the hospital pasture to check on Cassie and Bitterroot. Pier had taken good care of them. Bitterroot's stitches were healing well and Cassie was well enough to use on slow rides. I would swap her for Breezy this next week. He was old and had been ridden too much lately. He looked used up. I'd give him a couple weeks off to rest, keeping Bitterroot company until she was completely healed. I had also noticed that Missy had severe cracked heels, or 'scratches' as they were commonly known. Both front pasterns were swollen, and she was favoring her front end. I needed to put some corticosteroid ointment on her scratches daily before they got any worse and the problem became chronic. I would ask Pier to put her in with the other two horses for a few days.

Chapter 42

The Cody Stampede was next weekend. Rimrock's mountain guides and wranglers planned to be around for at least a couple of the days as guests and workers alike enjoyed the fun. Dustin had called Saturday night saying he was returning with his guests on Wednesday and would have three days free—"Can we meet up Friday and Saturday and take in the Stampede?" he'd asked.

"You bet, Rimrock guests will spend all day Saturday in Cody so hopefully we can be together Friday night through Sunday morning."

He called again Wednesday night, and we agreed to meet at Cassie's for dinner and dancing. We would stay the night in Cody to be sure to catch the start of the big parade and take in all the festivities of Cody's Fourth of July Celebration. He said Chad would take care of his horses and mini-ranch in Pahaska.

We met in the parking lot, embracing as if we hadn't seen each other in months. Cassie's was our favorite restaurant. The atmosphere was always amiable, especially tonight as the waitress put us in a dim-lit corner of the restaurant. We ordered T-bone steak with garlic mashed-potatoes, Caesar salad, freshly made bread, and topped it off with a bottle of good Merlot. We talked over wine, catching up on what had happened in each our lives while waiting for our meal.

There was nightly dancing and entertainment. Tonight there was a local four-piece country/western band playing called, the Park County Country Boys, and the place was filling up quickly.

"Let's go to the lounge and get a good table," Dustin suggested.

"You find us a table. I need to visit the ladies room."

After powdering my nose, I went to join Dustin—and there was *Janey* sitting at a table with him, all smiles as she nudged him playfully with her shoulder.

"Oh, hi Pat. I didn't know you were here," she said impishly.

"Nice to see you too, Janey," I responded politely. "And what are you up to? Or should I ask?"

"I just thought I'd come chat with an old friend. But if you two want me gone, just say so."

I thought to myself, *What an actress! I know her game and I intended to spoil it, if Dustin didn't.*

Dustin pointed out, "Janey, we're here on a date, so . . . nice to see ya. Bye."

"See ya later." Then she was off to visit another table, like a butterfly flittering from flower to flower.

"What is it with that girl? She just can't leave you alone," I said, disgustingly.

"She was just trying to be friendly, I guess."

"Well, I don't have to *guess* and she wants to be more than *friendly*, believe me."

Trying to avoid further conflict, Dustin said, "Let's dance, shall we?"

The band played their rendition of one of my favorite songs, *Bless the Broken Road* made popular by Rascal Flatts . . . reminded me of meeting Dustin. It was a long, slow dance and all thoughts of Janey disappeared. Dustin was a good dancer, and I loved being held in his arms. My foot was bothering me a bit so as the evening went on we did more observing than dancing.

Janey must have noticed us sitting and came fluttering over, slightly tipsy from too much to drink.

Taking Dustin's hand and pulling him toward the dance floor, she said, "Oh Dustin, don't be such an old fart. Come dance this fast swing with me like we used to?"

He looked at me and I gave a helpless shrug and said with a smirk, "Go for it. I need to powder my nose anyway. I'll be back."

He was sitting by himself when I returned. He said softly, "Do you mind if we leave now? I'd like some alone time with you."

"Mmmm, me too. Let's go."

We had other priorities in mind that night, and Janey's blatant behavior wasn't worth mentioning.

* * * *

Cody's Stampede Parade began promptly at 9:30am. We found front-row seats on a tree-shaded bench near the Cody Chamber of Commerce building—perfect to see the parade— and rest my injured foot. This year's parade theme was Wyoming or bust.

Entries including a multitude of antique vehicles, four bands, community-sponsored floats, youth groups, clowns, cowboys, cowgirls, Indians, and a variety of horse-drawn carriages. There was an old fire engine hauled by four magnificent Clydesdales, imitating the famous Budweiser Clydesdales, a pair of beautiful black Morgans pulled a funeral hearse and prancing gray Arabians showed off fancy family carriages. Horses of all breeds were represented: Quarter horses, Arabians, Morgans, Thoroughbreds, Palominos, Pintos, Paints, and Percherons, all decorated with red-white-blue ribbons, polished and groomed until they glistened. There must have been at least 150 different entries, taking over two hours to parade down Sheridan Avenue. The Cody Stampede Parade was known to be among the biggest and best in Wyoming.

We browsed the Wild West Extravaganza featuring arts, crafts, and a trade show, set up between the Cody Chamber and

City Park, as we headed toward where Alice had told us to meet for lunch.

Rimrock's picnic in the park after the parade was for all employees and guests. I took it to mean Dustin could eat too—after all, he'd previously been employed there as a pack-trip guide, and he was *my* guest. Glenn greeted him with a handshake and Alice with a warm embrace, so I assumed it was okay.

Grilled hamburgers and hot dogs, along with tomatoes, pickles, potato salad, coleslaw, chips, and Marla's peanut-butter cookies for dessert were served buffet style on one of the park's many picnic tables. The air had a chill to it, however it was a nice day for festivities . . . better than rain or temperatures of 100°F. I introduced Dustin around. He knew most of the employees, or their families who lived locally. We socialized awhile before walking over to the park's staging area to watch "The Swinging Lines", a western dance club, perform line-dancing routines and swing-dancing.

They wore appropriate costumes of bright red, satin-stitched shirts with white fringe sewn on front, back and down their sleeves. Short blue skirts for the ladies and tight blue jeans for the men added to their crowd appeal.

"I wish I could dance like that, although just watching them makes my ankle hurt."

"Let's save the ankle and stroll over to the art show at the Big Horn Gallery," Dustin said. "There is supposed to be silver work, saddlery, and other forms of cowboy art on display, along with western paintings and sculptures."

"Oh wonderful, I found this beautiful sculpture of a wild horse being roped when your mom and I went touring Cody this spring . . . if it's still there, I think I'll buy it." The *same* statue was not there however, so I purchased a similar but different pose of a wild horse fleeing capture. It reminded me of Jaalam's heritage.

It was getting to be late afternoon when we walked to the Silver Dollar Saloon, a favorite cowboy hangout, for a beer.

We literally *ran* into Chad and his wife Loretta as we entered the bar's swinging doors; they were exiting. "Whoa," Dustin exclaimed. "Hey nice *bumping* into you! Chad, Loretta, this is my girlfriend Pat, who hails from Maine. She's working at Rimrock Ranch this summer."

"Howdy ma'am," Chad replied. "Welcome to the west."

"Please to meet you, Pat," Loretta added.

"Same here," I said. "Nice day for the festivities, isn't it? Were you here for the parade?"

"Yep, we arrived just as it began so we saw most of it. No matter how many times I see it, I never get weary of the bright costumes, beautiful horses, and all the excitement," Loretta exclaimed. "We don't have parades like this over in the back woods of Idaho where I come from."

"Nor in Maine, either. Are you leaving or would you like to join us for a beer?"

"No thank you. Loretta here gets a little tired these days, and I have Dustin's horses to tend to, so guess we'd better be going. Nice meeting you."

"Yes, and congratulations on your pregnancy."

"Thanks . . . baby's due in two months. I'm getting pretty big as you can see and I get tired easily carrying around these extra pounds. Hope we meet again. See ya."

"Bye now."

"Chad, I'll see you tomorrow morning around nine. I'll feed up and start packing. Guests are due to arrive by ten thirty; I hope to be on the trail by eleven thirty."

"Yep, 'til then . . . have fun."

We ordered a couple of beers and two bowls of chili with sides of slaw and rolls. "You're right, Chad seems like a nice guy, and I liked his wife too. She seems awfully young, is she?" I asked.

"Yes. I kid him about robbing the cradle, but he takes it in stride. They met a couple of summers ago when she was a senior in high school working over here in Cody at McDonalds. They married last fall and now a new baby's coming along. That's a lot of responsibility for a young girl, but he being older, they'll do okay."

I was not looking to discuss marriage so I excused myself to find a ladies room. Dustin introduced me to some old friends who chatted with us until out meal came.

It was going on seven o'clock when someone said, "'Bout time to head over to the rodeo . . . supposed to be some kick-ass riders over there tonight." And, like a herd of cattle, everyone left—including us.

* * * *

The Stampede Rodeo, known throughout the world as one of the Best in the West, featured professional cowboys and cowgirls battling for an expected purse of more than $75,000. Stampede night brought out the best animals and the best competitors for traditional events like bull riding, bronc riding, calf roping, and barrel racing.

At halftime, Dustin left to get us cups of coffee while I watched tonight's rodeo specialty act: intricate patterns performed by the historic Santa Rosa Palomino Club of Vernon, Texas and the Pikes Peak Range Riders. When I'd belonged to a 4-H horse club as a teenager, we'd formed a drill team and performed at horse shows, but this far exceeded our maneuvers in difficulty and precision. They were talented *and* entertaining.

When Dustin returned with our hot drinks, he said, "You'll never guess who came over and talked to me at the concession stand."

I ventured a guess. "Some of the Rimrock crowd?"

"Nope. Janey."

"Surprise, surprise, she pops up like a bad dream." I was trying not to sound jealous, but it wasn't working well. "What does she . . . follow you around?"

"I don't know and don't care; we're here to enjoy the

rodeo. I'm having fun, how about you, cowgirl?"

"Yes, only I'm getting a bit chilly," I said as I snuggled a little closer.

Leaving the rodeo grounds was always a hassle. Too many people headed in the same two directions—east and west— and there was no system to merging traffic lines in the parking lot—just bumper-to-bumper confusion. While we waited to get back onto the Yellowstone Highway, Dustin suggested that we first pick up my car parked at Cassie's, and then I could follow him to his home. That way he wouldn't have to bring me back to Cody in the morning. He could start packing for his trip into the mountains, and I could leave for Rimrock whenever I wanted. Sounded reasonable to me.

As I pulled in to Dustin's mini-ranch, I spotted a small compact car parked in his yard. I thought it might be Loretta's car and she or Chad planned to get it tomorrow. Dustin was already out of his truck storming up the steps to the front door. Still not understanding what was happening, I followed a few strides behind.

Dustin turned on the lights and, there was Janey— stretched out on the couch.

Dustin's first words were, "What are *you* doing here?"

"I came to keep you company tonight. I didn't know *Pat* was coming with you. I thought she lived at Rimrock."

"You *don't* think, and that's the problem. You act first and think later."

I'd stayed quiet as long as I could, finally I said, "Listen *Janey*, I know you have the 'hots' for Dustin, but he asked *me* to be here, not *you*. You had your chance with him and you blew it, so why don't you salvage what little dignity you may have left and leave us alone? He doesn't want you—get it?"

"*You* don't get it. We loved each other, *very* much. We were engaged to be married for God's sake. I'll believe he doesn't still want me when *he* tells me, not *you,* bitch."

"OK, that's enough. *Out*—Janey," he said, pointing to

the door. "And don't come back. I tried being civil to you, but you just won't back off. Understand this: I do not want you here; I do not want you anywhere. Can I say it any clearer?"

Enraged, she flew out the door, yelling obscenities all the way to her car.

"Dustin, I can't take anymore of her. I don't want to be acting like a jealous shrew—it's not who I am—but you two *do* have a history together that we don't have. I just want to go back to the ranch." I turned around to leave.

"Please stay. I don't want you being angry with me when I have no control over what she thinks or does. I love you, babe. Please trust me."

I'm a sucker for a sweet-talking cowboy and I stayed with Dustin until Chad arrived in the morning. I drove morosely back to the ranch thinking *déjà vu*. Too often in my past relationships I'd been lied to and cheated on—been there—done that—didn't know if I wanted to let myself be vulnerable again.

I *did* know that if she did not stay out of our lives, we weren't going to make it through the next few weeks.

Chapter 43

Chief told me that I would be going on the pack trip, as a mountain wrangler, leaving next Saturday. I was ecstatic, even though it meant Dustin and I might not be in contact for another two to three weeks. Maybe this was a good thing as we needed some time apart to get our priorities straight—at least *I* did.

Two female friends from back home in Maine and three other guests were going on a six-day trip over Ptarmigan Mountain into Hardpan Basin. I picked up friends Janet and Ann at the Irma Hotel in town early morning and brought them out to the ranch. We would trailhead from there. My friends were a little older than I was and were avid horseback riders. Janet owned and trained Arabians and Ann owned her own horse. I'd warned them the ride might be dangerous and that they needed to be in fit condition—"Don't worry about us," Janet had said. I also told her the ride over Ptarmigan was a once-a-year event and was bound to be both beautiful and exciting—no one knew then just how exciting it would become.

The other three guests were Tim Carden from Ohio and his two college age sons, Mark and Roy, who had driven to the ranch the night before. They'd done some riding before and were in good physical condition from hiking.

Ryan was switched to Gerald's pack outfit to wrangle with Trampus; he and Trampus were friends and worked well together. Mike was pulled back to the ranch for a week; he would get his fill of pack trips that fall. Griz was our guide; Lisha was cook, and Cort the other wrangler. My job would be to help round up the horses in the morning, put halters on them, saddle all the guest horses, and help set up tents or gather firewood as needed.

Nine riders and eight packhorses headed south following Canyon Creek trail toward Ptarmigan Mountain. The mountain stood over 12,000 feet at the north end of Wapiti Ridge looking down the twelve-mile canyon to Rimrock Ranch. We saw patches of snow still atop the mountain. We were a little anxious.

I was astride Beauty, a spirited but sound black mare upon whom I'd had my first wrangle experience galloping down a steep bluff amid a hundred other horses last year. I trusted her. Griz led with Cowtown, Lisha rode Nick, Cort rode Nemo, Janet rode Waco, Ann rode Dixie, Tim rode Nick, Mark rode Zane and Roy rode Earl. The black Percheron packhorses were: Elvira, sisters Dolly and Polly, their half-brother Ebony, and Sundown. Sambo, Sankey, and Satan were sturdy black quarter horses.

After a cold lunch, we began climbing switchbacks up Ptarmigan though thick wooded conifers of the Shoshone National Forest. We climbed slowly for the remainder of the afternoon until we neared the tree line. There we stopped to camp in a large open area consisting of flat ledges—a few hundred feet below the mountain's peak.

The scene from our camp was spectacular; we had an eagle's view of the surrounding mountaintops, hills and valleys. However, most guests were quiet and subdued—partly from fatigue and partly from altitude sickness. Janet complained of dizziness, Ann and Tim both had headaches, while Mark was having stomach problems and was nauseous during the evening. After nightfall a thunder and lightning storm descended upon the Wapiti Range. The heavens exploded around us. The storm was so violent that each roll of thunder shook the very ledges under us like an earthquake. The skies lit up like fireworks and shown as brightly as daylight even through our canvas tents. The horses, sheltered in a nearby crevice overnight, seemed to fare better than we did.

At breakfast Tim expressed worry about his son being well enough to travel over the mountain that day. We were also concerned as none of us was eager to remain camped there another night. Unknowingly, the worst was yet to come.

However, Mark said he felt well enough to travel, so after packing up, we remounted and began our ascent over open terrain to the mountaintop. I was riding drag; Janet and Ann were in front of me. Suddenly Janet started to dismount. "Janet, you need to stay on your horse," I told her—to no avail. "You can't get off here, it's too dangerous."

"Pat, I have to," Janet replied. "I'm dizzy and I think I might fall."

"We've got problems back here, Cortney. Can you hold up? Janet's off her horse."

He called back, "Stay right there, we'll get these packhorses to the top and I'll come back to help."

In a few minutes, Cort came walking down to us. Janet was on her hands and knees, disoriented and refusing to stand upright. Ann continued to ride ahead of me while I led Waco, Janet's horse. With Cort's arm around her holding her up, she finally managed to walk the remainder of the way to the rest of the group.

We rested there for a couple of hours before proceeding. Janet recovered and seemed relieved when she learned that we wouldn't be *riding* the horses across the apex, or down the other side. I'd never encountered a trail too difficult to ride. *I* was apprehensive.

The trail across the top seemed a meager eighteen inches wide with steep drop-offs on either side. Room enough to walk single file, certainly not the place for a misstep. Lisha, the guests and I crossed first. I thought, *Well at least I'm being paid; I certainly wouldn't want to be a guest paying to feel this afraid.* Janet led her horse; the remaining horses followed on their own. Cort brought up the rear.

Suddenly Cort yelled, "Horse down! Horse down!"

"Pat, here take Cowtown," Griz said anxiously as he tossed his reins to me. "Lead him far enough ahead to allow the remaining horses to cross." He rushed back to see what had happened.

Sambo was wedged between two boulders after tumbling thirty feet down off the trail. Luckily, he was on his feet. The packs had acted as padding as he rolled and caught on the huge rocks, saving him from falling several hundred more feet to the tree line.

Griz returned to our group, saying, "Pat, Cowtown will ground-tie. You and Lisha catch a couple of mares and hold onto them; the other horses will stay close. We're going to climb down and see what we can do."

"What happened?" Tim asked with concern.

"Nervous animals. Polly was in a mountain accident a couple years back and lost an eye. Looks like she got anxious and nipped Sundown's rear, who in turn jumped ahead into smaller Sambo. He couldn't regain his balance after his hind feet slipped off the trail and he rolled. He's now stuck between two boulders."

Griz and Cort carefully made their way down to the wedged-in horse. Cort tied an extra rope around one of the boulders then to the pack to keep it from sliding down the mountain, while Griz severed the horse's rope-hitches, freeing Sambo to find his own way down the best he could.

With the help of the men guests forming a line, the pack items were passed up to the top where only the absolutely necessary items were redistributed among the other pack animals. The panniers were left behind, one tent, and the comfortable, but unnecessary, sling-back chairs.

The descent from the top was still scary, but not quite as dangerous for the horses as they each picked their own way down to the valley below. Griz and Cort slapped the rear of some horses to get them started down, and tossed pebbles at others who had done this before and hesitated to do it again. The horses slid on their rumps in places, occasionally having to drop down from ledge to ledge—there was no trail. The rest of us were sincerely relieved to be climbing down and not up. We slowly but surely made our way to the west end of Hardpan Basin where the horses were grazing contentedly. Sambo was with them, showing only minor scrapes on his legs and nose.

Increasingly, I admired these western horses for their diligence and resiliency.

After washing and putting some antibiotic salve on Sambo's abrasions, he was re-packed and we were once again on our way. Griz told us that because we had taken so much time rescuing Sambo, we would have to ride into the evening to make the campsite near the conflux of Elk Fork and Cougar Creeks. "At least," he said with a smile, "we won't be climbing up or down any more mountains today!"

We were all extremely thankful for that.

After a late supper, Griz gave the guests a choice: #1—Have a layover day the following day to rest and recuperate, then ride three full days. #2—Ride half days for the next four days. Or #3—ride two more full days, have a day off to fish or ride, then ride a full day back to the ranch. The guests selected the latter.

What a pleasant ride we had the next day compared with the day before. The weather was perfect and the riding easy as we followed the Elk Fork pack trail crossing four creeks instead of climbing mountains. We made camp late in the afternoon at the far end of Swede Creek Meadow sheltered by the Wapiti Range.

Around the campfire, Janet gazed at the rugged peaks and said, "I suppose you're going to tell us we're going to ride over that ridge tomorrow, right?"

"Well yes, sort of," Griz replied. "We will climb some wooded switchbacks. However, there's a pass through the range which will take us no more than a half day before coming down onto a trail leading around Citadel Mountain to Hardpan Basin. That's where we'll spend our layover day. It'll be a good ride—the highest elevation will not be over 9500 feet, and there are no open ledge areas—you'll enjoy it."

And, he was right, after climbing Ptarmigan, nothing would ever look as intimidating again—we were now all seasoned mountaineers. We enjoyed the views and the challenges the mountain range offered, though we were certainly glad when we finally arrived at our campsite on Hardpan Creek. The men guests had opted to walk and lead their horses the last mile. I would have liked to join them, but pride and the sentiment that I should 'cowgirl up' kept me from stretching my legs and resting my butt as they had. Anyway, I figured tomorrow should be an easy day.

It was nice to sleep in and rise without rushing around to gather the horses. Tim and his sons decided to take a cold lunch and hike up to Hardpan Lake to fish. Janet and Ann wanted to take an afternoon ride. Cort said he would rope Waco and bring him in from the meadow after lunch for Janet to ride. He always kept Nemo tethered, as he was a hard horse to catch. We had picketed the two mares, Dixie and Beauty, nearby, and I saddled them while Cort was catching Waco. Four horses were all we'd need for the day.

Cort, Janet, Ann and I started riding up the Basin headed to Hardpan Creek where we were going to explore a waterfall that was supposedly a few miles down the creek—we never got there.

We were riding over a small crest near the end of the meadow, and there ahead of us, right in our trail—was a grizzly. The bear looked monstrous; it stood up on his hind legs and roared. Cortney yelled, "Run!" We spun the horses around and *run* we did. We ran, scared the entire length of the meadow. At one point, I turned my head to see if the bear was following—it wasn't—but we didn't stop until we reached our camp.

Was I scared? You *bet* I was. Janet and Ann might laugh

later when they told the others what happened, but I am sure they were frightened at the time. Cort and Griz were concerned. They rode out toward Hardpan Lake to escort Tim, Mark and Roy back to camp, hoping the bear had not headed their way.

That evening, just in case the bear tracked us and came into camp, we hung the food containers high and between trees. We moved our personal tents into a circle far away from the cook tent, and built a large fire in the center of our circle with a supply of logs stored nearby. Griz warned us to have *NO* food in our tents, and to keep the flaps zipped and to stay inside—no matter what. Cort and I tethered six horses instead of the usual two, reasoning that there would be safety in numbers.

Griz and Cort had been sleeping in the cook tent since leaving one tent atop Ptarmigan, but tonight they intended to stay awake and patrol the camp's perimeter. Griz carried a 30-30 lever-action rifle and Cort had his own 44-magnum pistol. Neither gun would be sure kill to a grizzly, however together they figured they could take one down if necessary. It was illegal to shoot a grizzly unless a life was being threatened, so their first shots would be over the bear's head should it decide to pay us a visit. After that, they would shoot to kill.

I didn't think I could possibly sleep, but at some point, I awoke to crashing and banging from the direction of the cook tent. "Oh no," I said to Lisha who was awakened also, "I think the bear's in camp!"

As if knowing a grizzly was around wasn't bad enough, it let out a roar that sent shivers down my spine. *Crap*, I thought to myself as I crawled deeper into my sleeping bag. The next thing I heard was a bang like an explosion, more crashing and roaring, followed by running and gunshots. Then . . . welcomed silence.

The bear had apparently scared itself as it bit into an aerosol can and it exploded. To scare it even more, Griz and Cort continued to shoot over its head until it was well away from camp.

Griz said, "It's safe to come out now if anyone's awake." Everyone was. We sat on logs around the campfire talking and drinking coffee until darkness turned into dawn.

The ride over Table Mountain and returning to the ranch the next day was thankfully uneventful. Before leaving, Janet and Ann thanked us and assured us that they would never forget *this* trip. Tim and his sons shook our hands, Tim saying sincerely, "Thank you, I assure you, this was an adventure of a lifetime."

Enough excitement for one week, I was glad to be back to the ranch.

Chapter 44

The first thing I did after our guests left and the horses were turned out to pasture was to call Dustin. He was not at Pahaska so I left a message on his machine saying that I'd returned from a pack trip and would like him to call when he could.

Life at Rimrock Ranch was still busy and hectic. The new wranglers were a mix of uncooperative and ineptness, and we hadn't yet gotten a good work-routine going. Scott had paired new wranglers with experienced ones to help them learn the horses and trails. Ted, being chauvinistic, was determined not to work with *me*, so I ended up—much to my displeasure— wrangling and guiding with either Tom or Brad.

Tom was an excellent horseman and good with our guests. However, he'd been a wrangler before and didn't want to learn or follow our set routines. It was a good thing for him that Scott was his boss—*I'd* have fired him for his insolence.

Brad was a hotshot cowboy who rode broncs in the Cody Nite Rodeo, not caring that Glenn did not want him or any of us to. He became our resident farrier. However, he was rough and impatient with the horses. I came back from a trail ride one afternoon to find an aging pinto, named Arapaho, hog-tied by Brad who was trying unsuccessfully to put shoes on him.

"What the devil are you doing to Arapaho?" I demanded.

"He wouldn't let me put shoes on his hind feet. Every time I tried to put his hoof up on the stake he'd kick and thrash around, so I tied him up to teach him a lesson."

"For God sakes, Brad, Arapaho is old and has arthritis real bad. He *can't* bend his hind legs, that's why he fussed when you tried to lift them high. Untie him right now, and if you can't put shoes on him, then leave him alone." I was almost in tears seeing a sweet horse like Arapaho down with all four legs bound with rope.

"Well, I didn't know."

"No, you *don't* know these horses, so why don't you ask next time?" I was frustrated and angry at his abuse.

* * * *

Work at Rimrock could change as quickly as the weather. I was still disgusted with the wrangler situation—maybe he sensed this—when Chief came to me and said, "I need a PR person to work with a production company from England next week. I told them our representative's name is Pat Gott. What do you think?"

"Wow! Who would I be working with and what would I be doing?" I replied eagerly.

"You'll be dealing with a Torri Yardman. The company's name is Court-Yard Creations. I don't know exactly how many are coming but they've booked the Artist Cabin that will hold eight people. All I know is that they will be here all week to film a documentary. You'll find out what they need and we'll furnish it any way we can.

"This will be great publicity for Rimrock in our overseas London market."

"Sounds interesting to me. I'd love to do it."

I had no idea what they required but I *was* familiar with the ranch operation, its horses, trails, etc., and Glenn must have figured whereas I had business experience, I could negotiate, schedule and coordinate. I was game to try, thinking this might open a completely new career for me—director? production manager?—It might have been a bit premature, but I could see my name in lights!

If Wishes Were Horses was to be a documentary for a British children's television station. Court-Yard Creations sent a film crew of three, four child actors, plus Torri their director. We met Sunday evening after our ranch program of introductions and briefings.

"So what do you envision or have in mind to film?" I asked Torri.

"We basically want to film our children participating in your regular trail rides and in all horse-related activities. The 'how and where' are what we have to work out with you."

"I suggest the crew set up their equipment to catch the children at the beginning of each ride, and then while their riders are out on the trail, move to a location near the end of the ride. That would eliminate their having to hike too far."

"Sounds reasonable to me. Where would we set up for tomorrow's ride?"

"Monday morning the guests leave on an introductory ride that begins behind the ranch house; you could set up just this side of the wooded area and film them riding out. Then move your equipment to the trail beside the wranglers' shed to catch them crossing the creek and coming into the hitching area to dismount at the end of their ride. I'll help them tie their horses to the rails."

"Great, we'll follow *you* tomorrow. Would you like to meet the children?"

She introduced me to the four stars. As I talked to them, I found out their riding experience and assigned them our available horses. They ranged in ability from beginner to intermediate; all rode English-style but were looking forward to learning to ride western. I assigned Katie, age nine, to ride Coke, Sam, age ten, to Guy, Elizabeth, age eleven, to Chance, and Anna, age twelve, to ride Happy.

"Okay, I'll see you all at the corrals at 8:45am. We'll make sure your saddles fit properly, and Glenn will instruct you in the round corral to see that you are getting on well with your horses. Torri, your crew might be interested in filming them at the corral as well."

Scott agreed to have their horses' saddled and ready ahead of the rest of the guests—knowing that their preferential treatment would be fine with Chief.

I asked Scott, "Will my working with this production company create dissention among the other wranglers? Or will they understand that they are too new here to be of much help and you are too valuable and busy with your job to cater to the troops?"

"Doesn't matter much what they think; it's not their call. But I'll explain it to them if they get too bent out of shape.

"By the way, if you need help with anything, like—a good-looking, guitar-playing, country music star—just ask, I'll be glad to accommodate," he said with a smile. He was a rare gem.

The children were all good riders for their ages and loved the security of their western saddles. When the other guests were on their float trip or playing softball, I took them on private rides where the scenery was special, but local, so the crew could film without hiking. We rode into the shallows of the Shoshone River, one day. I took them on a short lope-ride under the roadside cliffs, another day.

The young girls had fallen in love with handsome Pier, especially after hearing him sing and play guitar during Wednesday night's cowboy sing-a-long. They asked if he could come with us on some rides. I ran it by Chief and he said, ". . . only if Pier's not needed to guide other guest riders."

Their request came to fruition on Friday as the rest of the guests were transported to Yellowstone National Park. Torri announced that the filming had gone so well that they planned to leave the ranch early Saturday morning. They would spend the day filming the children shopping in Cody and visiting the Buffalo Bill Historic Center before flying back to England on Sunday. I said, "And miss our Saturday ranch rodeo? Oh no!

Guess we'll just have to have our own rodeo on Friday. Maybe I'll ask Pier to help." They were thrilled. I knew he did not have a U.S. driver's license so he wouldn't be driving guests to Yellowstone, and his usual day off was Sunday, so he'd be available. He readily agreed to help out his 'fan club.'

Pier and I put the child stars through their paces in our large rodeo arena on Friday with a horsemanship class and the usual gymkhana games. Elizabeth won the horsemanship class; Chance could be the perfect horse with the right rider. She also won musical bags with him. Happy was the fastest horse, and Anna placed first in barrel racing. Sam won the steer-roping contest, and thanks to Anna, who unselfishly held her own horse back, Katie won the egg and spoon race.

Whereas Pier had done most of the legwork, the girls gave him three cheers when the rodeo was over. He and I both received big hugs from them when they left the next morning.

"Thank you, Pat, for your assistance," Torri said. "You were wonderful. I'll send you a copy of the documentary after it's edited and ready for the telly."

"I'd like that, thank you. It was a pleasure meeting and working with you. Have a safe flight home."

Although it looked like it was not my fate to become a film director or producer, I had had an interesting week with Torri, the crew and the children. It had given me a welcomed break from my usual wrangler routine.

Dustin called Saturday night and asked me about coming to his place the next day. I had Sunday morning off so I said I'd be there early . . . we had a lot to talk about.

Chapter 45

It took a half-day for Dustin and I to relate all that had happened to us since we had seen each other. We swapped war stories until lunch. I had missed him more than I'd realized; he was so much a part of my existence that being with him now seemed as natural as life itself.

After catching up on our personal needs, we ventured out to the corrals to see the horses. There were only three. Reena was looking fit and her attitude was still curious and friendly. Dustin said she'd been on four pack trips over the past six weeks, ". . .ridden by experienced equestriennes only," he added.

"Where are the rest of the horses?"

"At D & L Ranch. And that brings up a proposition I have for you."

"What would that be?" I was eager to hear what he had to say.

"Boulder Basin Outfitters wants to combine our resources and do a pack trip from Cody to Jackson Hole and return to Cody, leaving the last week of August. The trip takes a week each way, which puts us returning in September."

"Sounds like great trips. I've done both legs, only in separate years. Rimrock said they don't pack to Jackson anymore."

"They don't. The last year I worked for Rimrock is the last year they did the roundtrip. It's only profitable if you have enough clients riding from both directions—which is hard to schedule, or clients willing to do the roundtrip—which is rare. That's why we agreed to combine guests this year to get the trip revived, and then they'd make it an annual trip in future years."

"What does this have to do with me?" I asked, wondering where this conversation was going.

"I want you to come with me. Two reasons: first, I miss you like crazy when we're separated, and second, we work well together and I could use you as an extra wrangler. Between Boulder Basin's outfit and my own, we'd have eight guests one way and seven the other . . . your help would be appreciated. What do you say?"

"Wow, let me think a minute. That would mean getting through at Rimrock a week early—which would be okay, I guess, as long as I gave Chief notice. Fill me in on some more details. I think I'd like to go—*IF* you'll guarantee NO grizzlies!"

He chuckled. "I can't promise you we won't meet grizzlies, cowgirl, but I *can* guarantee your safety . . . with my life," he added. With that, he swept me up and swung me around. "I was hoping you'd agree to come—yee-haw."

"Put me down and talk to me," I said, laughing.

"OK, here's the deal: Boulder Basin has four guests going to Jackson and three different guests coming back to Cody; I have four hardcore riders who want to do the roundtrip. We'll trailhead from the Southfork, over Marston Pass into Turpin Meadow Ranch, Moran—just outside of Jackson. We'll return by way of Two Ocean Pass, the Thorofare, where I know you've camped before and said you loved, and over Eagle Pass to the trailhead on Eagle Creek."

"You've done a lot of planning. When did you decide all this?"

"I met up with the owner, Carl Sauerwein, an old friend from Rimrock days, at the Cody feed store. We got talking trips and came up with the idea to combine our guests and talents to do this pack trip.

"The main problem was figuring out whose horses and

equipment to use—you shouldn't try to mix horse herds on pack trips—and mixing equipment wouldn't work either. So, we decided to use *me* as guide, Chad as cook—he can also shoe and vet horses—you as wrangler, and take just our three *personal* horses. The remaining guest and packhorses will be from *their* herd. We'll use *their* equipment, and two of *their* wranglers. That will free Carl and his wife to run their regular trips while we're gone."

"You've put a lot of thought into this . . . can I ride Reena?"

"Yes, of course you can ride her. And I've *needed* to put a lot of thought into the logistics of this trip, coordinating with Boulder Basin Outfitters and Turpin Meadow Ranch for supplies, guest accommodations, and guest airport transportation, besides horses and pack equipment. They both have been great to work with and very cooperative. This is the last week to get things in place."

"Well, sorry to leave you, but I have to head back to Rimrock. I need to talk to Chief about my getting through work, and it's Scott's and my turn to fit this week's arriving guests to saddles. I'll pack up during the week and meet you here Saturday night, okay?"

"I love you, babe," he said after a long slow kiss.

"I love you too. See ya Saturday."

* * * *

Glenn understood my leaving early, he said, "That roundtrip to Jackson is a beautiful scenic ride. We stopped doing it five years ago only because it was too hard to find enough riders for both directions.

"So Dustin's guiding; he's a good man."

"Yep." I couldn't have agreed with him more.

"You know you're welcome back here anytime," Chief said.

"Thanks, I appreciate that. I've had some great times working here. I'll never forget Rimrock, or you and Alice." I gave him an unexpected hug.

Next, I talked to Scott.

He chuckled when he said, "Chief finally fired Brad last night. I don't know what he did, or if Chief figured he didn't need him or his hotshot attitude anymore."

"With the ranch already down one wrangler, then why was Chief so agreeable to my leaving early?"

"Probably because Gerald's pack outfit is through with trips this week. That means that Ryan and Gerald will be back to the ranch, available to replace both Brad and you. Trampus is going home to spend some time with his mom and family before going college."

"I *thought* Chief was being too easy. Oh well, at least your job will go smoother with some of the old crew returning. I'll sorta miss working here, but then, I'm really looking forward to trekking to Jackson and back."

"I don't blame you. What'll you do after that," Scott inquired slyly.

"Hmmm, that's the big question, isn't it? And, I don't have an answer yet. We'll see.

"Anyway, I may not get another chance to say this . . . 'It's been great working with you again. Good luck, Scott'."

"You too." We shook hands goodbye.

I packed up during the week and said similar goodbyes to Alice, Ryan, Pier, Trampus and Gerald, hoping I'd see them again sometime. Cort, Mike and Griz were out on a pack trip.

With a mix of regret and anticipation, I left Rimrock for Pahaska.

Chapter 46

As soon as the sun rose, Dustin and I loaded our three horses in his trailer, threw our tack and personal gear in the truck bed and headed to the trailhead on the South Fork of the Shoshone River. Carl's two wranglers, Dale James and Bob Lipkin, had transported *his* horses and equipment the day before. Chad's wife Loretta dropped him off at the trailhead as we arrived. Dale and Bob had already fed and watered their stock.

While Bob helped Dustin and Chad pack the horses, Dale and I began grooming, saddling and bridling the riding horses. Boulder Basin had some fine-looking horses—I hoped they acted as good as they looked. However, I was still glad I had brought Reena along to ride. Dustin brought Cochise for himself and Big Sadie for Chad. It was beyond me to learn the names of all twenty new horses; I would have to rely on Dale and Bob to help me remember their riding horses that I would be dealing with daily.

It took more than three hours to pack up the string of ten horses. At 7:30, Dale left to pick up the guests at the Mayor's Inn in Cody. I continued tacking up the riding horses; Bob came to help me and we finished just as the guests arrived.

Dustin's guests were experienced riders: Rose was a dressage instructor and her husband Terry, an equine vet and horse trainer. They were looking for adventure via horseback. Anna and Debra, two female friends from Rhode Island, were horse owners and booked the trip for rest and recuperation.

Carl had told Dustin that *his* guests were all novice riders, and advised him which horses to put them on. Two brothers, Don and Mike, were mountain bikers from Indiana and wanted to experience horse trekking. Hanna and Bill were hikers vacationing in Wyoming and decided to ride over the continental divide instead of walk.

This trip was a near perfect pack trip, albeit not as exciting as my last, hopefully. We followed the South Fork of the Shoshone River past Carter Mountain, riding narrow rocky catwalks along the base of Boulder Ridge, camping at Needle Creek our first night and at the base of Wall Mountain the second night. The days were clear, the land pristine and beautiful, and the nights chilly. I was glad to be sharing a tent with Dustin, to keep me warm.

We crossed the continental divide at Marston Pass, 9800 feet above sea level, leaving the Washakie Wilderness and entering the Teton National Forest. Although the ascent was steep, the trail was wide with no sheer drop-offs, and it opened to rolling meadows on top. It was very windy riding over the pass, and a storm was brewing in the west. Before we could descend to the protection of tree line again, it started thundering, lightening and then pea-size hail commenced.

I overheard Mike remark, "I don't think I like riding out in the open like this when it's lightening and hail coming down."

Don answered, "I don't think the guide cares what you like or don't like, right now."

"You're right," I said. "We have to make the campsite in time to set up and have dinner before nightfall. We'll travel no matter what the weather."

Luckily, the storm was only a quick Rocky Mountain afternoon weather disturbance and stopped as suddenly as it had begun. That night we camped at 9500 feet, on Lake Creek just below Ferry Lake. As we gazed up at the stars from around our campfire, they shone so brightly and looked so close that it was as if we could reach up and touch them. We made a game out of who could spot the most manmade satellites amidst nature's own wonders.

Dustin decided to layover a day here to rest the horses, workers and guests. Layover days were relaxing for everyone as there was no wake-up bell ringing, and Chad served breakfast any time up until nine o'clock. The sun brought another glorious morning to the Rockies; the horses grazed contentedly, ghostlike in the ground mist covering the meadow below our campsite. Two small deer drank from the creek at the far end of the meadow. I sat under the open flap of my tent observing this scene wondering, *who could ask for a more peaceful sight than this.*

Dustin moved in behind me and started massaging my shoulders. "Hey, babe, how're you holding up? Want to ride with me today to Ferry Lake and take whichever guests want to ride with us?"

"Sure. It looks like a lovely day. What's at Ferry Lake?"

"Cutthroat trout, lots of colorful wild flowers in the high meadows, and you can see all the way to Yellowstone from a high-point."

Dustin told the guests they could ride or hike three miles to Ferry Lake, or just kickback and stay at camp for the day. The bikers and hikers opted to hike; the riders said they would ride with Dustin and I.

While we were gone, Bob and Dale were going to set up the sun shower Boulder Basin had thoughtfully made available for the guests' convenience. They would also replace shoes on a couple of the packhorses. Chad said he'd begin preparing a pot roast dinner—he'd use a cast iron pot buried in-ground and surrounded by coals for long, slow cooking. He promised us fruit cobbler for dessert.

Ferry Lake was crystal clear and cold, as it was fed by snow runoffs. At the edge of the forest, there were remnants of lupine and bluebells prevalent. The meadows were still alive with red, Indian paintbrush, white phlox, and yellow asters among others I could not identify that looked like small daisies.

Bitterroot and alpine primrose were starkly defined on the high rocky and grassy slopes. The wildflowers were almost magical in their vibrant colors and abundance of blooms. They were also very fragile.

Dustin warned the guests, "Please enjoy the flowers from the trail. You can photograph them—but do not pick them. The law is: leave them as you find them."

"Pat, I'll stay with the horses, why don't you take the guests and climb that crest?" He pointed to a small hill with a couple of boulders on top. "You can see Yellowstone Park to the northwest. You'll be able to identify it by the smog that hovers over from all the visitors' vehicle emissions."

That was the sad reality of our times.

The next day we had a long descent to Pendergast Creek and a longer afternoon following the creek to the South Fork of the Buffalo River. We made camp there for the next two nights.

Dustin and Dale took the guests on a day ride to South Fork Falls the next day. While they were gone, it was such a warm, beautiful day I figured I would stay back at camp, swim and wash up in a pool I'd spotted in the river nearby. In the heat of the sunshine, I'd forgotten that the water was yesterday's snow! I stepped into the river water without caution and jumped back out in a hurry—yes, it was cold—frigid. I managed to wash strategic body places and soap and rinse my hair—not scalp—before huge horse flies drove me back to camp. Of course, I could have used the sun shower, but that would have been too easy. I read and dried my hair by the fire until the riders rode in.

Mid-afternoon, the guests returned from their trip to the falls all 'oohs' and 'ahs' describing its beauty. They'd also seen a beaver and a beaver house in the swamp on the way to the falls, and a large cow moose hiding in the bushes along the trail—no grizzlies.

We celebrated our last night in camp with a steak dinner accompanied by a couple bottles of wine Dustin had secreted away for this occasion. Campfire conversation lasted well into the night as we relaxed from the wine and anxiously talked about tomorrow being the last day on the trail for some and a turnaround point for the rest us.

Turpin Meadow Ranch was in Moran, Wyoming, about 20 miles north of Jackson. The ranch had a magnificent view of the Teton Mountains from their corrals, picture window in their lodge and from their guest cabins. We arrived late afternoon. The general manager greeted us with a smile and a handshake and indicated which corrals we could use to contain our horses for the next couple of days. A ranch hand showed the guests to their cabins. Rose, Terry, Anna, Debra, and our crew would spend two nights at Turpin Meadow before beginning our trek back to Cody.

It was customary to get together for a farewell dinner, so after showering and cleaning up, we all piled into one of Turpin Meadow's vans, and Dustin drove us to Jackson. We agreed to 'pig out' on pizza and fresh salad at Pizza Hut. We later had drinks at the famous Cowboy Bar, where saddles topped stools around the bar instead of seats.

The next day while Dustin, Brad and the wranglers unpacked from one trip and repacked for the next one, I drove Don, Mike, Hannah and Bill to Jackson Hole Airport and picked up our three new arriving guests.

LuAnn traveled alone. She had been on several pack trips throughout the southwest and was looking forward to riding the Rockies. A married couple, Jan and Fred, lived on a houseboat off the coast of California and were more interested in photographing landscape and wildlife than riding horses. They wanted to do a photo documentary of crossing the continental divide and figured riding horses was easier and less dangerous than walking—they might change their opinion after the trip.

Chapter 47

September first arrived. The day temperatures were chilly—I wore my winter jacket, gloves, and lined boots. The horses were packed, the guests ready and Dustin was anxious to get under way. He thanked the Turpin Meadow Ranch management and employees for their help, and we began our trek back to Cody.

Our first night on the North Fork of the Buffalo River was cold—the water in my canteen froze. The next day we enjoyed a casual lunch at Two Ocean Pass, where the Atlantic-Pacific Creek split into two: one flowing west to the Pacific, the other eventually flowing to the Atlantic. This natural phenomenon is the only one of its kind on the North American continent. Jan and Fred took many pictures of this unique divide. The elevation of the Pass was 8200 feet, not above tree line nor was it steep or rocky.

Dustin said, "Enjoy the rest because we have a long afternoon ride ahead of us. I want to camp at the lower Thorofare tonight, and it's another five to six-hour ride from here. Sooooo, in a half hour be ready to mount your horses and ride."

Although the ride was long, it was a beautiful trail. Fred was now riding in front of me. I chuckled when I saw him riding on a pillow and couldn't help chiding him a little. "Hey Fred, what's with the pillow?"

"My butt is sore, that's what's with my pillow. I'm not a landlubber or horseback rider like the rest of you. I live on a boat and usually walk to places to do photography.

"Hey Jan, whose idea was this anyway?" he asked his

significant other.

"Yours, I believe." She smiled.

We followed Atlantic Creek through the marshy lowlands of the Yellowstone River, crossing the river before skirting the edge of Bridger Lake. Hawks Rest Meadow was a couple of miles long with the trail winding through tall grasses. Most of us dismounted and led our horses—much to Fred's relief—a mile or so to the Thorofare where we remounted and rode to our campsite.

It was late evening by the time our meal was finished. The night air was cold and low clouds slid by the moon covering any stars. Dustin announced, "Sorry folks, but we'll have to move again tomorrow. You see that ring around the moon . . . a pretty sure sign of snow coming soon and we need to be over Eagle Pass by the time it falls."

"Will we make it?" I asked him quietly.

"I hope so," was all he said.

Guests and crew crashed early; it had been a long day.

The morning brought heavy frost; it added a quiet elegance to an already sublime river valley. The valley where we camped was about fourteen miles long north to south and three miles wide. It's known for its remoteness and beauty. I had camped here before and remembered it as my favorite campsite. I had looked forward to a layover day here to ride around Bridger Lake or up Pass Creek, until Dustin had—sensibly—decided otherwise.

A short ride to the west was the Thorofare Ranger Station, considered the most remote place in the continental United States. The log buildings and corrals are historic structures and quaintly huddle next to a hillside. I loved it. Riding another mile, we came to the Yellowstone River and followed it north as it meandered through this long valley just as free and wild as it did 200 years ago. This region was called the Thorofare because it was easy to travel, and for centuries Indians, fur trappers and mountain-men like Jim Bridger, for whom Bridger Lake was named, used this route.

We made good time riding up the valley, then we turned northeast crossing Mountain Creek toward Eagle Pass. Dustin said he would have liked to continue over the pass but it would have meant traversing the top and down the switchbacks on the other side at dusk, which he figured was too risky. Instead, we set up camp at what's known as 6D5 Yellowstone. We had had a good riding day which helped alleviate the worries of an upcoming storm.

Dustin went to sleep still anxious about the weather.

There is a saying: 'What you fear, you'll create.' Whether that is true or not, there were snow flurries in the air when we awoke the next morning. Dustin's concern was foremost for the safety of his guests. He trusted his own surefooted horses, however, climbing up and over a 9700-foot mountain pass, in snow, with seven guest riders, four crewmembers and twenty horses that were not his, was another matter.

He woke everyone early and at breakfast announced, "Be sure to dress warm today, we may run into some rough weather, and if you've got winter walking boots—wear them."

Seeing the concerned look on my face, he said, "Don't worry, babe, trust your horse, she'll do her best for you, and so will I."

"I know you will, I'm just looking forward to getting down into Three-Mile Meadow on the other side."

"So am I. Now let's get this group up and over the hill."

Sometimes, 'Ignorance is bliss', as the novice riders actually seemed happy that they would get a chance to lead their horses instead of ride. It would not turn out as easy as they figured.

The trek up the switchbacks went well until we neared the summit where the flurries had turned to serious snowfall.

Dustin halted and passed back word to: "Untie your lead-rope from around the saddle horn, dismount on the uphill side and lead your horse the rest of the way to the top."

The horses all had on western shoes with toe and heel grips. It was the chance that the novices would perhaps panic and disrupt their horse's concentration and balance that concerned him.

The going was steep but the forerunners had packed down the snow by the time we, at the end, made it to the summit. Dustin had had forethought to leave a shovel unpacked, and he sent Dale ahead to clear the snow from the exposed ledges, just over the apex, on the Eagle Creek side of the pass.

The experienced riders said they were okay with continuing to lead their horses *down* the switchbacks; the novices were not. Jan said, "Fred and I are struggling to balance our camera equipment in our backpacks *and* keep our footing. We don't want to lead our horses over open ledges."

"We don't either," chimed in Don and Mike.

I asked Dustin, "Would it work if I tied a breakaway knot from each of their horses' lead-rope to the saddle stirrup of the horse in front of it? —like a string of pack animals. Reena and I could lead them and one of the other wranglers could follow with the guests."

"Good idea, but . . ." he looked at me and hesitated.

"What? You said to trust my horse—I am. Now, trust me. We can do this."

"OK. Let's get it done. I want to get down to the meadows before wind is added to this snow."

Cautiously we made our way across the ledges and down the steep switchbacks that followed. Luckily the snow decreased as we descended. Halfway down the mountain, Dustin stopped at a clearing with space to tie our horses to the trees and take a break. We gave each other 'high-fives' for making it down safely and welcomed remounting and riding our horses, instead of walking, the remainder of the way to camp in Three-Mile Meadow.

At the evening meal, Dustin said heartily, "Congratulations to all of you for being real troopers today. The climb over the pass was not easy, but you did it in style—and for that, you deserve a layover day, providing we aren't socked in with snow tonight. The clouds look like they are thinning, so I think our luck will hold and you'll have a nice day to rest, ride, or hike tomorrow."

The usually quiet Chad said, "And let's have a cheer for our captain who got us through the storm unscathed."

"Hip, hip, hooray," they all yelled.

Later in the privacy of our own tent, I told him, "You look like you've been rode hard and put away wet."

"Worry comes with the territory, babe. Snowstorms can blow into the mountains any time from mid-August. Guides hope that *if* that happens, we can get our guests, crew, and horses through safely."

"And you did, cowboy. I'm proud of you."

"You're a true cowgirl yourself, although I couldn't help but worry about you leading that string across those slippery ledges."

"As a wrangler, that was my job, right?" Dustin hadn't realized that when I'd insisted on doing my job, I was, in a way, testing him. I wanted to see if he respected my judgment and independence enough that he would not try to dominate and control me—he passed with flying colors.

"Yes, but I was still worried. I care so much for you that if something happened to you, especially on *my* trek, I'd never forgive myself."

"We all make choices, my love, and live with the consequences."

"You're right, and this is getting too philosophical—my head hurts, let's go to bed."

Morning brought sunshine, albeit cold. The guests, tired from their yesterday's adventure, slept late. Bob, Dale and I fed the horses half of the remaining grain cubes when they came around late morning. We took the opportunity to check for injuries. Four of the packhorses had superficial scrapes on their lower legs. This was from scrambling back onto the rocky trail after slipping in the snow. I sprayed some Blu-kote antiseptic on their wounds. The riding horses, without weight to carry, fared better with only one scraped fetlock.

The guests didn't seem eager to ride, so I suggested we hike to the old gold mine shaft that Dustin had shown me when we camped here last year. The marshes around the creek were only partially frozen, so we skirted around them to reach the slope. It was a lovely view of the three-mile valley from the shelf where the mine was located. Jan and Fred spied two young moose with their binoculars and took several pictures with their 500mm zoom lens. Anna and Debra found obsidian arrowheads in the area. I reminded them to return the artifacts where they'd found them after taking pictures as proof of their find.

Our last night on the trail was celebrated with baked meat-and-mushroom lasagna, garlic bread and bottles of Chianti Italian wine. Warmed by the roaring fire and plenty of wine, conversation centered around exaggerated tales of our snow trek and tomorrow's last day of riding. Dustin assured the guests the ride back to the trailhead would be an easy one compared to what they had already been through.

And it was, with only a stray moose or deer here and there and patches of remaining snow to catch our attention. Eagle Creek's water flow was swift, high and cold. Dustin's three horses were strong and trustworthy, and Boulder Basin's horses had proven themselves capable under all previous circumstances. We crossed with a little anxiety and a few wet boots, but no accidents.

Carl and Michelle, Boulder Basin Outfitters, were there to meet us with a van to transport the guests back to Cody. There would be no farewell dinner later, as most of them were going on to Billings tonight and flying out from there tomorrow morning. The guests gave our crew warm and friendly good-byes. Jan and Fred said they took some incredible pictures crossing Eagle Pass in the snowstorm and would be sure to send us some. They all agreed it was an unforgettable ride of a lifetime—we took it to be a positive comment as we received larger than normal tips.

Bob and Dale would trailer their horses to their ranch on the North Fork. We fed and watered our horses, and then Loretta and Chad gave Dustin and me a ride to the South Fork trailhead to pick up his truck and horse trailer.

It was on our way back to Eagle Creek that it happened.

Chapter 48

We were driving through the tunnel under Rattlesnake Mountain, leaving Cody toward the North Fork when Dustin said, "I've thought about this the whole trip but didn't think the time was right to say it to you."

I was more than a little nervous at what was coming next. I looked at him and said, "Continue. You have my full attention."

"It's time to fish or cut bait, cowgirl. This trip was the final proof of how well we work together. We play well together, we do everything well together.

"Damn it; I love you so much. I want you as my partner in life, for the rest of my life. I don't want to play house and just live together; I don't want to be engaged; I want us to be married. Will you marry me?"

He looked at me and I opened my mouth to say something, but only a scream came out, as out of the corner of my eye, I saw: an oncoming a car cross the centerline heading directly toward us. That is all I remember.

* * * *

Headlines in the Cody Enterprise newspaper read:

Two Injured, One Dead in Tunnel Accident
Cody – According to the Park County Sheriff Department, Carol Lyman, age 82, from South Springs, Colorado died

from a heart attack before crossing into the oncoming lane in the Rattlesnake Mountain tunnel, crashing into a truck and horse trailer driven by local outfitter, Dustin Lee of Pahaska and passenger, Pat Gott from Maine. They were transported to West Park Hospital, Cody.

I awoke to bright lights and someone in white leaning over talking to me. "Good, you're coming around. How are you feeling?"

"I don't know, okay, I guess. My head and shoulder hurt, and my whole body aches."

"You have a mild concussion and a separated right shoulder."

I looked around. "What happened? Where's Dustin?"

Leena was there and she asked the doctor if we could be alone. "Welcome back, Pat. We were worried about you. Do you remember anything?"

"No, only that I saw a car coming toward us in the tunnel. Where are we? And where's Dustin?" I asked again, panicking.

"We're in Cody's West Park Hospital. Dustin's hurt, but the doctor says he'll mend."

"Where is he? I need to see him." I tried to get out of bed.

"He's in a room down the hall. Dan's with him. You can see him later. Right now, why don't you lie back down and rest a while longer?"

"Just until I can see straight," I said dizzily. "The horses, where are they? Who's taking care of them? How long have I been here?"

"Slow down. One question at a time. Chad got worried when you and Dustin didn't show up at the corrals, so he went looking for you. He called us when he found out what happened, and I asked him to bring the horses to our ranch. Dan and I came immediately."

"How bad is Dustin hurt?" I asked tentatively, afraid of the answer.

"The car hit his side of the truck. He has a bad concussion and a couple of cracked ribs, his left leg is broken and he has numerous cuts and bruises on his arms and face—he doesn't look pretty. However, the doctor says he has no internal injuries and will mend. He's hurting and sure won't be riding for a while, but it could have been worse. I'm so happy you're both going to be okay."

"He . . . he asked me to marry him just before the car hit us." I sputtered, tears spilling down my face like a waterfall. "I never had a chance to answer—I have to see him."

"I'll help you to his room. Wait here." Leena was back shortly with a wheelchair. "No more tears now," she said as she wheeled me down the corridor.

"Dan, why don't you come with me and we'll go get some coffee," she said as she winked and whisked Dan out the door.

Dustin's leg was in a cast and elevated in a sling; his chest was wrapped, and he had a bandage around his head. He looked like he was sleeping as I leaned over him and whispered, "Hey, cowboy, I never got a chance to answer your question— *Yes, I'll marry you.*"

His eyes fluttered open and a smile crossed his lips. "Yes?" he whispered. "You will?"

"Yes, yes, yes. I love you and want to be your wife, forever. But first I need to return home to settle my affairs."

"Remind me, how far to Maine?" This was an inside joke from when we parted last year.

"About 2500 miles too far," I answered with a smile, repeating what I'd said the previous year, then added, "but getting closer all the time."

Acknowledgements

Thanks to **Jay F Kirkpatrick, PhD.** Director of The Science and Conservation Center in Billings, MT for his knowledgeable suggestions and input regarding the Pryor Mountain wild mustang's history and his contribution to the PZP equine vaccine-based fertility control program

George Hooper of Bryant Pond, ME, who specializes in breeding Blue Star Arabians, supplied information on in-breeding and Arabian line-breeding programs.

You will find, as I did, **John Lyons'** books *Bringing up Baby* and *Lyons on Horses* excellent reading for training young horses.

Debby Deshon from South Paris, ME, who raced endurance for twelve years, including the IROC team competition in Venezuela where the U.S. got a bronze medal, lent her expertise concerning endurance riding, racing, training and pit crewing. I also obtained useful information concerning endurance riding from **Karen Paulo**'s book *America's Long Distance Challenge*. **Jan Stevens** from Ashland, MT provided data on the Fort Howes Endurance Races.

Janet Brunjes from Norway, Maine gladly supplied details of her thrilling pack trip over Ptarmigan Mountain, and having a grizzly come rampaging into their campsite one night.

I'm grateful to my longtime friend, **Laura Wiley Ashton,** for her suggestions in designing and illustrating the book cover and for helping me muddle through my first draft. In addition, I appreciate my friend **Rebecca Dowse**'s editing skills.

Thanks to the following people for allowing me to use their true names: **Carl and Michelle Sauerwein,** owners of Boulder Basin Outfitters; **Alice Fales** of Rimrock Ranch, whose husband Glenn died in 2000; and **John Davis**, local Wyoming artist. **Turpin Meadow Ranch** is located in Moran, Wyoming.

Patricia Gott Riding one of her Arabian Horses

About the Author

Patricia Probert Gott is a retired businesswoman and author of sixteen books. From her home in western Maine, her adventures have taken her to five continents, twelve countries and forty-seven states, from several horse pack trips in the American West, weeklong horseback riding adventures in Australia and Hungary, an exciting horseback excursion in Egypt, and a ten-day horse safari in South Africa, to rafting down the Grand Canyon, volunteering to Tanzania, walking on the Great Wall of China and visiting the Potala Palace in Tibet. For several summers she was a ranch wrangler and trail guide at Rimrock Ranch, Cody, Wyoming.

Ms Gott owns two Arabian horses. She began riding at the age of eight, and she has owned, raised and trained horses ever since, accounting for her knowledge and experience with horses as detailed in her cowgirl books and horse stories. You may visit her web site at *www.prgottbooks.net*